T0301114

THE
WEEKEND
GUESTS

Also by Liza North

Obsessed

LIZA NORTH

THE WEEKEND GUESTS

CONSTABLE

CONSTABLE

First published in Great Britain in 2024 by Constable

A CIP catalogue record for this book is
available from the British Library.

ISBN: 978-1-40871-624-3 (hardback)
ISBN: 978-1-40871-625-0 (trade paperback)

Typeset in Sabon by SX Composing DTP, Rayleigh, Essex
Printed and bound in Great Britain by Clays Ltd, Elcograf S.p.A.

Papers used by Constable are from well-managed forests
and other responsible sources.

MIX
Paper | Supporting
responsible forestry
FSC
www.fsc.org   FSC® C104740

Constable
An imprint of
Little, Brown Book Group
Carmelite House
50 Victoria Embankment
London EC4Y 0DZ

An Hachette UK Company
www.hachette.co.uk
www.littlebrown.co.uk

For my dad, Harry, the perfect companion
for discovering the Dorset coast

Afterwards

Dorset, 2019

The last caller had dropped his keys down the gutter. The one before had stubbed a toe. This was different. A bad line, dropping in and out of signal. A woman's voice gasping panic, gabbling sentences he couldn't decipher. Then something that might have been *he* or *she* or even *they*, and three words, suddenly clear, that gouged through a year's experience.

'. . . took the children.'

The call handler felt his mind empty, immediately, as if it had been shaken upside down. He stretched out fingertips and balanced them bloodless on the desk. Through the phone, he could hear the shriek of the wind, then the woman gibbering in incomprehensible snippets. From the next desk, his colleague turned to him, eyebrows up. He shook his head, speaking into the handset. 'Can you tell me where you are?'

The woman yielded a phone number, an address. Her voice held ice-still, then disappeared into the crackling line. The words emerged isolated, distorted. 'A gun . . .' His mouth seemed to dry of itself. He held his breath to catch every whisper. 'Please help us. Please.'

The handler keyed words into the computer, recalling his script with an effort. 'Help is on its way.' Did she even hear him? *He* heard only the wind, a wild drumming like stones on metal, and a high keening that could have been a baby's cry. Then that serrated breath, close to the phone.

'The others . . .' The rest of her words were lost. The handler heard himself barking questions, sharply efficient. Around him, as in a different world, he could see lines light up. More calls coming in.

'It's so dark,' the caller said. 'I can't see . . . I can't see anything.' Then the voice was clearer, high as a scream. 'What if they're all dead?'

Triassic

The continents are fused: one vast land. This stretch of desert is not yet Dorset. It is not yet England, or even Europe. Later, they will call this the Wessex Basin, lined with the accumulated sediments from aeons of geological history, Permian to Palaeogene. The red deposits draw a line like sand in a jar, to last for millennia.

1

Brandon

Dorset, 2019

The weekend, which would flirt with farce and end in horror, began with a kiss.

Brandon stood by the panes of what his wife called their second home, congratulating himself that the setting, at least, was proof against modernisation. Above him, the Dorset countryside that was alternately Cornwall wild and Cotswolds tame. In front, the English Channel. Grey as tin on this late winter day; deep sapphire when he'd seen it first. Despite everything, he was bewitched by this piece of coast. He would go to his grave loving it.

Aline came to him with her lioness walk and stood before him like a figure in a poster: pale hair and long legs, with floor-to-ceiling glass and that unreal view behind her. Beyond the panes, the ground dropped almost at once into crag and scrub. Far below, unseen from here, it rose and fell and fell again, landing at last in the oatmeal curve of the bay.

'God,' she said. 'We were so right to do this.' She indicated the glass, the opaque stretch of sea, with one hand. 'It's like you could run straight into it.'

'Fall into it,' he said. Fifty metres down, those tilting waters.

She slid her fingers down the back of his jeans, nudging long nails into his buttocks. He twisted his head and his lips touched the scented sheet of her hair. She turned him to admire her handiwork. Ripped-out walls and an interior stripped and started again. Wood and glass, white space, and what their architect had called a statement staircase, rising from the shining floor. Blue-edged lilies in a vase the colour of the sea on a table carved of driftwood.

A designer's dream. Aline's dream.

'It's perfect,' she said.

'It should be,' he said. 'It cost enough.'

He yelped as she ripped her hand away, nails scouring skin, and swung off to the table. He thought how strange it was that the same pain, caused by the same movement by the same person, could be entirely erotic or entirely not. Upstairs, he heard his children fighting; behind him, the rain starting.

He watched her set a bottle of Bollinger on the table and arrange about it the crystal flutes that had been her grand-mother's, getting the right angle for a photo. She showed him the picture gleaming on the screen and the message she'd typed to go with it.

I have champagne. And surprises.

'OK?' she said.

'It looks great.'

'You could sound more enthusiastic.'

'You know what I think.'

She laughed, pressed send. 'It's too late to argue.'

'Aline . . .'

She turned back to him, so close that he could almost taste the cherry gloss on her mouth. Nearly seventeen years together, and she was still the sexiest woman he had ever met – and the most frustrating. 'Anyone would think,' she said, 'that you didn't want to see our friends.'

'It's not that.'

'If you're worrying about how Rob will react . . .' She ran her lips down the line of his jaw. 'Then don't. He has his new girlfriend.'

'I know.' He hesitated. Her breath was berry-sweet, distracting.

'You don't suppose either of them feels the same, after all these years?'

He let her mouth move onto his. 'I'm not sure,' he said, while he could still speak, 'and I don't believe you are either.'

She laughed softly, into the kiss.

2

Darryl

Edinburgh, 2001

Saturday 15 September

The latest undergraduates are moving in next door. Their landlady came yesterday with yellow bottles and her own Hoover and all day the smell of bleach spilled onto the shared landing and down the communal stair. I do not care. They will not change my life.

I heard her again today, out of breath but talking up all four floors. In the brief intervals, I heard rattling keys and an intermittent low bass. Male. A very neutral English. Polite. I put my eye to my peephole and caught a distended glimpse before they disappeared through the burgundy door. Two men carrying boxes. One older, one young; both ordinary-looking. I turned to tell Phyllis, but she was in the bedroom, resting. She's always resting.

For hours afterwards, I stood at the bay window with the shutter half open, drinking and watching the smooth curve of the crescent. The tall bay-fronted tenements; the cars far below in their parallel lines. I saw the Volvo vanish onto Marchmont Road with the older man in it, and the next student turn up minutes later. He was tall and thin, wearing glasses and carrying two backpacks, and I guessed he'd walked from Waverley station. The first lad went along the street to meet him, and they half hugged, half thumped each other in the way I have noticed male students doing. The shorter one wrestled the smaller rucksack from his pal and put it on his own back.

I watched them along the pavement, chatting easily, then on the short weed-strewn path to the tenement door. Afterwards, I stared for a long time at my computer screen, unable to summon enthusiasm for my PhD, and wondering who the final room was for.

Sunday 16 September

The third tenant is a girl, and beautiful. Serendipitously, I was on my way back from the shop when they were unloading her belongings, so I got a first look undistorted by the peephole.

The Audi had found a space immediately outside the building (a miracle of either luck or determination), and at first I registered only that the pavement was filled with golden giants. Closer inspection revealed that only three were blonde and only two tall: the man at the open boot, who looked as though he belonged in an advertisement for Scandinavian outdoor wear, and the girl now hugging the shorter of the two boys I had seen before. She was – she *is*

– magnificent, laughing with white teeth and bright, swinging hair in a high ponytail. A sunflower on the drizzly street.

No question this goddess had her looks from her father: the older woman, unloading boxes, had a greying brunette bob and a placid, unremarkable face. The younger girl was fair too, but somehow more ordinary, as though the gilt pen had run out by the time they got to her.

I didn't want to walk past them carrying my plastic bag with its milk and bread and tea and a packet of mince for later, but I made myself do it. I held open the front door and they went past me in turn, legs bumping the carrier bag, all carrying one box except the Nordic-god father, who had three stacked on top of each other. I received five polite, very RP thank yous. I produced five company smiles, then waited until they were two flights up before I followed.

Phyllis was slumped in an armchair, facing the desk where I should be working on my thesis, still in the clothes she'd worn the day before. My smile tightened. I said, 'The girl next door looks like a Botticelli Madonna.'

I gazed into Phyllis's silent, purply eyes, waiting for a reaction. But she can play this game too well.

3

Michael

Dorset, 2019

He drove the narrow roads with Radio 4 playing quietly. *Front Row*, half attended to. In the back, his daughter jolted upright, cried out, then dropped into her dream again. In the dark, he couldn't see her in the driving mirror, but he pictured her as he knew she must be: one pink cheek pressed against the side of the car seat, curly hair going every which way and a plush mouse clasped, dribble-covered, in one fist. Behind him was his baby son, downy-headed, round-cheeked, lost in milk dreams.

Nikki slumped in the passenger seat, covered in a down jacket with her head awkwardly against the top of the seat belt. Seeing her, he felt a rush of affection and gratitude, and made a mental note to buy her a travel pillow, one of those that blew up and went round your neck. Sleep was precious to her now, guarded, grasped at, gobbled like a drug.

He thought about the invitation that had brought them here: the *come and see what we've done with the house* that had appeared out of the blue in his inbox, brightening and disturbing a January day at the office. He thought of the conversation in the kitchen that night, conducted in tense whispers against the smell of cooking, while he paced with Rufus unsettled on his chest.

'If Aline and Brandon want to see us,' Nikki had said, 'why not see us in London?'

Because that's not how it's worked out. It had been months since any of them had met, and then it had just been him and Brandon for a hasty drink in the city, not long before Rufus was born. Aline had sent a Harrods teddy bear for the new baby, a personalised 'big sister' doll for Chloe, but they had not visited.

'It's a long way,' Michael had said. This was true, if also disingenuous. They lived on opposite sides of that vast city: he and Nikki on the south-eastern edges, scrabbling to hold on, and Aline and Brandon in Hampstead.

'Not as far as Dorset,' Nikki had said. But she had agreed at last to this weekend, with its long drive and late nights. She had done it for him.

The road narrowed and grew darker, branches kissing above them. The headlights picked out skeleton twigs. Michael thought he could hear the sea, but surely that was his imagination, anticipating what he knew lay ahead. He changed down a gear, took a corner with careful precision.

They left the road and bumped along a rough track, coming to a choice between a shut farm gate and a sharp downward turn to the right. Memory tugged him. Nikki blinked, struggling to sit upright.

'Where *are* we?'

'Almost there.'

The car turned, jolted, slid steeply down. Nikki pulled the coat tighter around her. 'I'm freezing,' she said. 'What time is it?'

'Seven thirty.'

'It feels like midnight.'

She was right. The sky was heavy jet; he thought he heard an owl. It was as though they had dropped out of time and space somewhere on that last long trek from the motorway. He turned again, sped up, then pulled onto flat, crunching gravel.

'There's the house.'

An outside light came on, flipping sinister silhouette to showy renovation. Grey stone and glass stretching into black space. Stone urns with clematis just coming into bud, climbing by the door.

'It's beautiful,' he said.

'Of course it is.'

He looked sideways, but said nothing. He drew up against the high stone wall. The door swung open and there was Aline, radiant as he had pictured her, with her arms out. Then he was out of the car, she was kissing him on both cheeks and then, laughing, on his mouth, and he was tumbled decades back.

He saw her running through the Meadows, her long plait the colour of sunflowers; in their Edinburgh flat, leaning forward in the half-light, alive with laughter, Rob sprawled on cushions on the floor. At his parents' house, making it more sophisticated just by being there. Turning her fair head, her face unreadable, until her eyes met his.

Promise.

He saw her laughing out at a sea that was like the Italian Riviera, not half a mile from where they were now.

Enough, he told himself.

Nikki got out stiffly, wriggling her neck. Aline kissed her, then pulled her into a hug. 'It's so wonderful to have you here.' Michael unstrapped Chloe and carried her, still sleeping, against his heart.

Brandon wasn't there. 'Gone to get my surprise,' Aline said. 'Well, one of them.' She set down the car seat with Rufus just stirring inside it. 'Oh, he's scrumptious. It almost makes me broody again, just being near him.'

The room was spectacular, extending over almost the whole ground floor and including kitchen, dining and living spaces, each complete in itself, every beautiful piece of furniture looking as if it had been made to be there. The stairs were a sculpture, so cunningly contrived from wood and metal that each step appeared to float in space. Fifteen pristine rectangles.

'Wow.'

'I thought you'd like it. And here's another surprise.'

Michael didn't know what he'd expected. Caviar, perhaps, to go with the promised champagne. Another expensive present for the children. What he saw was a teenager with straight dark hair, eyes the colour of wet slate, an I'm-meant-to-be-here smile, and a pile of towels in her arms.

'Hi,' she said.

'Hi,' Nikki said. Her eyes were bemused.

'Childcare,' Aline said. 'You both look like you need it.' And then, to the girl, 'Milly darling, these are my friends Michael and Nikki. Would you show him their room, and help put Chloe to bed?'

Michael followed the narrow legs upstairs, his daughter half waking in his arms and Aline's voice carrying up after them. 'Milly's my Girl Friday. Our two love her.'

'How nice,' Nikki said.

The bedroom was so exquisite that he was ashamed of their scruffy holdall, plastic bags stuffed with baby paraphernalia. He asked, 'How long have you worked for Aline?'

Milly reached out her arms for Chloe, who wriggled contentedly into them. 'A while,' she said. 'Are you old friends?'

'Very,' he said, and he felt obscurely sad.

Downstairs, he found Nikki feeding Rufus on a shining sofa, looking faintly shell-shocked and holding a flute of champagne. The baby's fat hand gripped her bra strap and he spat her nipple out at intervals, sending beady glances round the dazzling room. Michael accepted a pale gold glass from Aline and sat close beside them.

'When's Rob getting here?' he asked.

'He texted,' Aline said. 'They're stuck in traffic.'

Nikki reattached Rufus. 'His new girlfriend must really like him. That's one hell of a drive just for the weekend.'

Aline shrugged, curling herself into an armchair. 'I suppose she does.' She glanced at Michael. 'Didn't they always?'

'Inexplicably, yes.'

15

He considered the gallery-perfect space, filling in new details. A vast oil in sea blues and greens on one wall; on another, floor-to-ceiling blinds the colour of winter mist. He permitted himself one long look at Aline's tilted face, as immaculate as any of it. Then he reached for Nikki's hand and raised his glass to them both.

The next surprise came twenty minutes later, walking ahead of Brandon into the house. A woman with hair like oak leaves in autumn (or *fall*, as she would call it), a long skirt, and a face Michael hadn't seen for nearly seventeen years. Behind her, two girls – near identical, perhaps five or six years old – surveyed the room with dark eyes.

'Jesus Christ,' he said. 'Sienna.'

The woman smiled. Realising that he had sounded more shocked than delighted, Michael added, 'What a wonderful surprise.'

'Isn't it?' Aline said, with her arms round the newcomer. 'She messaged me on LinkedIn and said she was in the UK for a few months.' She stood back, hands on Sienna's shoulders, smiling into her face. 'It seemed an unmissable opportunity to get us all together again.'

Briefly, Michael was back in his own tiny kitchen with the smell of ragu and that conversation that had only just not been a quarrel. '*Why* did Aline ask us?' Nikki had persisted. 'Why now?' Well, here was her answer.

Sienna hugged Michael, waved a greeting at Nikki. 'Cute baby,' she said. 'Gorgeous space.' But she said it not as though she saw them; as though she was looking through the spotless walls, waiting for something else. Michael took a bag from Brandon, hugging him in turn, and murmured in his ear.

'She knows Rob is coming?'

Brandon nodded, almost imperceptibly.

'And him?'

A wry face, a shake of the head. Michael saw Nikki watching them and shot her a too-bright smile. Sienna spun back to her children, as though wrenching herself from a hold. 'My two,' she said. 'Astrid and Luna.' Her accent was exactly as he had remembered it. Pure California.

Aline swooped, squeezing the little girls to her. 'Well, aren't you gorgeous?' Michael noticed how Astrid returned the hug, but Luna held herself apart. Aline turned away, still smiling, and pulled more champagne from a fridge that appeared to be full of it. The teenager padded down the stairs on silent feet, holding out a hand to each child.

'I'm Milly,' she said. 'We're playing cards. I'll show you how. Then we'll get you to bed.'

They hesitated only a split second before they went with her, Luna clutching her sister's hand.

Sienna settled onto a sofa and accepted a bubbling glass with a long exhale. 'Well, that was *much* easier than I thought it would be. Your nanny's a witch, Aline. Where did you find her?'

'London, of course. She's a student at LSE.'

Michael hardly listened. He was studying Sienna's now-smiling face, fingers translucent on the stem of the flute, and thinking – it was not an original observation – that it was she who could be a witch. An Avalon mystic, red-haired, long-robed. Insidiously attractive.

All this time, she had been gone. Even while the rest of them had stayed close – and they had, for several years – she had been conspicuous by *not* being there. In crossing the Atlantic she had vanished from their lives as completely as the early pilgrims must have done. Of course, she had had her reasons.

'It's going to be fantastic,' Aline said, 'to be all together again.' She smiled, Guinevere to Sienna's Morgaine, proffering a crystal glass.

Michael pictured Rob somewhere on a packed motorway with yet another girlfriend they had not met, and over the voices and the clinking glasses he formed another question. The same one Nikki had asked about Aline.

Why now? If Sienna had had good reasons for staying away, what had changed?

He pushed the thought from him. The past was a long way behind them. And Aline was right: it *was* wonderful to see her.

4

Darryl

Edinburgh, 2001

Saturday 22 September

A disturbed and unpleasant night. I was up late grappling with the thesis, and then I was woken, it seemed instantly, by a strident blare. I had at first a hazy, news-fed fear that the city was under attack. Then I thought it was my alarm, but the dark was too unyielding for that. I turned on the pillow and checked the time. 02:06. The sound came again, clamorous and rude, from inside the flat. I realised it was the buzzer for the intercom, which I hear so rarely that I had almost forgotten it.

I switched on the bedside light and sought blinking for my dressing gown, my mind veering between outrage and concern. I glanced at Phyllis, an unstirring lump with untidy hair on the pillow beside me, but I did not disturb her.

The voice at the other end of the wire was somewhat familiar, and very drunk. 'Please . . . please . . . let us in . . . pub . . . key . . . buzzer . . .'

I knew who he was then, though I still had the option of pretending not to. Oddly, I could detect his accent better in these disjoined fragments than in the complete phrases I had heard from time to time as he passed my door. Manchester, I thought, or possibly Lancashire.

I'm good on voices; you don't have to look them in the face.

I was still deciding how to reply when a girl's voice, laughing, replaced him. 'I'm so sorry to disturb you,' she said. She spoke the English of BBC period dramas, of Cheltenham Ladies' College and the Henley Regatta. 'We're your new neighbours. Idiot Rob forgot the key and our buzzer is broken. Could you let us in?'

Clearly she had no doubt of my answer. Probably no one had ever told her no. For a moment, I considered becoming the first to do so. But I must live next to them, all this academic year.

'Didn't forget . . .' Rob could still be heard, dimly, in the background. 'Lost . . . Oh shit.' From the intercom there issued the sounds, unmistakable and prolonged, of someone being sick.

I spoke sharply. 'Do you have any idea what time it is?'

'Christ, Rob.' The girl was still half giggling, half reproachful. I wasn't sure she had even heard me. Then she spoke back into the intercom. 'Oh God, I'm so sorry. We'll clean it up first thing, I promise. Could you just buzz us in?'

I pressed my finger hard on the button, heard her still-laughing thank you, and the door swinging open. Then I slammed the receiver down.

My feet were cold, my nerves rubbed raw. I didn't sleep until long after they had come upstairs, him groaning, her hushing him; after they had banged and banged on their own door and been let in and clattered around running taps and bumping things and finally collapsed, presumably, into their beds.

I was only faintly cheered, at my window at eight this morning, to see the girl and the other lad – *not* Rob – on the path far below, armed with what appeared to be a washing-up bowl of soapy water and several towels. No sign, down there, of the wrongdoer himself, but from the adjoining flat there issued the faint noises of continued vomiting, followed by groans and the toilet flushing. He was not, after all, unpunished.

Later

I am adding to this at the kitchen table, fortified with a cup of tea (stronger than usual), after a most surprising interruption. I am tempted to add a drop of whisky to the tea but I have resisted. Phyllis is not with me – I've barely seen her today – but it is as though I feel her reproachful eyes. Besides, I do not need the stimulant. I am not unhappy, though I am not entirely sure what I am.

The knock on the door was at first another irritation. Midday on a Saturday, when in theory there was still time for the day to be redeemed. For me to take a long walk, talk things over with Phyllis, or complete that overdue chapter of my thesis.

I sighed. I put this diary inside the desk drawer and shut it. I knew my hair was brushed, my shirt and trousers ironed, because they always are. I did a mental scan of the room and found nothing out of place. I had no intention of allowing anyone in, but something made me want to be prepared.

I opened the door and was almost knocked backwards by the smell of roses. Then by the look of them: yellow and white, absurd in their abundance, all bundled together in green and silver paper, in the arms of the beautiful girl. Rob stood beside her, sheepish of expression, wet-haired and soap-scented, though his face, behind the glasses, was still faintly green. He was carrying a bottle of wine.

'We've come to say sorry,' the girl said. 'The landlady swears the buzzer will be fixed next week, and Rob will never be trusted with the keys again.' She held out the flowers and I received them awkwardly in both hands. 'I thought chocolates,' she said, 'but then Michael said Rob here was playing Sebastian Flyte, so we decided on flowers.' She gave her companion a look that conveyed both mild contempt and undoubted affection. 'Although he didn't actually hurl into your window.'

I found I was smiling. I thought it was her, not the lad, who had the entitlement of Waugh's patrician youth: his beauty, but without the underlying vulnerability. Nor could I detect any Botticelli soulfulness up close. Her face might be timeless, but she is all modern.

'Wrong city,' I said. She raised her eyebrows, and I felt my face redden. I had only wanted to show that I understood her *Brideshead* reference, but she must have thought I was correcting her. I said quickly, weakly, 'Thank you.'

She elbowed her companion and he waved the bottle at me. 'Sorry,' he said. 'If it's any consolation, I've felt like shit all day.'

I considered telling him I already knew and decided not to. I stood there in the doorway, still holding the roses, with no free hand for the wine.

'So,' the girl said. 'Are we forgiven?'

'Of course,' I said. And then, despite myself – almost to my own horror – I heard myself say, 'Won't you come in?'

They followed me into the hall, the boy immediately dumping the bottle on my mother's Victorian side table. Châteauneuf-du-Pape, I noticed: better than most students buy. Better than I can afford, come to that. Something told me that she had chosen it. I waved them into the sitting room while I got a jug for the flowers and stood a while at the sink, running water from the cold tap over my wrists, wanting to splash it onto my face. I was cursing myself for letting them in.

I would have to offer coffee now, then make conversation while they drank it. I would have to keep them from meeting Phyllis, who is not good with strangers. Still, with the roses spouting from the Wedgwood pitcher that had sat unused for years and the thought of the wine waiting for later, I discovered that I was not entirely regretful. The first flowers in the flat since my mother left it. Perhaps I should have brought some for Phyllis. Perhaps she would like me better if I had.

I carried the jug through and set it blooming in the empty grate of the fireplace. 'Perfect,' the girl said. They were almost as radiant as her, and a great deal less unsettling to have about me.

'I'm Aline,' she said. 'And this reprobate is Rob.'

'Darryl.' I felt simultaneously reluctant and elated, yielding this minor intimacy.

Rob was looking out of the window, across the tall pale walls, high slate roofs and turret windows to the hills of south Edinburgh. I knew them without looking. Blackford Hill, andesite lava; the Braid Hills, ice-eroded volcanic stone; the spiny Pentlands forced into being all those millennia ago by a crack in the earth's crust.

'Cool view,' he said. 'Ours is the same.'

Aline scanned the room: the books in the Edinburgh press, my parents' paintings still adorning the walls, their Laura Ashley wallpaper peeling at the corners. I thought of cream paint and Scandinavian furniture, and wished, for the first time, that I had redecorated.

But perhaps that didn't matter. Rob's gaze, leaving the window, had settled on the small, round mahogany table and the one thing that I would never let go: my father's Isle of Lewis chess set, reproduced in meticulous ivory on a polished wooden board. He lifted a knight, holding it up to the light.

'Nice,' he said. The girl joined him, touching the figure with long, tanned fingers. Her nails were carnation pink.

'Do you play?' she said.

'I don't usually have anyone to play with.'

I regretted it as soon as I had said it, then despised myself for caring what they thought. Aline looked surprised. Then she laughed. 'Well,' she said. 'Now you can have Rob. Any time you like.'

5

Sienna

Dorset, 2019

He had barely changed. The years that had turned Brandon from all-American hunk to the kind of executive plied with phone numbers on corporate jollies and Michael from introspective boy to sagging businessman had left Rob the same tousle-haired nerd he had been at twenty-two. Still Jarvis Cocker sexy.

He arrived late, well after Aline had laid the table with heavy linen napkins and what she said were wedding-present glasses: when the children were in bed and Brandon was opening a fourth bottle of Bollinger. He shrugged off coat and scarf and dispensed half-hearted apologies, muttering about traffic. He accepted kisses, a flute of champagne, and all the time Sienna waited in the background for him to notice her.

She had had too much to drink. She was no longer used to it and the champagne seemed to rise straight to her brain, bursting like the bubbles in the glass. But it was something

25

to do with hands and mouth and nerves that wouldn't stay still.

After thirty seconds, those nerves failed her. She stood up. 'Hi, Rob.'

His hand jerked. Fizz splashed expensively onto his black jumper. He said, 'Sienna,' but not the way Michael had said it. Then he said, 'Aline is full of surprises.' He kissed her – almost but not quite as he had kissed the others. A second later, he added, 'How *are* you?'

Once, she had felt his face against her hair, heard his sharp breath in crisp winter air, tugged his red scarf around her own neck so it warmed them both. He had said, 'You smell of mangoes,' and she had laughed and told him it was her shampoo. What did she smell of now? Calpol and Bollinger, probably.

'I'm very well,' she said. He paused a moment with one hand on her arm. His fingers were hot. Her face felt scarred, tattooed by his mouth.

Behind them, Brandon said loudly, 'You must be Cass.'

Sienna saw Michael carrying bags and a woman following him through the open door. Sienna's first thought was that she was young, maybe ten years their junior. Hair dyed a gaudy bronze, skin the creamy, uniform smoothness of heavy foundation, curves pulled in sharp at the waist. Eyes that darted about the room.

'Your girlfriend?' she said.

'Something like that,' Rob said with a grin. The new-comer flinched. He looked away from her, and from Sienna, around the polished room. 'This place has changed,' he said.

He's still a bastard. And then – irrationally, on three glasses of champagne – *I still want him.*

Cass hesitated, then stepped inside. Brandon kissed her, proffered Bollinger, fussed with bags. The nanny, Milly, appeared fleetingly at the top of the stairs, then turned away.

Sienna pictured her girls, tucked up now on their mattresses on the floor, sharing an attic room with Lexie and Jimmy. She saw their tilted noses, heavy lashes on brown cheeks, the Afro hair she had finally learned to style. She thought of the husband she had left in San Francisco, hurt and bewildered and trying to understand.

'Tell me this isn't forever, Sienna?' he had said, when he drove them to the airport.

'Three months max,' she'd said, wilfully misunderstanding. 'Like I told the school. You know they're fine with it.'

'Of course I do,' he had said, impatient now. 'I was there, remember.'

'I wouldn't keep the girls from you any longer, even if I could. You know that too.'

'I don't know *what* I know any more,' he had said, suddenly defeated. 'And I wasn't just talking about the girls.' She had looked away then, unable to reassure him. She gripped her glass now, not looking at Rob. She felt woozy with booze and a new guilt. She must not be distracted.

She had contacted Aline a month since from an Airbnb in Glasgow. She'd meant to take the girls to Edinburgh, but had flunked it.

While they slept, cuddled together in a stranger's sofa bed, she had returned for the thousandth time to the photo on Aline's LinkedIn profile. A designer suit, hair in an immaculate bun. The name was changed, double-barrelled, and the accessories were more expensive, but it was the same silver-screen face.

Sienna had sat for a long time with her eyes glazing, holding her own wrists, reminding herself that she had crossed an ocean, thrown up her life, dragged her children into a mad backpacking escapade that she had told them would be an adventure, just so that she could find Aline, and all of them. She had to do it. And at last, while the night hung black outside the windows and hail pounded on the panes, she had typed her message.

It's been so long, but I'm in the UK. I keep thinking . . . She'd deleted that last bit, typed, *I need to talk to you*, then deleted that too. *I'd love to see you all.* That would do. She had pressed send, fast, before she could change her mind again.

Aline's reply had come twenty-four hours later, all warmth and enthusiasm, with the invitation to Dorset. *I'll get the old gang together*, she had written, as though it was the most natural thing in the world. And now Sienna was here in this unrecognisable house, show-home beautiful. She was with them all, enduring a pain she had not properly anticipated as the woman called Cass snuggled onto the sofa beside Rob and rested her hand on his thigh.

She drank again. The champagne was incredible: the taste of another world. She looked across at Michael, smiling at her with his old mix of kindness and minor awkwardness.

'I've missed you,' she said, and amidst a maelstrom of more complicated emotions, she realised with relief that this was true. She was glad to see him again, glad to meet his nice wife.

Cass swigged as at a pint. 'I needed this,' she said. 'What a drive.' She gazed round the brilliant room, then beamed at them all. 'It's amazing to meet you guys at last. Rob's so reticent. This is the closest I've got to meeting his family.'

Rob scowled. She giggled. 'You'll have to tell me all his secrets.'

Aline smiled. 'Oh no,' she said. 'We all know how to be discreet.'

6

Darryl

Edinburgh, 2001

Wednesday 3 October

More change. I am made uneasy by it, but also, perhaps, excited.

My supervisor's office is on the tenth floor of a 1960s tower that must be a contender for the least attractive building in this magnificent city. I went there reluctantly today, knowing what I had sent her to be inadequate, and anticipating causticity (or at best, indifference). The lift was clogged with undergraduates, so I walked up flight after flight of stairs and arrived out of breath.

My supervisor didn't get up when I opened the door, but spun her office chair around to face me. She's a large woman in her late thirties, so heavily pregnant that it is almost impossible not to stare transfixed at the distended orbs of belly and breasts. Today, all were insufficiently contained by a dress that I can only describe as a clinging green sack, rendering this more difficult still.

She regarded me with what appeared (unusually) to be concern. 'I took the stairs,' I puffed. I looked over her head to the window. Close to, it yields a panoramic view of the city, but I could see only cloud-packed sky.

'Good God,' she said. 'Sit down.'

'I've made some comments,' she said, while my lungs recovered. She waved a hand, swollen and with its rings removed. I saw my few pathetic pages almost covered with blood-red ink. 'But first we should talk about logistics while I'm on maternity leave.'

She placed a hand on the green sphere. I glanced down and saw it distorting under her gigantic fingers, like an alien trying to break out. I looked away again. 'Normally,' she said, 'I would just put the second supervisor in charge, but as yours is in a different school, it feels important to have someone else based here, to support you.'

As though left unguided I would slide into the maw of geosciences, never to be released. I could have told her there was no danger of that, since it always takes at least three emails to rouse my second supervisor from whatever it is that absorbs him so completely in the labyrinthine tunnels of King's Buildings. But there seemed little point. My interdisciplinary PhD, much approved of in theory, is in practice treated by both my instructors as an unexploded bomb, full of ill-understood parts and liable to lead to disaster. Or perhaps they just think badly of me.

She was still talking, though I only caught the tail end. '. . . more so since there are concerns about your progress.'

I sighed, but said nothing. 'So my new colleague has kindly agreed to cover my leave. I'll take you to meet her now.'

Her.

I got up again – it had hardly been worth sitting down – and followed her jolting rear and greying hair out of the door and along the drab corridor to another door. *Dr Gemma Harris.* A light voice called us into a room so small I suspected it of having been a broom cupboard in a former life. Once my supervisor was inside, belly first, there was barely room for anyone else.

'Gemma.' Her voice was brisk, as always. 'This is Darryl. We've discussed his project . . .'

Ominous.

'. . . Darryl, this is Dr Harris.'

The other woman got up. The first thing I thought was how young she was. Surely barely past her own doctorate. Then I clocked her prettiness and, disquietingly, that she reminded me of someone, but I didn't know who. She is a slight woman (although she may have seemed more so today, by comparison with her colleague), with freckled skin and soft brown hair that hung in waves to her narrow shoulders.

'Dr Harris is here on a two-year lectureship,' my supervisor said. 'I'm sure she will have some very helpful insights.'

Gemma Harris held out her hand. She might even have been younger than me. She said, 'I'm looking forward to working with you.'

Her accent was soft, all lulling echoes of the far north. I said I was looking forward to it too, although in truth I wasn't sure. My current supervisors may be (respectively) astringent and unreliable, but at least they have seniority.

~

Returning to the stairs after three quarters of an hour dissecting my inadequate wraith of a chapter, I passed Gemma Harris's door again and realised who she reminded me of. Phyllis. I couldn't decide if this was disturbing, or auspicious.

I dawdled back along the tree-lined avenue that crosses the Meadows, with cyclists rushing past and students clustering either side on the grass. Then along the tall Marchmont streets. As I went, I thought about my thesis, and a deep gloom settled on me, like an old, damp blanket, so my limbs felt heavy with it.

Aline was coming down the stairs in our tenement wearing trainers and leggings and a university sweatshirt. She didn't stop, but greeted me cheerfully. Rob was at their flat door, letting himself in.

'Hi,' he said. And then, surprising me, 'Fancy that game of chess?'

I noticed he was carrying a six-pack of Carlsberg under the arm not unlocking the door. I hate lager. I started to say no. I do not socialise. Besides, I didn't know where Phyllis was. Instead I found myself saying, 'Give me half an hour.'

'Sure,' he said.

When he arrived, nearly an hour later, the flat was quiet and tidy and Phyllis was well out of the way. Rob settled down on the sofa, apparently at ease, evidently already thinking of the game. I pulled a low chair close to the little table and sat across from him. I held out the two pawns in my closed fists and he picked one without speaking. Black.

It was a strange, half-forgotten pleasure to pick up the fragile pieces and play against someone other than myself. A stranger pleasure still to be there with anyone who was not Phyllis. Rob played well; I saw that at once. I opened with the King's Pawn and he responded almost immediately with the French Defence. He didn't talk much, though once, when he was waiting for my move, he looked around the room as though he were taking it in for the first time.

'Fancy place for a PhD student. Do you live here on your own?'

I avoided the question, but inadvertently opened myself up to more. 'It was my parents' flat.'

'Wow. All right for some.'

I let my hand hover over a knight, then moved it away. 'They're dead,' I said.

Another silence, less comfortable than before. 'Fuck,' Rob said at last. 'I'm sorry.' I thought he would ask more, but he didn't, and I was mostly relieved. I didn't want to talk about how they died. I didn't want to think about what happened afterwards.

Towards the end of the game – when it was becoming clear to both of us that I would win this time but need not always do so – we heard footsteps, a door opening on the landing, voices. Aline called, 'Rob?'

'In here,' he yelled, and then, to me, 'You don't mind?'

I did, but I couldn't say so. I got up unwillingly and let them in. Aline, flush-faced and in running clothes, and the other boy in jeans and a jumper that looked home-knitted.

'This is Michael.' She was still lovely, even with sweat soaking through her T-shirt. 'I'm a bit stinky. You sure it's OK?'

34

I thought about Phyllis, then swallowed and said of course it was, and to come in. 'I'll get you some water.' I remembered I'd never offered Rob a drink and asked him too. He shook his head, not looking up.

'I'm good,' he said. 'Well, I'm screwed here . . .' He gestured at the board. 'But fine otherwise.'

Aline and Michael sat on the sofa beside Rob, watching us play, drinking the water and eating some crisps I'd found at the back of the cupboard. Across the room, the flowers she had brought me still bloomed in the fireplace. They wouldn't last much longer, but for now they were beautiful.

I felt disturbed, bewildered, by the speed of this step towards . . . what? Friendship? Intimacy? Amazed that these almost-strangers could sit there on my mother's sofa in their socks and Rob could caress the chess pieces that had so long been mine alone, as though they were his.

I closed my eyes. I saw teenage faces alive with malice and big, laughing teeth. *Did you really think we'd be friends with you?*

I told myself, *This is not then.* I brought my attention back to the board and saw that I'd made an idiotic mistake. Rob was lifting my queen from her square.

'Careless,' he said.

I swore, but inside my head. We played on, Rob grinning at his unexpected advantage.

'It was a good run,' Aline said. 'You should have come.'

'This is mental exercise,' Rob said. 'Besides, I'm tired.'

'I bet you are,' said Aline. I presumed this was a reference to a girl I'd seen leaving their flat this morning (by no means the first), and was proved right when Michael asked, 'What was her name?'

'Saoirse maybe. Or Siobhan.' Rob yawned. 'I know she bollocked me for pronouncing it wrong.'

Aline crunched the last crisp. 'She seemed to have forgiven you by the time you crashed into the flat together. Seeing her again?'

'She left her number.'

'I see.'

Rob smirked.

After the checkmate, I congratulated him, hiding my irritation. 'I shouldn't have won,' he said, and I didn't correct him. He got up, stretching long limbs like a spider. 'Thanks, though. I'll give you a rematch soon.'

The others took this as their cue, pushing themselves up from the sagging sofa. I suddenly wanted them to stay longer, but I dared not ask. Besides, I had nothing to offer them. Even the wine Aline and Rob had given me was gone, drunk last night as I sat tense and unspeaking in front of the TV with Phyllis.

Tonight, when they had left and I had her back with me, she sulked. I watched her pallid face with its spots of pink blush. I noticed that her eye paint could do with some repair and felt a pang that was at once affection and irritation.

I said, 'Are you jealous?'

Jealous that I have friends now. If that's what they are.

She said nothing. I ran a fingertip down her unyielding cheek. I thought passingly of Gemma Harris. 'Don't worry,' I said. 'I still need you.'

7

Rob

Dorset, 2019

After the Bollinger, there was Chablis, then Bordeaux. Then whisky: Scottish and Japanese, single malts. Brandon arranged them like chess pieces on the gleaming coffee table, as though he was laughing at himself. Rob gazed determinedly at the ostentatious array because the alternative was to look across the table, to Sienna.

Sometimes, when circumstances seemed especially to provoke him, he made lists in his head of the ways in which Brandon's life was better than his.

Amazing job. Tick. The hedge-fund directorship, complete with astronomical salary, versus a medium-level tech job that no one ever wrote home about.

Whisky splashed into Rob's glass. All around him was the glitter of money well spent.

Multiple homes. Tick. The house in Hampstead, the buy-to-let investments, and now this fucking house on the cliffs, landed in their laps while he, Rob, had one new-build flat in Edinburgh.

'I won't,' Nikki said, to Brandon's proffered tumbler. 'Rufus won't know what's hit him.'

'I will,' Cass said, leaning heavily on Rob's shoulder.

A perfect wife. Tick. And that was it. The real issue. He didn't want Aline. Almost alone among their straight male contemporaries, he had never wanted her. But he had lost the woman he *did* want, while Brandon had taken whatever it was that he and Aline found together in the heat and craziness and near desperation of that student summer, and had made it real. Or maybe Aline had. They'd kept it, too, despite everything.

While Brandon discoursed on the merits of Island versus Speyside malts, and Michael took forever to choose between them, Aline outlined her plans for the weekend. 'I thought Durdle Door tomorrow. We'll have a picnic, weather permitting. Games on the beach.'

Organised fun, irredeemably competitive. That was very Aline.

'Then back here, settle the kids with a movie—'

'And start drinking?'

Aline gave Rob her cat's grin: the same one she had given him in an Edinburgh student bar the night they first met. 'That would be far too dull. I've other plans for the grown-ups, or at least those who are feeling intrepid. Outdoor plans. *Then* dinner, and yes, you can drink.'

Cass sipped her whisky, distaste flickering across her face then vanishing into a polite smile. Nikki looked sceptical.

Michael accepted a generous measure of Laphroaig and looked over it at Aline.

'Sounds interesting. And Sunday?'

How like Michael, too, to want it all mapped out.

'Something local,' Aline said. 'Lazier. Maybe our beach here. But remember, I want you all in posh frocks, or the equivalent, for the evening. That's the third surprise.'

Rob sniffed the Talisker, heady and peaty in his glass, while Michael and Sienna asked the expected questions.

Bloody Aline and her surprises.

They might not see each other as much as they had in their twenties, the regular weekends when he had visited them in London, or hosted them for the Edinburgh Festival, dwindling to the odd drink when he was down for work. They might, if he was honest, have precious little in common nowadays. But Aline had been there in Edinburgh with Sienna and him when they were students. She had lived with them, for Christ's sake. And while she had always been high-handed, she had never been stupid. She had known what it would mean, springing Sienna on him like this.

And Sienna herself, landed among them like a living ghost? What did *she* want from him, from any of them, after years of silence? Years in which she had presumably found a partner, certainly had babies, and now, it seemed, turned up to play catch-up. Just as if they were any old friends.

'I'll never forget you,' she had said, looking like death on the station platform. Had she?

Rob sighed, raising his glass to his mouth. Might as well enjoy it.

~

The whisky dropped in the bottles. Conversation rose and fell and rose again. Nikki went up to her baby, and stayed there. 'She's knackered,' Michael said, as though he was explaining something away.

Aline gave an earth mother smile. 'You don't need to excuse her. We know what it's like.'

'Those *nights*,' Sienna said, tucking pale feet under her long skirts. 'My boobs still hurt thinking about it.'

There was a pause in which Rob tried not to look at her breasts and conspicuously failed. Cass downed what was left in her glass and said, too fast, 'So tell me how you guys met? Rob said it was at uni.'

'Yes,' said Aline. 'Edinburgh. Rob and Michael and I were friends from the start. Sienna was a visiting student one semester. As for Brandon . . .' She looked at her husband, the way she never looked at anyone else. 'I guess I just picked him up along the way.'

'All those years and you're still pals. That's so cool.'

Rob kept his eyes on the bottles. Had Cass emphasised the *all*? It hardly mattered. He was conscious of Sienna shifting in her seat, then settling again. Cass waited as though for a reply, and when none came, she got to her feet. 'I'll go to bed too. It's been a long day.'

She leaned over Rob and kissed him on the mouth. He could taste the Yamazaki she'd been drinking, vanilla and sandalwood. 'See you soon,' she said.

Her feet sounded heavy on the stairs, then across the landing. Aline bit into an apple, poised on the arm of the sofa. 'It's nice to meet her at last. She seems sweet.'

Rob scowled. If Aline hadn't lobbed the real Sienna so unexpectedly back into his life, would he have felt what he did now? Pity and irritation and a deep consciousness that Cass did not fit in here. Would he have noticed that she – like all the others – was just a pastiche version, a cheap imitation of the girl he had lost?

'It's not that serious,' he said. 'Me and her.'

Aline laughed. Her pale hair slipped across his forehead. Her peach nails tightened on his shoulder. 'God, you're a shit.'

Sienna considered them across the fire-tinted bottles, saying nothing. Michael plucked grapes from the bunch and spun the last amber drops round his glass. 'Poor Cass,' he said. Was he being sarcastic? Impossible to tell.

Aline let the words hang, then raised her tumbler to the room. Sienna started to speak, then stopped.

'What?' Aline said.

Sienna's eyes glistened. Her chest rose and fell, full curves under fluid lace. Her skin was so pale that the lamplight seemed to shine through it. Rob had given up trying not to look at her.

'What shall we drink to?' she said.

'The past?' said Brandon, his voice unreadable.

'The future,' said Michael, too loud.

'The future,' said Aline, crystal bright. 'To being together again.'

'The future,' said Rob. He leaned forward, chimed his glass against Sienna's and tipped twelve-year-old Talisker like Lucozade down his throat.

8

Darryl

Edinburgh, 2001

Tuesday 30 October

Working with Gemma is a revelation: what I thought academia would be but it never was until now.

But I should start at the beginning. I walked to George Square with Aline and Michael, who were late for a ten o'clock lecture. I say walked, but in fact we all strode at her take-no-prisoners pace: along the crescent and Argyle Place and a blustery Middle Meadow Walk. The leaves, turning now, were starting to fall. Rob, of course, was still deep asleep, probably with another girl beside him. The current one (*not* Saoirse or Siobhan) has lasted a whole fortnight, but Aline thinks she is on the way out.

Aline has a boyfriend, met last summer and studying in Durham. This much I have learned. She has been down once to see him, and he has been up once, but I had only a glimpse of a heavy-muscled type, sandy-haired and tall enough to walk down the street with his arm around her shoulders. Michael is single. Sometimes I see him looking at Aline and I wonder what he thinks of the boyfriend.

We parted in George Square. I thought of the many times I had made that walk alone and had no ally to shout goodbye to. I got the lift, arrived unflustered, and Gemma Harris smiled as though she were truly pleased to see me. I called her Dr Harris and she said, 'No, please, Gemma is fine.'

I gazed around her cupboard office, no longer crammed with a pregnant professor, and observed the rows of books and notepads, a framed print of the Colosseum and another of Alexandria, the spider plant in a pot and photos tacked to the corkboard above her desk. She had almost made it nice.

'Sit down,' she said, and removed a pile of printouts from the only spare chair. 'Isn't it lovely about Caroline's baby?' I tried to remember if I'd had an email announcing this happy event and decided it was best to pretend that I had.

'Gorgeous name, too,' she said. I made a mental note to track down the possible email later and find out what it was. I still haven't.

'Coffee?'

I nodded, almost too surprised to speak, even though I prefer tea.

She made the coffee in a cafetière she kept on a shelf, going out into the communal kitchen for hot water and milk. While I waited, still in shock at this courtesy, I studied the photographs on the board. Holiday snapshots of a coastline I thought might be Cornwall but could have been Brittany, and more of what was undoubtedly Skye. Venice, the Pyramids, something rainforesty, and a woman who looked like but was not Gemma, holding a toddler. The same child gurning on what appeared to be a specially printed card with a banner headline saying *GOOD LUCK AUNTIE GEM!*

In a frame on the desk, I saw Gemma herself in a green dress, holding hands with a man in shorts and sandals. They wore sunglasses, and the sea behind was a brilliant aquamarine. I felt irrationally deflated.

When she brought in the coffee, my eyes slipped to her hands. Short, unpainted nails. One pretty ring, as she passed me the mug, but it was on her right hand. She raised the other one, unadorned, and pushed her hair behind her ears. I looked down at my cup.

I was there for two hours, during which my doubts about her inexperience erased themselves and were replaced with exhilaration. It could have been the coffee, inflating me with caffeine, but it was more than that too. Her comments were pertinent, positive. She understood what I had wanted to do, what I *want* to do. Every detail of my chapter was pored over until I wondered how many times she had read it. For the first time in almost a year, I felt that the PhD might not have been a mistake.

Gaining courage, I asked her before I left if she liked Edinburgh. She said she loved it. 'So beautiful. So friendly. I can't get over my luck in landing this post.'

So friendly. That had not, until recently, been my own experience. I asked where she was living, and she said, 'We're renting a place in Stockbridge. It's gorgeous.'

I registered the *we*, which I had half expected, with an internal sigh. I reminded myself that I had Phyllis.

At the open door she asked, 'Any plans for Halloween?' I told her I didn't know but would probably do something with friends. She smiled and I smiled back: two normal, sociable people, discussing their lives.

Wednesday 31 October

Another unexpected evening.

Whatever I told Gemma, I had no plans for Halloween. I never do. We sit together at the back of the flat, lights off at the front. Phyllis is afraid of the guisers, even though (or perhaps because) they are children. I am not afraid exactly, but I never know what they will want.

Tonight, though, it was different. I saw Rob on the street in the late afternoon and suggested chess. He said he couldn't because they were going out. Then he looked back, two strides ahead of me, and said, 'Why not come too?'

'Me?'

'No, Hugh fucking Grant.' He stopped, waiting for me to catch up. 'Of course you. Wear walking shoes and something warm. Make it a costume if you like. Do you have a head torch?' I shook my head. The words were so uncharacteristically efficient that I wondered if he was quoting one of the others, and what he said next seemed to confirm it. 'Oh well, Aline probably has a spare.'

'OK,' I said. 'Thanks.'

I have very few clothes, and those I do have are almost all the same. In the end, I found a pair of jogging bottoms that had belonged to my father and a fleece I had worn at school. I put on trainers, also from school days.

'Don't,' I told Phyllis, eyeing me from the bed. 'Don't say anything.'

She didn't, but she was angry. Three times this week I have found her there with her face in the pillow, radiating fierce sorrow. Each time, I wanted to shake her, tell her I'm allowed my own life, but I didn't dare.

I was ready long before they knocked for me. They were all also in outdoor clothes, though Aline had her face painted like a cat and Michael as a ghoul. Rob was a skull: deep hollows and shaded white, incredibly convincing, above a blood-red scarf. I gestured to my bare skin with a sound of disappointment. 'I'm sorry,' I said. 'I should have . . .'

But what should I have done? Gone out and got myself face paints, created some grotesque masterpiece – or, more impossible still, persuaded Phyllis to do it – all in the half-hour that Rob had given me?

Aline smiled. 'Don't worry,' she said. 'Give me a moment.'

She was back in their flat before I could protest, then out again with a plastic box containing circles of waxy colour. She stood before me in the light of the hall, as tall as I am, a fine brush in her long fingers. Her cat face was only inches from mine, still strangely magnetic with its white teeth nipping red lips. I felt her power to change everything.

'Close your eyes,' she said. The brush flicked across my forehead, my cheek, my chin. 'There,' she said, minutes later. 'Perfect.'

I went inside to look at the bathroom mirror, while she returned the paints to their flat. She had drawn a spider's web, stretched black and silver, across the left half of my face. The spider squatted, black and red and sinister, on my right cheekbone.

We walked fast through the streets, evading gaggles of small witches and skeletons, crossing Marchmont, then Newington. 'Where are we going?' I asked, and Michael said, 'Can't you tell? Arthur's Seat.'

'We could have gone up next week to watch the fireworks,' said Aline, 'but everyone does that.'

It was the strangest experience. I know Arthur's Seat. I often went up it as a child: my father and mother first carrying, then persuading, finally following us up. I have hiked it alone since. I have made a study of its geology: the ash and basalt, the sandstone and dolerite. I have learned to revere it as a pinnacle in the history of science, the living (or dead?) lab in which James Hutton, one of this city's finest sons, worked his geological wonders. But being there in the dark, with these transformative new players in my life, I felt that I had never known it at all. The steps, ill-lit by torchlight. The lights of the city, further and further below, and the darkness, all-consuming, making the familiar strange. The last, scrambly summit, finding holds by touch and torchlight, feeling the rock cold and sharp and steep on my chill fingers.

At the top, I looked round at their faces, at once macabre and striking, head torches bizarre above the face paint. We switched them off and stood there a while with only the lighted windows like yellow dots below and the thin moon to tell us where reality was. Rob dug in his pocket, fished out a metal water bottle, swigged, and passed it round. At my turn, I nearly choked, for he had filled it with whisky.

My mouth and throat burned. Tears started in my eyes. But the stinging passed and then there was only a hot glow, pressing out my chest and running through tired arteries to the tips of my fingers and my toes, which were already numb in the old shoes.

I thought of the past. I looked at the shadows who were now my friends and felt a fine strand of optimism weaving into my heart. I thought of Gemma Harris, whom I will see again in a few weeks' time. I tried not to think of Phyllis.

I washed my face, three times over, before I let her see me.

9

Michael

Dorset, 2019

Michael stood with his son on his chest, watching the light. He looked down through oak and ash and sycamore to the tilted roof of Aline's house. Beyond, the sea was a pale line, fluorescent-edged in the silver dawn. He dipped his head and kissed Rufus's woollen cap. He smelled normality, milk and lavender oil.

'You little horror,' he whispered. 'You sleep *now*.' He heard the baby snoring: tiny rising snuffles, like a mouse. He remembered Nikki in the double bed, head gripped between shaking hands, whimpering for rest. He drank in the stillness, the cool, clean air, heard the impatient call of an early chiffchaff. Then he heard footsteps on the damp ground, and a voice beside him.

'*If I have seen one thing, It is the passing preciousness of dreams.*'

Sienna. It had to be Sienna, and it was her, in a mossy shawl and Aline's Dubarrys. Michael had forgotten her habit of throwing quotations at any occasion that seemed to her appropriate. In her unembarrassed Californian, it was almost endearing.

He looked the question.

'Thomas Hardy,' she said.

'Still the literature major?'

'Still the bookworm. And this is Hardy country.'

Michael twisted his neck. It crunched horribly. He looked up the tree-lined track and thought of the rolling hills beyond. 'I suppose it is,' he said. He had never studied Hardy, somehow. 'I always think of him as inland. Bog and heath and depression.'

Sienna laughed. 'Not always. He wrote a poem about Swanage. The luminous spray and standing there holding hands with his wife. It's kinda lovely.'

She stopped. Her face, still rosy, was careworn, and she breathed as though she had been prescribed it. Rufus jerked his arm from the sling, rearing up his head. Michael glanced at Sienna. He had always liked her, but disquiet seemed to wrap itself about her now, about them both, insidious as the morning mist. Again he wondered why she had come, but it seemed too intrusive to ask.

Instead he said, 'How does it feel to be back?'

She hugged the shawl closer; the trees throwing spiky shadows on her pale face. She moved her lips, but said nothing. After a long moment, she spoke on an unconvincing laugh. 'Strange.'

'I missed you too,' he said, as though it had been one continued conversation from the night before. 'I understood why you left, but I missed you.'

I understood.

She froze, just an instant. Rufus stirred again, half squawking, then settled. Michael said, 'I was afraid we'd never see you again.'

She smiled rather sadly. 'That's what I thought too. I thought I had a whole new life.' She'd told them about that new life last night. Her work for an NGO supporting refugees, low-paid but rewarding. Her 'hippy liberal' life choices (her phrase, half mocking, half not). Of her marriage, she had said little. Only that her husband was a human rights lawyer and a 'wonderful person'. He had wondered at her reticence last night: she, who had always been so open.

He heard her words again. *I thought I had.*

'Sienna,' he said. 'Are you OK?'

She turned from the silvery horizon and looked him full in the face. 'Not really,' she said. 'But I'm not ready to talk about it yet.'

He nodded. She leaned her copper head against him, so close that he could see the first grey hairs threading through. He wanted to ask what had changed, whether anything had happened to force the past onto her. Instead, he stroked her back, as though she were Chloe.

'Thank you,' she said, at last.

As they walked on, she reached out, touching Rufus's clear cheek with pale fingers. 'He's so adorable. My girls are with Milly.' She paused, finding her smile again. 'Aline really is the hostess with the mostest, isn't she?'

He said, carefully casual, 'Do you think she's changed?'

Sienna gave him a look. 'She's matured along exactly the trajectory I would have expected. Nikki is lovely,' she added. 'I'm so glad you found her.'

'Yes,' he said. 'I'm very lucky.'

'It's good that you're happy,' she said, at last.

'Thank you.' He waited a long moment, moving past the whispering trees. 'Sienna?'

She turned from the rising green to the path in front of them. 'Yes?'

'Did you come back for Rob?'

She spoke when they were almost back on the pale gravel of the drive, and he had thought she would not reply. 'I'd be an idiot,' she said, 'if I had.'

He crunched across the drive, pushed open the door and let her through in front of him, reflecting that this, in fact, was no answer at all.

There was a photo montage on the wall of the landing, framed in pale wood. Michael stopped, stared at Aline on her wedding day, fair as an angel, with diamonds in her hair. At her flushed and triumphant with a newborn Jimmy, flanked by Brandon and toddler Lexie. Michael had taken that photo. Then he had left them, taken the Tube across London and got drunk alone in his flat. He could still taste the cheap gin and the despair.

Two weeks later, he'd been dragged to a colleague's brother's house party in Clapham, only to spend all evening on a sofa beside a girl with humorous eyes, a blue top and a bottle of tequila. He'd drunk the tequila, or most of it, and the next morning he had woken up beside her. The woman had been Nikki.

10

Darryl

Edinburgh, 2001

Monday 26 November

Rob's latest is called Melissa. She's blonde and attractive but in exactly the opposite way to Aline – plump and unintimidating – and prone to hanging around the flat at all hours. Sunday has become our chess night, and she turned up to watch yesterday, fiddling with her turquoise nails, alternatively offering facile opinions on the war in Afghanistan and asking us questions.

I was annoyed. Rob was playing well and I needed my head clear. Still, she is always friendly to me, so I tried not to show it. He mostly ignored her.

Today, on the way to George Square, I asked Aline if she thought it was serious between them. She laughed as if I'd made a joke, so I tried to look as though I'd meant it that way.

'Yeah, right,' she said. After a while, she added, almost seriously, 'Still, it might outlast me and Johnno.' Johnno is the beefy Durham boyfriend.

I was surprised. I glanced sideways at her faultless profile, topped now with a striped bobble hat. Then I looked away to the trees that were barer by the day, the students and workers hurrying up Middle Meadow Walk. She'd never confided in me like that before. I don't think anyone had. I didn't know the script.

I said nothing, but she replied as if I had. 'It's just, you know, not quite right.'

I didn't know.

'I'll give it until Christmas,' she said. 'Then I'll decide. There's no point in wasting time, is there? His or mine.' I agreed that there was not. I thought of the fraught silences at home and envied Aline her clarity.

As we turned into George Square, she looked me up and down: a friendly, interested glance. 'You're looking smart, Darryl. Going somewhere special?'

I was wearing a long wool coat I'd found in a charity shop and a tartan scarf that had been my father's. I tugged at the scarf, hiding my gratified smile. 'Thank you,' I said, 'but I'm only seeing my supervisor.'

'This is excellent,' said Gemma.

I glowed.

She didn't look especially smart, but she did look lovely in faded jeans and a burgundy sweater that I think was cashmere, sitting snugly on her slight form. Her hair has grown a little since I first met her, and she wore it in a ponytail today. She leafed through the printout, indicating sections she'd marked with stars.

'You should think about working these bits up into a journal article. You can't think too soon about getting published.'

She hadn't commented on the coat or scarf, but this was much better. I studied her soft smile and decided I had wronged her in seeing a likeness to Phyllis, whose resting expression lies somewhere between resentment and animosity, and who – increasingly – only drags me down.

I said at once that I would write the paper before Christmas. 'Will you read it for me?'

'Of course.'

Later, when I had my chapter in my bag with all her careful notes on it, she asked if I had considered tutoring next semester. 'It's good experience,' she said. 'Important for the academic CV.'

I visualised a room full of undergraduates, as clever as Aline and as scathing about their unfortunate instructors as Rob invariably was. 'I don't think I would be very good at it.'

'I'm sure you'd be great. And you won't know until you try.'

I knew. But I didn't want to refuse her. 'I guess I could do with the money.'

She nodded. She had my student profile on the computer screen now, and was scrolling through it. I felt a brief, unreasoning panic at what she might find there. 'I did see that you're self-funded. That can be tough.'

'I inherited some money from my parents, a while ago. It won't last forever, but it's just about enough for now.' I decided not to mention how much I had used up already, the lost years barely leaving my flat, living on their money, before I stumbled back into education.'

'I'm so sorry.' She really sounded it. 'Sorry you lost your parents.'

'Thank you. It was a long time ago.'

Eleven and a half years. Is that long? 'They were killed in a car crash.' I swallowed, dragged out the rest. 'My sister was with them.'

'My God.' Her eyes were huge: full of sympathy. 'You must have been very young.'

'I was fifteen.'

'What happened to you?'

'I was sent to Mum's cousin in New Zealand. I stayed six months, then came back here.'

Full stop. New sentence. And everything that mattered in the space in between.

My mother's cousin lived with her family in what must once have been a town in its own right but was now a carbuncle on the edge of Auckland. They had a white house in a row of other houses, with space around the sides, picket fences and a small, very green garden. They had two teenagers who were between one and two years older than me. 'Irish twins,' their mother regularly said, with a laugh that was half smug and half rueful.

That first evening, when my body still thought it was morning – or no time at all, because I had been lost in my dark grief and the artificial light of the flight – those kids seemed like creatures from another planet. For long after, I was awed by their tall, leonine glory. And yet if I try to put it on paper, I cannot capture what it was that made them at once so unsettling and so irresistible. I can say only that they had tawny hair, deep tans, and yellow flecks in their eyes. And that, once written down, seems like nothing at all. Perhaps it is closer to the truth to say that they, like Aline, were impossibly confident, and I was not.

They hugged me when I arrived, one after the other. The boy patted me on the back, said, 'I'm so sorry, bro.' The girl held me longer.

'You'll be all right,' she said. 'You'll be happy here.'

I felt the warmth of her. I smelled coffee and jasmine and thought that I would be, *must* be, happy if I could have them for my friends. The very thought, at the time, felt like a betrayal.

I remembered all this with a shiver as I trudged down many stairs and out of the building, my face flayed by the furious wind that seems always to channel through George Square. Then I spotted Michael and Rob emerging from the library, and hurried to catch up with them.

Rob greeted me with what at least passed for pleasure, Michael with more subdued politeness. I matched my pace to theirs, pushing away the past, catching ends of sentences. 'What are you planning?'

'A Christmas party,' Rob said. 'It was Aline's idea.'

Michael cut in, too quick and too loud. 'It's only a thought. Nothing definite.'

Discomfort clouded me, fed by memory. Aline is always definite. We crossed the cobbles in silence, until Rob veered off northwards. 'I have to meet Melissa,' he said, without enthusiasm.

I considered Michael as we progressed unspeaking into the Meadows. I am considering him still. He is neither as relaxed as Rob nor as extrovert as Aline. I have been sorry for him, because of what I am increasingly sure he feels for her, but now I am inclined to save my pity. He looked at me today as though he saw a different Darryl from the one Rob and Aline interact with, and did not trust what he saw.

I want to say he observes less than them, but perhaps it is more.

Wednesday 28 November

I caught Aline on the landing while she laced up her running shoes. 'I heard you're planning a party.'

She nodded, still looking at her feet. 'A week Friday,' she said. 'You should come.'

I said I'd love to. I went into my flat and told Phyllis that I would be going. She sulked all afternoon.

11

Aline

Dorset, 2019

By day, the windows dominated the room, so it seemed all sky and sea. Brandon stood by the high panes, bouncing Rufus in his arms. Beside them, Nikki was looking over the edge. 'What's down there?'

'Crag. Earth. Plants. Boulders. Eventually the beach.' Brandon grinned, as though he loved it all: clay and stone and wildlife together. Aline smiled too, because she had given all this to him. Nikki flinched, full (no doubt) of imagined disaster. Sienna turned in her chair, until she stared outwards through the shining glass.

'It's incredible,' she said. 'The sky and the sea, just *there*. But it must be terrifying in a storm.'

'It's exciting,' said Aline.

Nikki shivered. 'It gives me vertigo.'

Aline resisted the urge to roll her eyes. 'Sit,' she said. 'Eat while you can.' She covered irritation with largesse: croissants straight from the oven, orange juice that surged from a glinting machine, fresh-brewed coffee with beans that she ordered in, whole, to her London house.

'This is lovely,' Nikki said, without emphasis. 'Thank you so much.'

Aline sighed. She had wanted to be close to Michael's wife. If she was honest, she could have done with a female friend who was *really* a friend: neither fawning colleague nor obviously jealous school mum. She had her sister, of course, but Clara had her own life, in another city. And at first, Nikki had seemed to fit the bill.

She had come into their lives nearly eleven years ago, when Jimmy was tiny and Lexie a wheat-haired toddler, and Aline had long since got used to thinking of Michael as permanently, disconsolately single. He had had girlfriends over the years, but never for long. They hadn't blazed out in a messy tumult of infidelity (his) and tearful rages (theirs), like Rob's did; they had simply fizzled into nothing, as though neither party could be bothered keeping the relationship going.

Nikki had been different, right from the start. They had been holding hands like teenagers the first time he brought her to visit, but it wasn't just that. He had been faintly defiant, but obviously happy. She had been warm, a little shy, admiring and enthusiastic about house and children alike. She had watched Michael, smiling, as he read *Meg and Mog* to Lexie.

'I think this one might last,' Brandon had said, after they had gone. 'I hope it does.' He had been holding Jimmy against his chest, just as he was holding Rufus now, watching Michael and Nikki from the window. Lexie had been making a tower of cushions, then pushing them to the floor.

'Perhaps,' Aline had said. 'She seems nice, and it's time he got over me. Now, what are you smiling at?'

'At you. Being you.'

She had kissed him hard on the mouth, while Jimmy kicked his little legs into both of their chests. 'After all,' she had said, 'he and I were never even a couple.'

'Perhaps that's why he didn't get over you,' Brandon had said, with the grin that always made her want to punch him, or screw him. Or both.

Now, she contemplated this woman who was still officially her friend but had never made her feel like it, and wondered what, despite her own efforts, had gone wrong. Then she discarded regret. She had Milly now, half extra daughter, half lifesaver. She might even have Sienna too, though that remained to be seen. Perhaps Nikki had been jealous. Perhaps she still was. After all, who could blame her?

Aline piled extra croissants into an earthenware bowl, hot and buttery and smelling of mornings on Alpine ski holidays. 'I've been longing to share this place with you all,' she said. 'Make it a real celebration. It's been such a labour of love.'

Rob, hung-over, was acerbic. 'A labour of money, don't you mean? I wouldn't have recognised it. Would you, Mike?' And to Aline, 'You've ripped everything out. Your gran must be turning in her grave.'

Aline dropped the smile. 'Granny was cremated.' Her grandmother never lived in the past. She would have expected Aline to do what she wanted with the house. And what the hell did Rob know, with his squalid single man's flat in Edinburgh and the endless stream of meaningless women who were never permitted to share it?

Nikki frowned at Michael. 'You've been here before?'

Michael shrugged, as though pretending it didn't matter. Milly appeared through the back door, a welcome distraction, looking for Lexie's coat. Brandon got up to help her.

'When you're done eating,' Aline said, 'I'll show you the garden.'

But Nikki, who claimed to love gardening, was still interrogating Michael. '*When* were you here?'

'One university summer,' he said, as though he didn't know the year. 'We stayed with Aline's gran.'

'Why didn't you tell me?'

'I guess it never came up.'

The moment hovered on the edge of awkwardness. Milly emerged triumphant from under a sofa cushion, wielding Lexie's down jacket, and made for the back door. Rob, with some smugness, pointed out a thin crack in the otherwise pristine plasterwork, winding above the window.

Bloody decorators. They'd cost a fortune, and they'd sworn that wouldn't happen.

Nikki took another croissant, still frowning, and reached for the jam.

The garden was sheltered on the inland side of the house, edged by high stone walls and the sloping hill behind. The rose bushes, unpruned for years, were now a tangle of prickly stems and red and green buds, fighting weeds.

Daffodils, superseding the last of the snowdrops, seemed scattered all about with no attempt at order. The paths were almost completely overgrown, the wet grass as long as Lexie's hair.

At the far end, the children played hide-and-seek, just as Aline had played it with Clara and their cousins. The morning sun, peeping through new leaves, cast bright patches onto Lexie's flaxen ponytail, Chloe's jacaranda curls and Milly's silk-dark head.

Nikki said wonderingly, 'It's like they're in a painting. A Monet.'

Aline said, 'It was lovely once, but it got too much for Granny in the end. I've got a landscaper coming in next time we're down.'

Nikki said, 'I think it's beautiful now.'

Michael took her hand. Sienna gave an exaggerated squawk. 'Aline, you can't landscape this. Where's your soul? It's a painter's garden, like Nikki says. Or a poet's. It's perfect.'

Aline rolled her eyes. Michael said, 'Oh Sen, you haven't changed.'

Rob gave Sienna a long look, as though he too found her unaltered. Cass turned away from them, examining a patch of campanula on the stone wall. Nikki reached out her free hand like a child in a sweet shop, until she was almost touching the pink bud of an apple tree.

Along the garden, Lexie was now high in another tree, stepping airily from it to the top of the stone wall. That girl would climb anything. Jimmy was on one of the lower branches, lying flat, while Milly held Chloe in her arms, eyes closed, counting aloud. Aline said, lightly, 'I never had you down as a gardener, Sienna. But you must tell me about yours, in California. Give me some inspiration.'

As a jibe, it was far more effective than she could have imagined. Sienna's pale face spread briefly pink, then white again. 'I don't have one,' she said. 'Not now. I don't even have a home, to speak of.'

'What do you mean?'

Sienna's eyes were clear, almost defiant. 'I've left my husband.'

Nikki let her hand fall from the apple bud. Aline glanced once at Rob, then away. Michael and Brandon made sounds of mumbled condolence.

'The children don't know,' Sienna said. 'Not yet. It's very new.'

Aline put an arm around her. 'Come and look round,' she said. 'Then we'll show you one of our more spectacular Dorset beaches. It's bliss to have you here.'

Sienna accepted the caress. Nikki watched them, absently plucking dead daffodil heads from their stems. Brandon was frowning. Aline turned from him, from them both, and tugged Sienna towards the trees.

Which of them? Which couldn't she trust?

12

Darryl

Edinburgh, 2001

Saturday 8 December

I write this with a cup of tea, strong and milky and soothing. The thin winter sun is illuminating the kitchen and Phyllis is cross and quiet in the back bedroom. Next door, no doubt, they are all sleeping. I wonder if Melissa is still tear-stained, lumpen-faced, as she was last night, or whether Rob has cajoled her into a temporary, satiated contentment. I wonder when Aline will get up, stretch long limbs and run round the Meadows. One steady foot ahead of the other, until she clears the last vestiges of alcohol from her athlete's body.

When it came to the point, I was nervous about the party. Perhaps this was unsurprising, given my experience of social occasions, but the result – ill-advised and also predictable – was that I drank too much. I remember it all, but not as one smooth, consecutive sequence. I remember knocking at the door, holding my bottle of adequate-but-not-too-good wine, and forcing myself not to disappear straight back into my own flat. Only the thought of Phyllis's triumphant eyes kept me there until a stranger opened it and waved me in.

I remember many undergraduates, young and drunk, squeezed into a space that was like my flat, but also not like it. I remember posters on the wall, Pulp and Radiohead and Le Chat Noir, and Jack Vettriano prints that must have been the landlady's because they were in frames. I remember the queue for the bathroom and music impossibly loud. I remember gaggles of them trooping downstairs to smoke in the shared garden, or leaning, like Rob does, out of half-open windows.

I remember Aline in a coral dress and Michael and Rob in Christmas jumpers. I remember Rob dancing with a black girl in a silver top and Melissa crying in a corner. I heard her tell Michael, 'I don't know why I put up with him,' and Aline, passing by with a jug of mulled wine, saying, 'I don't know either.'

I remember the smell of orange and spice and the smoke that didn't all float outside, and the kitchen so full of people that I could hardly get into it. I remember how fast and loud they spoke, and how they all seemed to know each other. In the other room, there were piles of books in corners and couples kissing on the sofa and two girls with tinsel earrings telling me to get up and dance. I remember Michael watching Aline when he thought himself unseen.

I squeezed in beside him. 'Johnno not here?'

He shook his head, not looking at me. Across the room, Aline was dancing with a brunette with stars on her top and heavy bangles on her wrists. They were both laughing. I thought about what she had told me last month, and wondered whether Michael knew it too. But I didn't break her confidence. Even if I'd wanted to, he didn't deserve it. He hadn't wanted me there.

Later – at least I think it was later – Rob shared the dregs of a bottle of cheap whisky with me and we had a conversation that I remember, unfortunately, all too clearly.

He was talking of Melissa, with disjointed dissatisfaction. 'She wants me to be serious.' He regarded me, blurry-eyed, over his mug of whisky. 'But I'm not, Darryl. I'm not like that. Why doesn't she understand?'

'You're serious about chess,' I offered.

'And music.'

'But not her?'

'Not any of them. Not yet.' He downed the whisky. 'God, that's rank. Maybe not ever.'

I looked about for Melissa, who had been wearing a distinctive (because too tight) crimson top and a tinsel crown. 'Where is she?'

'In my bedroom.' Rob exhaled heavily. 'Sulking.'

I laughed. The horrible whisky was already heating my veins. 'Sounds like Phyllis,' I said.

Rob looked surprised and, briefly, interested. 'I didn't know you had a girlfriend.'

My face was burning. I would have done almost anything to swallow the words. I said, 'Yes, well . . . It's complicated.'

I grimaced, though it was meant to be a smile. Rob laughed. 'Isn't it always?' He raised his mug, then seemed to realise it was empty and abandoned it on the windowsill.

'Well, I'll have to make it up with her,' he said, 'if I want any sleep.'

When I got home, I pulled Phyllis up from where she lay, face down and resentful in the spare bed. I examined her face in the overhead light: wide eyes deliberately dull, hair that was almost like Gemma's but in need of a brush.

'I told someone about you.'

Well, that was stupid.

I took a clump of hair and pulled it so hard that her whole head jerked towards me. I wanted her to cry out, but she didn't. It was me who cried, dropping to my knees before her, telling her how sorry I was. And all that time she watched me, not lifting a finger to repair the damage, because she knew that would make me feel worse.

There is one comfort: it was Rob I told, who will care little and may even have forgotten it, given how drunk he was. Aline would have been harder to fob off.

I will have more tea and try not to think about it.

13

Sienna

Dorset, 2019

The beach was draped with slow drizzle. Sienna's daughters, California-bred, quivered in their new winter jackets. Sienna stood in a borrowed Burberry and her own dampening trainers, their hands in hers, staring at the improbable rocky arch of Durdle Door.

'Impressive, isn't it?'

She turned, smiling, to Brandon. The word was both appropriate and inadequate. She thought of Hardy, sheep teeming over a precipice. She thought of herself, teetering on one. She thought of Aline's house with its glass wall; the ground dropping sharp and sudden to the shifting sea. She thought of the moment last night when the five of them had been alone and she could have said what she had come to say, but had not dared. She heard Aline's voice, clear and imperious, carrying across sand and breeze.

'Come on! Before we get cold.'

Along the shore, she, Lexie and Jimmy were hauling bat and ball and posts from a big bag, setting up for rounders. Brandon rolled his eyes, then jogged towards them. 'Take your time,' he called back to Sienna. His laugh carried, faintly dry, on the salt breeze. 'We don't have to do everything she says, you know.'

Sienna considered these words, wondering if they were true. Astrid tugged at her hand. 'Mama! Can we go?'

Sienna looked down at her daughter. Eyes wide open, freckles patterning her soft brown skin. 'Of course,' she said. Astrid ran, towing her twin after her, small feet sure on the brittle ground. Sienna called after her, 'But no going in the sea.'

The waves were half-height, cresting and rolling. Californian surfers would have despised them, but they seemed fierce enough to Sienna on this inclement day. And they were: Brandon had warned them repeatedly about the rip tide. She shivered, hugging Aline's coat tighter around her.

'You always wanted kids.'

Sienna jumped. Rob was beside her, his gaze following her racing children. She turned her head and saw Nikki and Cass still staring out to the arch, the rest now pressing posts into the ground. Out of earshot.

'Well, aren't I lucky?' she said. 'I got what I wanted.'

Rob hadn't wanted kids, or had said not, but they had been too young then for it to matter much. Besides, she had understood. He had told her little of his own childhood, even in the months when they had been inseparable, and those few facts had emerged reluctantly, each cajoled out of him like a stuck pearl. But they had been enough for Sienna

70

to construct an image that was probably not so far from the truth. A clever, lonely boy, playing pawn in an endless game between a disinterested father and a possessive mother. A game no one, least of all him, could win.

Had he changed his mind about children in the intervening years? She couldn't know.

He said, 'I'm glad Aline organised this weekend. I'm glad she found you.'

'I found her.' The words were automatic: a smokescreen. She thought, *Am I glad? I'm not sure.*

They walked together towards the shore. She told herself, *Think of your children. Think of what brought you here.* Because whatever Michael thought, it wasn't Rob. *Think of the beach. Think of Hardy, and the sea.* Underfoot, the ground seemed halfway between sand and stone and shell, flecked with dying brown seaweed. Ahead, Aline was marking out bowler's and batter's squares with sticks.

Rob said, 'I thought about looking you up myself. I thought about it a lot, over the years.'

Sienna abandoned Hardy and thought instead of *Persuasion* and Captain Wentworth. A handsome head among flowers and candles in a Bath drawing room. *If I had then written to you* . . . She almost laughed. At the comparison, and at herself for making it.

Rob said, 'Only I didn't know how you would react.'

Would I! That was how Anne Elliot had responded, wishing away years of separation, revealing a heart unequivocally devoted. But the scenarios were, in all other respects, entirely unalike.

The sea rolled and dropped, the sound rising and falling so it seemed to fill her whole consciousness. Water turquoise grey and the foam impossibly white. She used to imagine she would fall in love with a man like Frederick Wentworth. Handsome, honourable, brave. Easily her favourite Austen hero. Yet when she had married one, she had not made it work. And here she was again, playing guessing games with a man who, for whatever reason, was none of those things.

Ten minutes later, Aline had them all collected for rounders as efficiently as she had once organised lethargic students to run races in the Meadows, or hike up Arthur's Seat.

'I'll watch.' Nikki had Rufus in the sling on her front. She stroked his head in its woolly hat, like a talisman. Milly coaxed Chloe away along the beach, collecting stones. Aline divided the rest into two teams. Herself, Lexie, Michael, Rob, Astrid; and Brandon, Jimmy, Sienna, Cass and Luna.

Brandon asked Cass, 'Have you played before?'

'Rounders? Never.'

Aline smirked. 'We'll go easy on you.'

'She's lying,' Lexie said. 'She never goes easy on anyone.'

Aline made a mock swipe at her daughter's head. Sienna took Luna's hand. 'Just do your best, honey. If you don't enjoy it, you can always stop.'

Beside them, Jimmy looked astonished. Brandon laughed.

From her post, Sienna watched him bowl with calm efficiency. She watched the growing waves and the implacable rock arch. Walkers paused to stare. She could have been in the Meadows again, part of a group that was always the centre of attention. But that was because of Aline, not her. She watched Jimmy, all anxious concentration, trying to cover both the backstop and the fourth post; the batters flying from post to post; Astrid standing very still with her small hands tight on the bat.

Don't let her get out first. Funny how she minded these things for her children, and couldn't care less for herself.

'Christ,' Rob said. 'I could do with a cigarette.' He had stopped at her post, stripped off his jacket.

'I thought you'd never quit.'

They had fought about it, time after time, in those months when they were all in all to each other. 'I won't let you kill yourself,' she had shouted, holding the packet from him, making as if to throw it from the top-floor window of his Marchmont flat. 'I love you, you idiot. I need you to stay alive.' How had it been possible to be so sure?

Rob shrugged. 'I guess I grew up.'

The twins played respectably; Sienna herself abysmally. A marauding dog caught the ball and they had an enforced break while the embarrassed owner chased it, fell over, got up, wrestled the ball back and returned it, still dribble-coated, to Brandon. Glancing sideways, Sienna saw Rob creased with laughter, and felt the years slip away.

They stopped for water, then swapped sides, while Milly and Chloe made an elaborate pattern of their stones.

Michael smiled reassuringly at Cass. She smiled back – looking suddenly very young – and hit the ball almost casually, as though she barely noticed. It flew fast and smooth and straight, halfway to the curved rock of the arch.

'Jesus,' Brandon said.

Cass jogged round the posts, still grinning. Her next go, Rob tried for a catch, missed the ball and ran swearing after it. Cass was round again before he could get it to the post. Then Jimmy, distracted, hit wide. The ball sailed out on a high diagonal, into the sea.

Aline glared. Brandon laughed. 'It was always going to happen.'

Sienna only half attended. She was watching Rob, still rumpled and faintly sulky, at the edge of the fielders. But Luna, seeing what the rest hadn't, cried aloud. Sienna swung round, following her terrified gaze. The waves were higher now, crashing down on sand and stone, and Astrid, the nearest fielder, had run straight into them, after the vanished ball.

It happened in less than a minute, but felt infinitely longer. Sienna heard herself yelling, and saw Astrid not hearing, the foam at her waist now. She ran forward, stumbling, with the shingle tugging at her feet. Behind, she could hear the others moving and shouting and all the time her mind revolved between numbed, relentless logic and desperate guilt. How far out had Brandon said it was before the tide got you? How *could* she not have been watching? Astrid turned, at last, to come back. Sienna half breathed. Then a wave hit the child and she vanished under the churning water. Sienna screamed, high as the gulls above them.

And then suddenly, miraculously, Milly was there, ahead of Sienna. She caught Astrid by the hand, then under both arms. A moment later, she had her up and through the boiling foam safe onto wet shingle. And Sienna herself, crying now, wrapped them both wet and shaking in her arms.

For the rest, the incident was over, and easily dismissed. Milly and Astrid were bundled into a motley collection of waterproof trousers and other people's jumpers, then fed hot chocolate from a flask. 'It's a good job we brought you this weekend,' Aline told Milly, with an arm round her thin shoulders. 'But I knew that already.'

Astrid wriggled out of her mother's arms, demanding to keep on playing. Brandon's team won the game, or rather, Cass won for them. Jimmy did a victory dance. Lexie hit him and was told off. Afterwards, yanking posts from the ground with unnecessary fervour, Aline said to Cass, 'You said you didn't play.'

'I *have* never played rounders. I was in my university cricket team.'

Sienna shivered, barely listening. She hated the sea. She hated herself.

14

Darryl

Edinburgh, 2001

Tuesday 18 December

I spent all this morning looking for a Christmas present for Gemma, and found it at last in a little shop on Morningside Road. A tiny painting of the beach at Portobello, square and framed in driftwood. Just the row of wooden posts, the sand and sea, a hint of clouds in the sky, and a woman in a white dress, barely outlined, at the shoreline. Something about that woman – the slim form, the sense of quiet content – made me think of her.

It was expensive, but she's worth it.

I walked back up the road, smiling for once at the Christmas lights, the windows full of cards and trees and gifts. In the post office, I bought green tissue paper, red ribbon, a pack of gold-edged gift tags, and Sellotape. It has been so many years since I gave anyone a present that I have almost forgotten what to do. Last of all, I saw a silver trinket on a chain in a charity shop and decided, on a whim, to buy it for Phyllis. We don't usually do Christmas gifts. We barely celebrate at all. But she still hasn't forgiven me for the party, and the holidays will be long enough without her being angry.

The staircase felt quiet when I came home. The building has several student flats and they have mostly left for Christmas. Michael's dad collected him on Sunday and they dropped Aline at a station somewhere on the way. Michael looked so smugly proprietorial as he opened the car door for her that I wanted to open my window and call down to him, 'She's not yours, you know. I doubt she ever will be.' Of course, I didn't.

Rob left yesterday after his last exam, thumping on my door to say goodbye. 'I'll miss you guys,' I said.

'Bollocks. You'll enjoy the peace.'

I was afraid he would mention Phyllis, but he went off with his giant backpack and a cigarette already in his hand, as though he had other things on his mind. I wonder what his family is like.

Today, I shut myself in the study to wrap the presents. There was enough paper left over from Gemma's to do Phyllis's too, and a spare tag. No ribbon, though. I hid Gemma's in my bag for tomorrow and carried Phyllis's through rather ostentatiously to the sitting room. We have no tree, so after some thought I put it on the mantelpiece beside my mother's china ducks and the three cards I've had this year. One from the postman, no doubt wanting a tip, and two unusual, exciting ones. An abstract picture of a Christmas tree, nominally from Aline, Rob and Michael but all written in her flamboyant blue cursive, with two kisses after the names, and a snowy mountain scene from Gemma, without kisses but with a longer message wishing me a lovely Christmas and a 'happy and productive' 2002. Nothing from New Zealand, where my only remaining family live. But that was to be expected.

It was Gemma's card, presented at our supervision last week, that made me decide on getting her a gift. I picked it up and read it again, then settled it tenderly beside Aline's. Maybe I'll do something this Christmas, even if it is just Phyllis and me. Get a turkey crown, or even a chicken. I could stretch to a plum pudding, a special bottle of wine. For the first time in years, I feel like I deserve it.

Wednesday 19 December

Gemma had a student with her, so I waited on the plastic chair outside her office, beside shelves of books no one wanted, union posters, and notices of long-past events. When she invited me in, she looked surprised and a little tired, but gave me her habitual smile.

'Don't worry,' I said. 'I'm not complaining about anything.'

I had wanted to make a joke, separate myself from the undergraduates who had, no doubt, brought the strained look to her sweet face. But she only looked baffled, so I added quickly, 'I just came to drop this off.'

The moment was not as I had planned. I held out the green and red parcel. She half stood, then sank down again, receiving it into her hands. 'Oh Darryl, how kind. But you really shouldn't have.'

'It's to thank you for all your help.'

'I've just been doing my job.'

'Go on,' I said. 'Open it.'

'It's so beautifully wrapped.' She turned it in her thin fingers, the silver ring shimmering under the fluorescent light. She examined the gold tag and a rosy glow showed below her cheekbones. It seemed to me that she was reluctant to undo it, but at last she untied the ribbon and folded back the paper.

When she saw the picture, she gave a little start. I wondered what she had expected. A box of chocolates probably. Generic, impersonal.

I said, 'I hope you like it.'

She held the frame up, frowning slightly, stroking the striped wood with her thumb. The lunula was a perfect white half-oval. 'It's lovely, Darryl, but really this is far too generous. I shouldn't accept it.'

'It's nothing,' I said. 'I just happened to see it and thought how kind you have been this semester.'

She said again, 'It's my job. I've wanted to help you.'

The tone was gentle, as it always was. But it grated. I wanted more. I looked at her wrists emerging from a grey wool dress. I glanced down at her ankles in black tights and lace-up boots. I said, 'Please accept it. You've made a huge difference to my project.' Then I smiled. It felt false, somehow. 'I might even be published because of you.'

'*When* you are published,' she said, with a gentle emphasis on the first word, 'it will be because of your own talent and hard work.' But she put the picture on her desk, leaning it against a pile of books so she could see it properly. 'Very well, then,' she said. 'Thank you. It's lovely.'

~

At home, I took the smaller package from the mantelpiece and unwound the wrapping myself. 'Happy Christmas,' I said.

Phyllis sat passive in her chair, shifting only fractionally when I fastened the chain round her neck. I got the hairbrush and ran it through her hair until it was almost lustrous again. I found a flannel and scrubbed the blotching shadow from her eyes.

'There,' I said. 'Look how pretty it is.'

I stayed there for nearly a minute, waiting for thanks that never came.

Tuesday 1 January 2002

I climbed Arthur's Seat today. I wanted to recapture the excitement and promise of Halloween, but it was only a shadow experience, friendless in the dwindling midwinter light of the afternoon, with the steps slithery and too many tourists still around me.

I leaned on the trig point and drank the whisky I had brought. I stared out at the darkening sea on one side, the city lighting up on the other, and imagined the volcano still active, casting its red fire and molten rock over everyone and everything. Over the families walking together before settling down to board games, the lovers who had shared New Year's Eve kisses, and the friends opening new beers over old hangovers.

I pictured rocks tumbling, lava pouring along the streets. I saw the city desolate, the rocks remade, lives preserved in death like those in Pompeii and Herculaneum. I saw the liquid fire lifting Phyllis, wrapping her, melting her. I imagined myself immolated like a prince-sacrifice, there in the heart of the furnace.

Saturday 5 January

I took down my cards from the mantelpiece and put the two that mattered in a drawer. First, I reread Gemma's, but the words had dulled with repetition. I traced Aline's confident script and thought how much one could tell about a person from their writing. Then I thought maybe I was only imagining that because I knew her.

I felt Phyllis watching me. I spun, staring at her ugly blue dress (long, to hide her misshapen leg), the cheap necklace on her hard chest.

'You're not enough.' I heard the words as if they bounced back to me from the walls. 'You'll never be enough.'

Against my will, I thought of New Zealand and how I promised myself afterwards that I was done with friendship. I kept that promise through the last years of school, the dead period that followed them, my undergraduate degree, my master's, and the first years of my PhD. I prided myself on it. But tonight, under Phyllis's pitiless gaze, I asked myself if I *had* kept it, or if circumstances – the indifference of other people – had kept it for me. I cracked soon enough when Aline and Rob stood with their flowers and their wine and their youth and self-assurance at my door.

Either way, I have friends now, and I don't know how much longer I can wait to see them. I don't think I could cope without them.

15

Milly

Dorset, 2019

They baffle me, these people. That's not the right word, but it will have to do. I don't understand them.

Of course, it's partly the money. The Linden-Millers are seriously rich. I knew that when I met Aline and I've known it ever since. There are the houses, for a start. This one was a building site when I first saw it, but the one in London made me so nervous that I nearly left without knocking at the door. Then there are the cars, the furniture, the clothes and toys and tech gadgets, the extra fridges just for wine. Everything screams *insanely expensive*, and doesn't stop screaming it, and Lexie and Jimmy prattle of holidays in Paris and Costa Rica, schools with piano rooms, sports pavilions, and Latin as a matter of course.

The only things in either house that don't look like they came from Harrods are the crocheted toys the children keep in their beds. Lexie has a dog, unravelling round the whiskers; Jimmy has a brown bear, which he calls Cuthbert.

He told me their aunt made them. Sometimes I look at those two kids, think of all the love and all the money and wonder if they have any idea how lucky they are. But I like them both, despite all that, and I like them most when I remember that these are their favourite toys.

Even the picnic today is a how-to of conspicuous consumption. Vintage champagne, rose lemonade, smoked salmon sandwiches, cold roast chicken, strawberries and vine tomatoes and little spotted eggs that Aline says are quails' eggs. I catch passers-by giving us looks of disbelief.

When I first started working for her, occasions like this made me want to run up to gawping strangers shouting that it wasn't anything to do with me, I was just the hired help. I've got over that now, but from the expression on Nikki's face, I'd say she feels something similar.

But it's not *only* the money that's getting to me. It can't be, because this weekend is the one with the atmosphere and these guests aren't exactly gold-plated. A very different proposition, in fact, from most of Aline's friends. Usually you can count on several rounds of My Totally Unnecessary SUV is Bigger Than Yours at every get-together, but Michael and Nikki's car looks like it's held together by gaffer tape and determination. Rob has made several barbed comments about the champagne and quails' eggs (although that doesn't stop him from eating them). As for Sienna, she works for a charity and dresses like she's the beneficiary of one.

I watch them chatting and drinking their coffee while Lexie and Jimmy scramble on the scrappy cliffs at the back of the beach. She climbs like a cat. He is much warier, like he always is, giving each move due consideration, staying closer to the ground. Astrid wants to climb too, but Sienna calls her sharply back. Chloe curls up on her father's lap with hot chocolate smears on her face. Luna has built a tower of round, flat stones.

All normal enough (or, in Sienna's case, understandable). And yet . . .

If someone asked, I couldn't put my finger on it. If they said it was just my prejudice, inventing what I expect to see, I wouldn't have a convincing defence. All the same, I can feel it. Perhaps it's just me. Or perhaps it's all the things that aren't being said.

16

Darryl

Edinburgh, 2002

Saturday 12 January

They are back. I could hear them through the wall all afternoon, a burble of chatter and unpacking and the seductive, melancholic music of Dido. (That must have been Aline's choice; it certainly wasn't Rob's.) I watched Michael's dad's Volvo as it disappeared along frost-crisped streets. I checked in the fridge for milk and wine and beer for Rob, my heart racing with anticipation while I waited for the knock on the door.

It never came.

At nearly six, I heard their door open again. I abandoned my laptop and hurried to the peephole, to be rewarded with a misshapen flash of smooth skin and striped hat. Aline. I grabbed my coat and keys and stepped onto the landing.

'Hi,' I said.

'Darryl!' she said, a few steps below me. 'Happy New Year. How was your Christmas?'

She looked glossy, at peace with the world, in an emerald coat that must have been a Christmas present. I thought of tense silences and the chicken I had never got round to buying.

'Quiet,' I said. 'Yours?'

'Lovely.' She said it as though it always would be.

'You all back?' I knew they were.

'Yep. Footloose and fancy-free.'

I studied her an instant, not wanting to get it wrong. 'How did Johnno take it?'

She shrugged. 'He'll survive. Best not to drag it out.'

I wondered how Michael had reacted. 'And Melissa?'

'Need you ask? Also in the past.'

We stepped into the chilly night. I wished I'd brought a hat. As the door shut behind us, she said, 'How about you? How's Phyllis?'

The wide street and the cars seemed to pivot about me. The thin path contorted. The untidy garden of the ground-floor flat split into unsteady diamonds. Rob hadn't forgotten. Drunk as he was, he'd remembered and told her. He'd probably told them both.

I blinked until my surroundings levelled again. Aline was out of the little gate, waiting for an answer. I made my mouth move. 'She's OK.' What had I told Rob? *It's complicated.*

Aline was heading to the shop. I'd meant to go with her, get myself asked in when we came back. Instead, I said goodbye and almost ran the other way, down the crescent, onto Marchmont Road. I stopped somewhere in the Grange, out of breath, staring past bare trees and lighted windows to the star-scattered sky, thinking of all the better things I could have said.

Friday 18 January

Aline has a new pal, or perhaps they all do. I was coming downstairs on Wednesday when they were coming up, Aline in her new coat and this other girl all curves, with lots of red hair and a face so pale you could almost see through it. I waited for them to pass, and they smiled and thanked me. The new girl's voice was accented. American, which does not predispose me in her favour.

Tonight, I heard it again, and Rob's in response. He was only letting her into the flat, calling out to Aline, but it made me uneasy.

Sunday 20 January

I was right to be apprehensive.

I waited for Rob tonight with the chessboard ready on its table and a bottle of wine on another one. I sat with my glass in my hand and watched the clock creep round. Five. Five past. Ten past. Twenty past. That wasn't so unusual. Twenty to. That was. And all that time, I heard their voices through the wall, prattling and laughing, and longed to know what they were saying.

At ten to six, I got up, paced to the door, then returned to my seat. Maybe he had the hour wrong. At five past, I rose again in one quick, angry movement that carried me out of my chair, out of the flat and onto the stone landing. Michael answered my knock with a smile, but it became fixed when he saw me.

'Darryl?'

'Is Rob around?'

He hesitated, but we could both hear Rob's laugh, so he had to let me in.

They sat there like a picture in a magazine. *Student life*, complete with striped throws and patterned cushions, posters and landlady prints. They had bottles of lager, crisp packets, and a game spread out on the coffee table. Green and blue boards, cardboard cards and what appeared to be dozens of small counters. Aline was on the sofa, the cushion beside her still squashed where Michael had been. Rob lounged on a beanbag on the floor. Next to him, in a low armchair, was the girl I had seen on Wednesday. She was leaning into him, asking something about the game. As I watched, they both smiled.

They saw me at the same time. She sat up straighter. Rob glanced at his watch and pulled a face of comedic despair. 'Oh shit, mate, sorry. I totally forgot.' I waited for him to uncurl his body from the beanbag, get up, go through with me to the board with my father's pieces and the wine I chose with such care yesterday. I waited for it, but I knew it wasn't going to happen.

Aline said, 'Darryl, this is Sienna. She's visiting from Berkeley for the semester.'

Sienna said, 'Hey,' and smiled again. She wasn't beautiful like Aline, and she was dressed as though she thought it was still the 1960s. But there was something about her. I could see it, although I didn't want to.

Michael sat back down on the squashed cushion and turned his attention to the game. He picked up his drink but didn't offer one to me. Aline said to the girl, 'This is our neighbour, Darryl.'

Our neighbour. Not *our friend.*

Sienna said, 'Nice to meet you.'

'Likewise.'

I kept looking at Rob. After a long pause, he said, 'Can we take a rain check? I'm doing this now.'

'Sure.' It's not an expression I ever use and I don't know why I did then. Perhaps because it, like this intruder, was American.

As I turned to leave, Aline said, 'Have a drink.'

If she had said it sooner, or more enthusiastically, I might have accepted. As it was, I glanced from Michael's carefully passive face to Sienna's, palely glowing, asking Rob her next question. I shook my head.

Back in my flat, their laughter leaked like acid through the wall. I sought out Phyllis where she lurked, waiting to mock, and shook her so hard I thought her limbs would crack. I took the necklace in my hand and pulled it until the chain snapped. Then I lifted the trinket and flung it across the room. It hit the wall, hard, above a chest of drawers and slithered behind it into dusty oblivion.

Afterwards, I thought I should have been grateful, at least, that none of them had mentioned her again.

Monday 21 January

Last night, I dreamed of my time in Auckland. It's not something I do often, and that is a mercy for which I should,

I suppose, thank someone. The Fates, perhaps, or the dour Calvinist God of my ancestors.

But this time I did.

The dream itself was a kaleidoscope of stretched, painful scenes, half memory and half fear, but the few moments after waking were almost worse. I recalled, with videographic exactitude, the moment I met my cousin's boyfriend. I saw her tumbled hair, her hand gripping his, the casual glance over her shoulder. He was a big youth with weightlifter arms and buffalo thighs; not handsome, as her brother was, but strong. He too looked backwards at me, with evident complete indifference.

'Hi,' he said. As they ascended the narrow stairs, he whispered something into her hair. She giggled.

I had been there two weeks, and his was the first dissenting voice in a choir of pity and welcome. I crept up after them and into the little room that had been hastily converted from a study to a bedroom. I sat on the bed, hearing her music through the partition wall. I shook with what I told myself was grief for my lost family, and was partly so.

I didn't lust after her. It is important to be clear on that. I wanted her friendship. I wanted to be part of her life. I knew, instantaneously, that this over-muscled lout stood in the way. I have decided not to ask myself why I have been troubled, just now, by that particular recollection.

17

Rob

Dorset, 2019

The picnic had warmed them, with its alcohol and hot drinks. Aline, typically, had even provided blankets. But the cold descended like a blight afterwards, sending fingers reaching for gloves and woolly hats, toes twisting in damp shoes. Michael had Chloe on his shoulders; Rufus was wailing in his sling. Jimmy and Lexie appeared to be wrestling each other to death, and Sienna's kids clung whimpering to her hands. 'I'm cold, Mama. I'm cold.'

Happy bloody Families.

Of all the things he envied Brandon, at least Rob had never coveted his children. Sienna's two were a complication he chose, for the moment, to ignore. Beside him, Cass was huddled in her waterproof, her face streaked. Another – and more immediate – complication.

'Why did you say you couldn't play rounders?'

'I said I *hadn't* played. That was true.'

'You know what I mean.'

'I thought it would be fun.' She glanced ahead, apparently measuring the distance between them and the others. 'I'm sorry,' she added. 'Aline was being so patronising. She assumed I'd be useless, so she put me in the other team. I wanted to show her up.'

He knew what she meant, although he resented her for saying it. It was, after all, the same emotion that provoked his own Brandon List. 'Another time,' he said, 'please don't.'

She took this in wet, reproachful silence. But back at the house, dry and warm in their room, with its geometric quilt, expensively simple furniture and pale grey walls, she went on the offensive.

'Why did you and Sienna break up?'

What the fuck? He yanked off his wet socks and rolled them into a ball, playing for time. 'What do you mean?'

'It's obvious you were together. What ended it?'

He threw the fetid bundle hard into the corner. 'It doesn't matter now.'

She changed tune, sitting close beside him on the edge of the bed. 'Rob,' she said, in a small voice, 'you wanted me to come here and meet your friends.'

'Not Sienna. I didn't know she would be here.' The words were incautious, regretted as soon as they were out. He felt her go tense and hurt beside him and was simultaneously annoyed with himself, irritated with her and furious with Aline.

He patted her on the shoulder, which was probably worse than doing nothing. 'Look, it's old news. Unimportant.'

'Did you end it?'

He sighed, wishing her anywhere else. 'Technically, I suppose she did. Now can we drop it.'

'Please, Rob. I would like to know.'

'Like Aline said, Sienna was a visiting student. She went home in the summer, as she was always going to, and that was it. No big deal.'

No big deal. Sienna with her red hair dirty, her eyes bloodshot, telling him, 'Don't write, don't email. It'll be easier that way.'

'It won't be easy,' he'd said, sulky and miserable. 'It won't be easy either way.'

He turned from Cass, reaching for dry socks, wanting to hide his face. She spoke to his back. 'I don't think that's the full story.'

He tugged the socks over his still-damp feet, pulled the ends of his trouser legs over them, and got quickly upright. 'Think what you fucking like,' he said.

Downstairs, Brandon was making tea. Michael and Nikki were on one sofa and Sienna on the other, her hair brazier-red on the cushions. Rob hesitated, then sat beside her. Immediately he was accosted by Lexie, imperious as her mother, carrying her great-grandmother's chess set. She placed it precisely on the small table beside him and pulled across an armchair for herself.

'Fancy a game?'

For answer, Rob reached for the box, opened it and started to put out the pieces. Sienna said, taut-voiced, 'You still play chess?'

'Sure.' He spoke without looking at her, his eyes on the smooth cream of the rook in his fingers. 'Why not?'

'He's pretty good,' Lexie said. 'He might even beat me.'

'Possibly,' Rob said, grinning, 'since I beat you last time.'

'I was nine last time.'

'I couldn't do it,' Sienna said quietly. 'Not if I were you.'

Aline said nothing. She stood watching the daughter who was almost her mirror image, confident fingers positioning each piece in its polished square. Michael got up, his footsteps loud on the hard floor, and stared out to sea.

'What is it?' Nikki said, but no one answered her.

'One game,' Aline said, although neither of them had asked her. 'Then Rob and I have things to do.'

Rob lifted two pawns in his hands and made a show of shuffling them behind his back. 'Ah yes,' he said. 'Your *outdoor plans*, as if we hadn't had enough of that for one day. Spill the beans.'

'A night hike,' she said, 'for old times' sake. Or maybe a night run.'

He glanced past her to the long windows. The room was bright and warm; the dimming grey outside was anything but inspiring. 'Fuck's sake, Aline, I've only just got dry.'

'You'll love it,' she said, in a tone that had once been daily familiar to him. 'We're doing the Pirate's Path.'

'In the dark?' Rob held out his closed fists to Lexie. He wondered if there was a way to opt out without losing face.

Aline, witch-like, appeared to read his mind. 'Turned coward in your old age?'

Lexie jabbed a finger into Rob's closed ones. He revealed the black pawn. 'I'll come too,' she said.

'Sorry, Lex. Dad says no.'

'Why? I've done it in the daytime.'

Brandon set down mugs of tea. 'Not after a winter of rain, you haven't. Anyway, night is different.'

Lexie glared. 'I'm not afraid.'

'You never are,' Brandon said. 'That's not the problem.'

'It's not *fair*.' Her voice, which held sometimes the reasonable cadence of a young adult, had reverted to the wail of a spoilt child.

Rob lifted his pawn, moved it two spaces forward. 'You're on,' he said. Lexie, competitive as her mother, turned immediately to the board.

Brandon said, 'I'm not sure any of us should do it. The forecast isn't great.'

Aline sighed. 'You're as bad as Rob. It'll be fun. Michael's in. I asked him earlier. And Sienna.'

Michael turned to glance at his wife, and Sienna pulled a face, but they did not otherwise contradict her.

'Well, I'm definitely *not* in,' Nikki said. Perhaps she meant to sound light-hearted, but it came out as angry. 'I think it's insane.'

Jurassic

The age of dinosaurs. Pangaea has split, tearing continent from continent, and the Wessex Basin has deepened. What was dry sand is now tropical sea. Starfish and lobsters and ichthyosaurs. Sandstone, mudstone and limestone, born of the salty water, lie atop the red base. A second line in the jar.

18

Darryl

Edinburgh, 2002

Monday 28 January

I am not teaching. I couldn't face it. I told Gemma today that I had missed the deadline for applying and would start in September instead. I wonder if she knew I was lying, because our meeting, which I had anticipated with elation, was subdued. Then, when I emerged, the snow had started.

I crossed George Square with special care, ignoring the squeals of excitement around me. A group of students were having a snowball fight in the Meadows, their quick feet and gloved hands ripping the white blanket even as it tried to settle. Turning into the crescent, I had a postcard view of the tall buildings with their doors in different colours, bay windows jutting out, floor on floor, floating snowflakes, and fat white lids on the parked cars.

The interloper, Sienna, stood at our open door.

She was all colours, flame hair, purple coat, green beret, exclaiming at the snow. As I came closer, I saw the dark tangle of Rob's hair behind her, his pale hands and maroon sleeves round her waist. She twisted in his arms, and they stood there kissing for a long time, like a film, while the snow fell on the ground in front of them and oozed through my father's scarf onto my neck.

He missed another chess game last night.

When they finally stopped, he stood at the open door, waiting, until she was out of the gate and had turned again to wave. I went on, as though I was newly there, and she walked almost into me. 'I'm sorry,' she said, but she didn't sound it. Her face shone. As she turned the corner, thinking herself unwatched, she lifted both arms, palms up to the falling snow, and laughed aloud.

Emotion throbbed in my temples, sharpened by cold. I told myself she looked ridiculous. I skidded along the snow-damp pavement and into the building. Rob was out of sight. Back in the flat; probably back in bed. I dragged heavy feet up the long stairs, thinking of Melissa and the ones before her, unthreatening, let out like stray cats onto the landing.

I turned my key in the lock, forcing it round. I thought of Phyllis, who never laughed. I yanked at the door as though it too would thwart me if it could. I needed to get inside, to find her and tell her how much she was letting me down.

Sunday 10 February

Rob turned up fifty minutes late today, when I had almost given up expecting him. I tried to ask him about Sienna

– he'd talked quickly enough about the others – but received only a complacent smile. He won (Sicilian Defence) and left immediately, barely finishing his wine, desperate to be back with her.

I recorked the bottle, though I wanted to drink it. I heard Phyllis's laughter as if it came from inside my own head. I hear it still. She seems, impossibly, to be in every room I go into.

See? You do need me. You always will.

I shut out her malign certainty, tell myself she is wrong. But I have no eloquence to silence her. Not when I can barely convince myself.

Still, Rob did tell me one interesting fact. Aline's sister is visiting next weekend.

Thursday 14 February

Before today, I had written two Valentine's cards. The first was early in my primary school career, a painstakingly drawn image of two children hand in hand in a wobbly pink heart. I bestowed it unwisely on an infant Medici with thick ebony pigtails and olive eyes, who gave me my first experience of rejection by laughing at my artwork and dropping it in the playground.

The second was to a quiet girl in my class at secondary school who sent me encouraging blue-green glances behind our copies of *Catcher in the Rye*, and whom the boy who sat next to me in maths and her on the bus had said fancied me. I didn't sign the card – perhaps I was still cautious after my earlier experience – but I hoped she would guess it was from me, and she must have because weeks later, the same boy said she had liked it and why didn't I just ask her out.

'She's almost as much of a misfit as you are,' he said. 'It's like you're made for each other.' The odd thing is, I think he meant it kindly.

I was going to ask her. I almost did. I even had the words planned, but less than a week afterwards, a reckless driver slammed into my parents' car and nothing about my life would ever be the same. The next year, newly returned from Auckland, back at my old school and living alone in this flat that I have not spent a night away from since, I could have tried again. But I never did. Instead, after a time, I found the unwanted blonde who was Phyllis's predecessor but one.

I have done well enough without Valentine's cards, from then until now.

I chose Gemma's card as carefully as I had chosen her Christmas present; as deliberately as I had selected that other card a dozen years before, for a girl who was, I now realise, remarkably like her. Perhaps it is a good omen. That one, I remember, featured a pink heart. This had a red one, small and embroidered on a plain cream background. It too was anonymous. I wanted her to wonder if it was from me, maybe even to hope it was, but I also needed deniability, so I bought a copy of *The Scotsman* and cut out letters from the supplement. Afterwards, I wondered a little how that would look, but it was too late by then.

This morning, early, before anyone else could be there, I took the red envelope into the department and put it in her pigeonhole. Quitting my flat, I saw that someone had left a bunch of yellow tulips outside Aline's door. On the way back, I met her coming out, dressed for running, with her plaited hair snaking down her back.

'Who were your flowers from?'

She looked surprised, then smiled. 'It didn't say, but I have some ideas. What about you? Any Valentine's plans?'

I thought of Gemma and of the card now resting on journals and university circulars in her pigeonhole. 'Nothing special,' I said.

'Poor Phyllis.'

I noticed the dryness of the words before I took them in, and then quick panic engulfed me. I took a surreptitious breath, found the prepared phrases. 'That's over. Like you said, life's too short.'

'Oh,' she said. 'Only . . . we've heard shouting a few times. We hoped everything was all right between you.'

I swallowed. I spoke with careful calm. 'I'm afraid she didn't take it too well. I'm sorry about the noise.'

Aline raised her shoulders, then let them fall. 'Don't worry on our account. We're noisy enough. So long as everything is OK.'

'It's fine,' I said. 'Thanks.'

It wasn't until I was inside the flat, replaying this dialogue in my head, that I realised that what I had taken for friendly concern could have been suspicion. Suspicion of me and concern – of all the ironies – for Phyllis.

Either way, I must be more careful.

Later

I have just seen Aline again, leaving the building with Michael. She smelled of a new perfume. I was returning from taking the rubbish out and would rather they hadn't seen me, but I was also curious. If this was a date, it was not a welcome turn of events.

Aline disabused me. 'We're going to the anti-Valentine's night at the union.' She didn't ask me to join them. 'Leaving the flat to the lovebirds.'

Lovebirds. 'That doesn't sound like Rob.'

She snorted. 'He's not *being* like Rob. I think he's finally clicked that women aren't all interchangeable.'

'I've hardly seen him.' I tried not to sound hurt, but she looked at me as though I had.

'Sen bought so many bloody candles that the sitting room looks like the waiting room for a posh spa, though I'm pretty sure that wasn't the vibe she was going for. I just hope they don't burn the place down.'

'I'll listen out for the smoke alarm.' I wondered if my hands smelled of the bins, and shoved them into my pockets. 'Did you find out who your admirer was?'

'The tulips?' Aline paused, then turned from me to the heavy front door. 'Not yet.'

I studied Michael's fixed expression and knew who had left the flowers. I wondered whether she knew it too, and was pretending not to.

Before she could leave, I said, 'Rob says your sister's visiting.'

'At the weekend, yes.'

'Is she like you?'

She gave me a sideways look. 'Not especially. She's the nice one.'

'Will I get to meet her?'

'Sure,' she said. 'Come round any time.'

I want to feel victorious because she said that, but I can't. I shouldn't have had to ask and *she* should have laughed and said of course, you idiot, you're always welcome. I wish I could hear what they are saying, through the thick wall between my sitting room and theirs. I wish it so desperately, tonight, that I picture a hole in the wall, round and hidden, yielding me their secrets. But I have been there before. I know where it leads.

19

Brandon

Dorset, 2019

The room was beautiful, made so by Aline and for her. The bed huge with creamy linen, the Victorian rocking chair upholstered in pale-yellow silk, the mirror with its ornate trim in which he could see the edge of her reflection.

Another gorgeous home, in his textbook life.

He hadn't wanted to keep this house. 'We could sell it,' he'd said. 'Split the money with your sister and cousins.' It wasn't fair that he and Aline should have this on top of so much else. No one in the family had said so, but they must have thought it.

'If Granny wanted them to have it,' she had said, 'she'd have left it to them.'

'OK, so we could sell it anyway, and buy something else.' He'd imagined something on his side of the Atlantic. A foothold for the children, a place for summers fishing and canoeing and seeing their American cousins. A diet of waterfalls and hiking trails and wide-open plains. If he was back there, he had thought, he could breathe.

But Aline, when she understood, had been implacable. 'This is my family history, and you want to flog it for some Disneyfied version of yours.' She'd gazed at him with her apatite eyes. 'How can you?'

How can you? he'd wanted to say. But he had not.

She'd smiled then, her hand gliding warm and strong into his. 'Anyway, you love the Jurassic Coast. You've always said so. I watched you fall in love with it.'

'You made me fall in love with it.'

She had laughed up at him, gestured around her at the designer wallpaper and antique mirrors of their London drawing room. 'Same thing,' she'd said. Then, with calm conviction, 'Our lives are here in England. I thought we decided that years ago. Let's keep it that way.' So they had, and now he stood in another carefully curated space, caught in this landscape that he both loved and wanted never to see again.

Aline hummed to herself, slid clothes off, lifted leggings and a Lycra top from a drawer. 'Aren't you going to change?'

'Why are you doing this, Aline?'

'What?'

What indeed? This crazy expedition? Or this whole weekend that she had told him was at once reunion and celebration of the renovation? He peeled off his jumper and undid his shirt.

'The Pirate's Path,' he said.

'I told you: it'll be exciting.'

'Nikki hates the idea.'

'So? She's not coming.'

'She doesn't want Michael to go.'

'That's up to him. She's not his keeper, and nor am I.' She dropped the clothes on the bed.

He removed his shirt. 'Really?'

She came close to him, in just her jeans and rose-satin bra. Her eyes laughed. Her fingers crept across his chest. He watched the top of her shining head: the clean, straight parting. He felt her lips on his collarbone, then the side of his neck. He saw her as she had been seventeen years ago, almost to the week. A tall, stunning girl in shorts and a white T-shirt. A hand reached out with surprising formality amid the stretching bodies and gasping breaths of the end of the race. He remembered the rush of elation, feeling long fingers close on his, looking into those green eyes.

'I knew then that I wanted you,' she'd told him, months later. 'I always get what I want.' Now she giggled. Her breath tickled his neck. 'You needn't be jealous.'

'I know that.'

He said it drily, but she only laughed again and kissed him on the mouth. 'You love it too,' she said. 'The thrill.'

He had walked the Pirate's Path first in June sunshine, feeling his life fall out of his own hands and into the keeping of the vibrant, unstoppable girl in front of him. Eighteen months later, he had run it with her and her dad on New Year's Eve. It had felt like a test of his courage, his right to be among them all with their power and charm and determination. Afterwards, Aline's grandmother, handsome and intimidating, had poured them all brandies and touched her glass to his.

'Welcome to the family,' she'd said.

He gazed down at Aline's manicured hands, fingers

spread on his bare chest, the single diamond on the left one, and the row of them glinting on the right. She called it an eternity ring.

'We have guests,' he said, without much conviction.

'So?' she said, again. The gleaming hands slid down, and he did not resist them.

Afterwards, pulling outdoor clothes onto hot, damp skin, he watched her again. She was in her sports bra and Lycra, smoothing her hair into a ponytail and smiling at her own reflection. He listened for the sea and thought again of the turning water and forest trails of Ohio. She saw him looking and came to him again. Warm lips against his ear, breath light as a benediction.

'I would do anything to keep you,' she said. 'You know that.'

Downstairs, the kids ate fish fingers and chips and peas that Chloe spun like ball bearings across the glossy floor. Lexie kept up a persistent campaign to be included in the hike, which Brandon and Aline ignored. Milly poured squash, replenished plates and swept the floor, moving quietly about them. She was so much a part of the family now that he hardly noticed her. Nikki sat on the sofa, also without speaking, with Rufus snuffling at her breast.

'Cass isn't coming,' Rob said. Brandon wondered whether he had even asked her.

Sienna wore a borrowed fleece and her own American trainers, darkened by British mud. 'I have no idea why I'm letting you make me do this, Aline.'

Because you always did, Brandon thought. *All of you. All of us.*

20

Darryl

Edinburgh, 2002

Sunday 17 February

'You've got to be nice when your big sister looks like
Grace Kelly and is better than you at everything. It's
either that or be the bitter, jealous one – and who wants to
waste their life on that?'

Aline's sister, Clara, said that last night. We were in the
pub, the Earl of Marchmont, squeezed together on one side
of a table. Clara had brought a friend with her, three lads
from Aline and Michael's course had turned up (apparently
uninvited), and other students kept stopping by.

I considered the comparison. Aline *does* resemble Grace
Kelly: the same clean, classic lines, the same composure in
repose. But she is more athletic, less winsome; less ethereal,
more real.

Clara sighed, exaggeratedly. 'Don't tell me you're in love
with her too?'

I laughed, relieved to be able to speak the simple truth. 'Not remotely.' My mind jumped to Phyllis, then Gemma. 'Rob and I are the exceptions.'

Rob was on Clara's other side. He shifted lazily, an arm round Sienna, speaking on a yawn. 'What about me?'

'I'm counting the men here who aren't obsessed by my sister. So far, it's only you and Darryl.'

Disparate snippets of conversation landed, distractingly, in the pause that followed. Whitehall memos, Britney Spears, the Milošević trial. Rob let his gaze slide over the three new lads, now downing pints and talking over each other about the winter Olympics, presumably for Aline's gratification. Briefly, he considered Michael, lurching on the edge of the trio, only half listening to Clara's pal.

'That's about right,' he said, at last. 'Definitely not me.' He twisted his fingers in Sienna's loose hair and waved his pint glass in my direction, splashing beer onto the table. 'And you, Darryl? Not even now you've ditched Phyllis?'

'Your ex?' Clara asked. She has her sister's trick of raising her eyebrows.

'Yes.' I gulped my wine, conscious of an enormous relief. In this one casual exchange, the Phyllis situation had been transformed from painful entrapment to a normal part of any youngish life. 'Not even now,' I said.

Clara raised her glass to the friend she'd brought with her, and the other girl lifted hers in response. She had straightened black hair and light brown skin and had appeared quite unremarkable until that moment. The look between them lasted so long it was almost embarrassing.

~

111

Hours later – when one of the other lads had gone, when we had returned to their flat and Rob had put on music unfamiliar to me; when Michael had called for pizzas and we had eaten them from the boxes, and the evening seemed settled into an alcoholic camaraderie that was also wholly new to me – Clara asked, 'Has she still got you doing night hikes?'

Michael laughed. 'Oh yes. Every month.'

I thought about how I had gone alone on New Year's Day. I'd never known they were a regular event.

'It was always our thing,' Clara told me. 'Part of the family lexicon. Trekking in the Peaks and Snowdonia, pitching camp in the dark, even when we were quite little. I was terrified, but Aline never was.'

'We could go now,' Aline said. She had been lying on the floor with her head on a cushion, but she was up like a cat, instantly alert. The two boys I didn't know made incoherent sounds of enthusiasm.

Clara's friend said, 'It's almost midnight.'

'So?' Aline said. 'Pick your hill, Clara. Edinburgh has seven of them.'

'Oh God,' said Clara. 'No. Why do you have to be *so* like Dad?'

Michael said, 'It's raining.' He opened the shutters, folding them back against the wall, revealing his own understatement. The rain hammered against the glass, wind-tossed and violent. It is always this way, high as we are in the building. Like being in a lighthouse above the crashing waves. Or how I imagine that to be.

Aline turned off the music. She stood in the curve of the bay window, apparently determined to be part of the storm and, being there, to make us all part of it too. Sienna uncurled herself from Rob and stood beside her. Aline reached out without speaking and took Sienna's fingers in hers. They stood there together as though they were keeping guard over the furious night.

'What a city,' Sienna said, when she sat down again.

Aline settled not where she had been, but on the arm of her sister's chair. 'OK,' she said. 'Maybe not now, but soon.'

'Yes, soon,' said Clara. 'When I'm well away from here.'

'Philistine,' Aline said, but she smiled. 'Do you ever think of the Pirate's Path?'

'Frequently,' said Clara. 'That's why I'm staying right here, in this warm, dry flat.'

'We'll go there.' Aline's smile took in Michael, then Rob and Sienna snuggled together among the sofa cushions. 'This summer, when we go to Dorset. I'll show you.'

This summer. The thought of it yawned ahead of me. Those weeks and months, far longer than the Christmas holidays. And when they came back, would they even stay in the same flat? I wouldn't think about it. Unless . . . The thought wormed into my brain, unbidden but irresistible. Unless I could go with them.

Alone in my bed, I spoke as though Phyllis were with me (and not, as was in fact the case, moping in the other room).

'You were wrong,' I said. 'They are my friends, and it will be OK.' But I lay a while unsleeping, and for some reason Clara's words repeated themselves on the radio in my head.

Who wants to waste their life on that? Was I bitter, twisted not by jealousy but by ill-usage and bad luck?

As I drifted off at last to sleep, a strange thing happened. The phone rang: as loud and unfamiliar as the buzzer had been that night that Rob had been sick. But by the time I got up to answer it, no one was there.

The First Postcard: December 2018

You think you have it all, don't you? You think you deserve it. But I know your secret, Aline. Do you really think you will be safe in your house on those tumbling cliffs? Do you still believe that nothing can touch you?

21

Aline

Dorset, 2019

The Pirate's Path ran from the easternmost end of the beach, starting up a wooden ladder propped against the rock, then winding its tortuous, precipitous way through thickets and along edges, and finally zigzagging up steep grass, past craggy outcrops, to the comparative safety of the coast path.

When Aline had been a child, her dad and uncles had run this perilous line after dark every New Year's Eve, coming in exhilarated and ready for champagne. Tall, fair, strong men, all of them, fearless even when the weather was wild. *Reckless*, her mother said. But Aline knew better. She knew they had faith in themselves and their ability to conquer whatever the world could throw at them. From when she was very young, she had felt her ability to be like them.

She had been told she could join them when she was twelve, but her teenage cousin had tripped on the steep slope the year before. He had been carried away white-faced, with wrist and ankle broken, by ambulancemen who spoke sternly to his father, and the next day Aline's mother had issued a rare edict. Aline had to wait another three years.

She had felt only resentful irritation. Her cousin had always been a clumsy idiot. *She* would not fall. She had not, and she would have let Lexie join them tonight. Her fearless daughter would be thirteen that year. But Brandon was almost as annoyingly risk-averse as his mother-in-law, and when it came to the children, uncharacteristically obdurate.

She ran on. She had always been intensely conscious of her physical self, and tonight, in the almost dark, this awareness seemed to extend to everything about her. To the sea, closer and louder than by day; the beach curving towards the scrubby headland. The tumbled clay-and-stone above and the pale crags made vast by the cloud-filtered moon. The lights of Portland across the black water, seeming near enough to swim. She felt as though she could run forever.

Waiting at the edge of the boulders, she breathed the sharp air and watched her friends by moonlight: so many scurrying shadows across the shore. Rob and Michael side by side, as they had followed her on night hikes up Edinburgh's scattered hills. Sienna, breasts bouncing and hair inadequately held back, so thick strands twisted and rose, pulled out by the erratic breeze. Brandon, who knew this way as well as she did by now, and loved it almost as much. He jogged slowly, so Sienna would not be left behind. Always the gentleman.

For a moment, she allowed herself to wonder what this expedition – this weekend – would have been like if she had not had to watch them all the time, forensically attentive, ready for signs of betrayal. But speculation, like regret, was pointless.

Michael came to a panting stop beside her, then Rob. 'Jesus, Aline. We're not running *up*. That would be a midlife crisis too far.'

They walked instead, fast after the shining boulders and the slippery wood of the ladder, flicking on head torches. What had been moonlit shadow became a bouncing bright circle, edged with the black unknown. To one side lay scrubby ground, dead tangled lines in the torchlight, though by day it was waking from its winter sleep. To the other side, the sea, somewhere far below, splashed against rocks.

They turned a corner, coming so close to the edge that Aline heard Michael gasp behind her. 'Christ,' Rob said, catching up. He did not sound impressed. She led them on again, back through lichen-covered stones, strands of bramble, the first of the nettles.

Behind her, Michael asked Sienna, 'Glad you came?'

Sienna laughed, though she was gasping for breath. 'Avalon,' she said. And she was right. With a twist of the path they had gone from heart-stirring exposure to glades silvered by the torchlight and waving silhouette trees. A winter fairyland.

They dipped down again, so steeply that Rob insisted they must be going the wrong way. Aline ignored him, following the narrow thread almost into a tiny rocky cove. She knew every step of this path; she could have walked it blindfolded.

'Is this where the pirates landed their boats?' Sienna asked. 'Hiding stolen treasure.' Aline smiled briefly back at her, then drew them inexorably on. Up and up again, past spikes of blackthorn and white boulders that seemed half buried in the earth.

The rain began, so cold it was almost sleet, and Rob's complaints rose high and persistent above it. He hadn't been this flaky on the Edinburgh hills. Aline did her best to ignore him, even as her running shoes skidded on wet dirt and water soaked her feet. Behind them, Brandon yelled, 'We should go back.'

Jesus, they were *all* flaky. She pictured her father as if he were running in front of her, their feet lifting and landing like the strokes of a metronome. She called without stopping, 'It's quicker to finish the loop than to go back now.'

The path darted towards the edge again, then veered more steeply up, back into the enchanted forest. They climbed on, out of the thickets, and came at last to a thin thread of path across desolate hillside, with the crags jutting above. At last, the rain paused. Aline stopped with it, letting the rest catch up.

'Turn your torches off,' she said. 'Just for a moment.'

The night wrapped around them, heavy as velvet, before the fine moonlight filtered through. Wet fresh air filled her lungs. Below them, the grass slope dropped like a waterslide, then cut off sharp, high above the black sea.

'This,' she said. 'This is what we do it for.'

Rob laughed, almost as he used to do. Beyond him, Sienna sighed, soft as the breeze. Then she yelled.

~

Aline jumped. Beside her, she heard Rob cry out, felt him slip, writhing in slick mud, grabbing at her arm. He wobbled an instant, on the edge of nothingness, then settled on his hands and knees on the path.

'Fuck,' he said. 'Jesus, Aline. This bloody place.'

Aline pulled him upright. 'What the hell, Sienna? He could have gone over the edge.'

Sienna was staring. 'I saw someone.'

'Don't be stupid.'

'I'm not.' She pointed up the hillside behind them. Her other hand fumbled for her head torch. 'Up there. There's someone there.'

Aline pressed her own torch on and swung her head from side to side, coolly illuminating the strewn boulders and scrappy white crag. Nothing else. She repeated the movement. She closed her eyes and saw words in blue ink under a first-class stamp. She thought, *This doesn't make sense.*

'You imagined it,' she said.

'I didn't.'

She had forgotten that about Sienna: her quiet certainty. It was there now, even as her voice shook. Aline said, carefully, 'Who the hell would be watching us?'

'I don't know,' Sienna said. 'You tell me.'

The rain intensified, hitting them in hard sheets, so they could see nothing above or below. Beneath her feet the path ran with mud. 'Come on,' Brandon yelled. 'Let's get out of here.'

22

Darryl

Edinburgh, 2002

Sunday 3 March

I woke early, sweating and clinging to Phyllis. I think she sought to comfort me, but I shoved her across the bed.

'You cannot understand,' I said. She didn't argue.

I lay there for hours, thinking of myself as I had been twelve years before. Of my dad at the kitchen worktop, making breakfast, talking through plans for the day. He had buttered my toast on autopilot, as though I was still a child. My mum had wandered in, yawning, in her cream silk dressing gown and fluffy slippers with a hole in the toe.

I went out as soon as it was light, because then I had stayed in. Perhaps I believed (wrongly) that I could trap the memories behind the slammed door of the flat. I paced round the Meadows, the loop the runners take, and saw Aline, ponytail swinging, at the front of a group of them.

She was turning her head as she ran, saying something to a tall lad in a Detroit Tigers T-shirt. She didn't see me.

I felt sick, so I found a bench and sat on it. I gazed at the grass thick with crocuses, the trees starting to bud, just as they had been that other year, and every year. I don't know how long I was out there, only that at some point I became very cold. I walked back like an old man, my limbs unyielding, and found Rob and Sienna on the stairs.

Their hands were clasped. They gleamed with love. They looked at me oddly, and Sienna said, 'Are you OK?'

'I'm fine.' I spoke to Rob. 'I'll see you this evening.'

He shifted, not meeting my eye. 'Sorry, mate. I don't think I can make it.'

The front door opened below us. I watched Aline's pale head rising up the stairs, and the line on the wall where the paint went from peeling red to faded grey. I felt Rob and Sienna edging away from me. I said, too fast and too loud, 'I could really do with the company tonight. It's the anniversary of when my parents died.'

I heard my words, and despised myself.

Sienna stared at me with her luminous eyes. Rob said, 'Fuck, I'm sorry.' Exactly the words he used when I first told him that my parents were dead. I don't think he'll get a job as a bereavement counsellor any time soon.

Aline arrived on the landing and wrapped her arms round me as though it was the most natural thing to do. I felt her, face and hair and limbs, satin and steel, and her breasts pressed against my chest. I stepped back.

Sienna told Rob, 'You play chess. I've got that Donne essay to finish.'

I don't know if I want him to come at her behest.

Later

In the end, they all came, bringing Michael, wine and a Chinese takeaway in cardboard boxes that seeped fluorescent colours onto my mother's table.

'Do you want to talk about it?' Aline said. I shook my head.

I was thinking of my sister, who had been spending the weekend with a friend in Perth. She'd been looking forward to it for weeks. Of how my mother and father had wanted me to come with them. 'We'll have tea on the way home,' my mother had said. 'Make an occasion of it.' I had refused, because my sister and I had fought the night she left and I had still not forgiven her.

I was hearing their called goodbyes, seeing my mum's round face appearing briefly at my bedroom door, blowing a kiss. I had been at my desk, staring into a book. I hadn't even replied.

Rob said, 'Do you want to play chess?' But we couldn't really, not when they'd brought food, so I said no, it was OK, and it almost was. We ate in the kitchen and Aline talked about her running club and Michael about his presentation for class next week, and they asked how my thesis was going. I thought of Gemma then, and that was a comfort.

Michael asked, 'What's your PhD about?' None of them had asked that before.

I gave my summary: rusty now, for lack of use. I should be going to conferences, networking, presenting my elevator pitch to any senior academic I could crowbar into listening, but even Gemma has not yet succeeded in bringing this about. I talked vaguely of geology and literature, the power of metaphor, interdisciplinarity. Words that sounded well enough until you saw how little I'd done with them.

When they were all gone, I looked at the clock: 9.29. It was 9.30 when the SUV overtook head-on into my parents' car. Or that was what they told me, those police officers who came to the door at midnight. My dad had tried to swerve and smashed into a tree. My parents were dead. My sister died three days later in hospital, never waking, our quarrel not made up.

Then, and for a long time afterwards, I imagined the screams.

23

Jimmy

Dorset, 2019

Jimmy lay uncomfortably in a triangular cupboard under the eaves in Milly's room with the small door pulled back in towards him. There was a fat armchair just in front of the cupboard, so it was a good hiding place. Lexie would have tracked him down in seconds, but Lexie wasn't playing. She had already been cross about not being allowed to do the Pirate's Path, then Rob had beaten her at chess, so she had stamped into the room they were all supposed to be sharing and slammed the door.

He could hear Luna, Astrid and Chloe running up the stairs, then banging on the other door, Lexie shouting at them to go away. The door to Milly's room opened and they must have put the light on because a thin yellow gleam appeared all round the entrance to his hidey-hole. But they didn't really look. They were too young. They whispered and giggled a bit, then their feet went thumping back downstairs.

He lay very still, listening to the disappearing footsteps, then the rain hammering on the eaves. His parents were out there somewhere.

Jimmy had been up the Pirate's Path last summer when it was dry and sunny, but the thought of doing it at night made his stomach twist. Nikki thought it was an insane, dangerous thing to do and had said so, repeatedly. He'd heard her shouting at Michael in their bedroom earlier. 'Do you want to kill yourself? Because that's what it bloody sounds like, and don't start making crap up because I know why you're doing it.' Jimmy didn't know what the last bit meant, but the first part had been clear enough.

He hadn't told Lexie he didn't want to go. There was no need because he wouldn't have been allowed anyway. She was afraid of nothing, like their mum. Like he should be.

He hadn't meant to sleep, but he must have dozed off because suddenly he was sore from the hard floor and he knew that something had woken him but wasn't sure what. He wriggled shivering to the door, pushed it open a crack and listened. A long way away, he could hear the thump of fists against wood. Then a baby's crying and Nikki grumbling from the floor below him.

By the time he was out of the narrow space, down the top flight of stairs and halfway down the next, the front door was open. A cold blast of wind and rain was rushing in, and with it his mum and dad and the other hikers, dripping wet and out of breath, crowding in from the dark. In his relief, Jimmy had been going to run all the way down, greet his dad with a hug. But he didn't, because his mum had the hard, cross look that made him wary of annoying her more. His dad was grim-faced, too, shutting the door with a loud click. Michael appeared worried, Rob sulky and covered in mud. As for Sienna, she looked as if she'd seen a ghost.

Rufus made cross noises from Nikki's shoulder. Cass brushed past Jimmy, hurrying down the stairs with her hair twisted up in a towel and smelling of orange soap. She said, 'What's wrong?' which was exactly what Jimmy wanted to know.

'Nothing,' Jimmy's mum said. Her ponytail dripped onto the shiny floor and she rubbed it hard with the jacket she'd just taken off. 'Just bloody awful weather.'

Cass looked at Rob. She sounded a little bit worried but mostly just annoyed: 'What happened to you?'

Rob looked up from untying his laces. 'I tripped,' he said. The next second he gave up on the laces and kicked the shoes off, crumpling the heels. One hit the wall, leaving a black streak.

Jimmy's mum would have killed him if he'd done that.

The other kids were in the snug, Lexie pretending to read a book but actually singing along to *The Lion King* with the rest of them. Milly was perched on the edge of the sofa in the leggings and jumper she'd worn the night before, one finger playing with a spiral of Chloe's hair. In the warm room, her face was pinker than usual. She looked up at Jimmy, smiling, and he smiled back. He liked Milly. Sometimes he thought he liked her better than his mother, but then he felt bad.

Lexie frowned. 'They're not dead, then?'

'No.' Jimmy plonked himself down, squeezing between Astrid and Lexie. A worm of worry wriggled through his mind, as if there was something he should have noticed, and hadn't.

Lexie scowled. 'I *said* it wasn't dangerous.'

But Jimmy wasn't really listening. He'd been wrong about Sienna, he decided. She hadn't looked as though she'd seen a ghost; she had looked as though she was one.

24

Darryl

Edinburgh, 2002

Wednesday 6 March

'You look happier,' Aline said, when I caught her and Michael on Argyle Place.

'Do I? Maybe I am.'

I was. I'd submitted my paper to the journal, and I was on my way to tell Gemma. We walked on together towards George Square. The sun shone almost whitely, spilling onto the pavement, Aline's hair, and the tall bay-fronted buildings. Emboldened, on the crest of my run of luck, I asked, 'Are you still going to Dorset?'

There was a pause. It seemed longer than ideal, but perhaps that was my imagination. Then Aline said, 'That's the plan, yes, but not till June.'

'I need to visit the Jurassic Coast for research.' I said it fast, so I couldn't stop myself. 'Maybe I could come with you.' It wasn't a complete lie: it might provide inspiration, being in that geological jigsaw.

Aline looked surprised. I went on, too quickly, 'I could drive us all down.'

I do have a car, although (for explicable reasons) I don't often use it. I pictured the road trip: Rob choosing the music, Aline passing me snacks from the passenger's seat, all piling out at service stations in one chatty, happy gaggle, so that other drivers would look at us and make eye-rolling comments about what it is to be young.

Michael said, 'But we're going for a holiday. I don't see how it would work.'

Aline glanced from him to me. 'We'll think about it,' she said.

I let it go. For now.

All the slow, stopping way up in the lift to Gemma's office, I set aside thoughts of Dorset and anticipated her pleasure in my news. I imagined her offering me a coffee and talking, long and intimate, about my future. But she was on her way out when I got there, hauling on her jacket and loading books into her bag. She seemed tired, her eyes bigger than ever, her smile slower to bloom. It made her look more like Phyllis, but I didn't want to think about that.

'Darryl? I thought we were meeting next week.'

I said we were. Then I told her about the paper. She smiled and told me well done. 'I'm proud of you,' she said, standing there with her blue scarf half wrapped round her fine neck and that sweet, soft look at last on her face. The moment was like a precious stone, laid into my outstretched hand.

But it was too short. Someone called to her from the corridor. She apologised, locked the door behind us both and hurried away to the calling voice. I walked alone down the many stairs, cursing myself for not holding on until we would be meeting anyway, when I could have had her to myself.

At home, the phone was ringing. I picked it up without thinking, still preoccupied by Gemma. By some fluke of fortune, I didn't answer the way I did on the other (rare) occasions anyone called, the way my father always had, with name and number. I said, 'Hello?' and a man's voice sounded back at me. Youngish; deceptively close.

'Darryl, is that you?'

I said nothing. He said, more hesitantly, 'I'm sorry, I hope I haven't got the wrong number. I'm looking for Darryl Arniston.'

I found my voice. It sounded much older than it had on my first hello, older than my father had ever got to be. 'I've never heard of him,' I said. 'You must have made a mistake.' I replaced the handset, precise as an artefact on a museum shelf. From the sitting room, Phyllis watched me.

'It was no one,' I said. I turned from her and walked into the kitchen. I stared at the cupboard doors and stretched out my fingers, hard, before they could shake.

Did I recognise the voice? I'm not sure. But I recognised the accent. Not Australian. In my months in Auckland, I had at least learned that distinction. It wasn't no one. It was very definitely someone. And he came from New Zealand.

Monday 11 March

There have been no more calls. I have counted off each day of silence, and I have started to believe there never will be.

Perhaps I imagined it. Perhaps I imagined it all.

And today there is a golden opportunity, throwing Gemma back into the central place in my mind; more than making up for last week's little disappointment, and almost for Rob's failure to turn up for chess last night. She has invited me to her flat. She emailed first thing and said she couldn't go to the office because her washing machine had broken and someone was coming to fix it. She said would I mind postponing our supervision. I replied at once and said I could come to Stockbridge.

She sent back the address – *Well, if you're sure* – and I memorised it at once, like a badge of intimacy. Later, she sent another message, saying she'd been thinking and it really was too much to ask of me and we should do next week at the office instead. I said of course I was coming, I said I would enjoy the walk.

Later

I did enjoy it. I passed through the Meadows, alive with spring flowers, along George IV Bridge, down the Mound, past the galleries, across Princes Street, then down again through the New Town. It was, as ever, almost unbelievably lovely, with its austere Georgian tenements and private squares with gardens bursting into bloom behind iron fences. I crossed Circus Place, cream and green and beautiful, and came at last into Stockbridge.

Gemma's flat is in the Colonies, neat little villas squeezed in cobbled rows perpendicular to the Water of Leith. They have bright doors and tiny gardens and exuded an ambience, on this promising morning, of pervading hope. I thought how they suited Gemma and how Gemma, opening the door to me in leggings and a long jumper that might have been a dress, suited them.

Inside, the flat was small, much smaller than mine, but it felt light and airy. I sat on the sofa taking it all in, while Gemma made coffee. The floorboards were warm brown and shining and the walls were painted a bright, deep yellow, which I suppose was the landlord's taste. The pictures were surely Gemma's, though: more framed photos of Venice and of the Highlands; an oil painting of a beach with steep rocky sides and a white-flecked teal sea. The books, too, had the stamp of personality. Victorian novels, biography and travel guides, their spines marked by opening, forced too many to a shelf into the Edinburgh press.

She set down white mugs on coasters with pictures of Edinburgh Castle on them and sat in the armchair across the coffee table from me.

I pointed to the painting. 'That's beautiful.' I didn't say what I was really thinking, which was that I was finding it altogether intoxicating stepping into this other part of her life.

'Thanks.' She lifted her coffee, took a sip. I watched her fingers, the silver ring, the way her sleeve slid back on her narrow wrist. 'Trebarwith,' she said. 'It's in Cornwall. My boyfriend's family are from there.'

I decided to ignore this.

She set down her cup. 'Right,' she said. She sounded very businesslike, and I was obscurely disappointed. I saw the outline I had sent her of my next chapter, printed out and neatly annotated on the coffee table.

'I know there's not much there,' I said. 'I was focused on my journal paper.'

'There's enough to talk about,' she said. Then she said something I wasn't expecting and didn't want to hear. 'I do think, though, that your next meeting should be with your second supervisor. There is a lot here where you need to engage with the actual geological scholarship, and I can't help you there.'

I didn't want to engage with it, not any more. I only wanted to write what she would read. I envisaged trudging down to King's Buildings, having my inadequate generalisations dissected and being pointed towards more and more impenetrable journals. My second supervisor distrusts anyone who isn't outside with a hammer, snow or shine, doing their research the old-fashioned way. He especially dislikes me.

I said, 'I'm going to Dorset with friends in June. The Jurassic Coast.' The words were out almost before I had committed to saying them. I hurried on. 'I thought I could make a field trip of it; get some inspiration.'

She gave a quick smile. 'I'm not sure you need a field trip for what you're doing, though I'm very glad you're getting a holiday. But your other supervisor can advise on that too.'

'He's very busy,' I said.

'It's still his job.' A frown formed on her forehead and moved down to her lovely eyes. 'Would you like me to email him?'

'No. It's OK.' I was remembering that in fact he had emailed me twice in the last few weeks – an unheard-of development – and I had replied to neither message. 'I'll get in touch.'

When I left, an hour later, she reminded me again to email him. I stared at a pastel sketch of a goldfinch on the hall wall, and thought of something that made my stomach slump. 'Does that mean I won't see you next month?'

'I don't think you'll need to.'

I'll need to. I wanted to rush back into that peaceful room, sit on her sofa, *make* her talk to me. 'Perhaps we can have coffee,' I said. 'I'd like to check in.'

'How about you pop by my office if you have any questions?' She opened the door and stepped aside for me to pass through it. My arm brushed softness in the narrow space. My fingers touched the back of her hand.

'Thank you,' I said, stepping into the bright, cool day.

'No problem. It's always a pleasure to see you, Darryl.'

The washing machine man was getting out of his van, double-parked on the narrow street. She smiled and lifted a hand in greeting. I was still tasting her last words, imagining ramifications, all the long uphill walk home. And when I opened my door, the phone was silent.

25

Sienna

Dorset, 2019

At bedtime, hours later than it should have been, the girls cried for their father. Sienna tried to call him, but the line rang out in his San Francisco office. She tucked her children into their improvised beds while Lexie and Jimmy lay reading beside them. She washed her tired face and plied it, like a doll, with make-up. She felt overwhelmed with loneliness.

Downstairs, they were still around the table, with only Nikki missing. The blinds were down, the night shut out, and music was playing on hidden speakers. Dido's *No Angel*, folksy, oddly evocative. How long since she had heard that album?

I cannot do this.

'I'd like a few minutes to reset,' she said. Did her smile look as unconvincing as it felt? Probably. 'I'll go into your lovely garden.'

Aline said, 'You'll freeze,' but Brandon found Sienna a jacket and hat from the back porch, opened the door and shut it behind her.

She stood a long time in the dark, wrapped in his coat, leaning against an apple tree. She saw the lamp-lit room she had left, all money and clean lines, thought of what she had come here to say and was afraid of saying. She recalled rain like hammer blows, shifting darkness, and a shape that she had not imagined, moving among the rocks. She saw Astrid, running heedless into high waves.

She turned away from the light, towards the uncontained plants and unpruned trees, her chill fingers gripping her left wrist and the tears dropping in warm streams that turned to ice on her face. She told herself she could leave, take her girls back to Californian sunshine and the life she had thought she could make real.

The door opened, then shut, and she turned from the hanging darkness to the yellow circle of automatic light. 'Brandon? Michael?'

Her borrowed layers moved with her, heavy and too big. Then she saw the man, pale in the pale light, and stood abruptly still.

'You,' she said.

Rob said, 'Are you OK?' He came closer, so close that he must see her swollen eyes and tear-streaked face. She sniffed, then pushed her fingers into the pockets of Brandon's coat. Fleetingly, he produced his old grin. 'I see you're completely fine.'

She laughed, then plucked out a question from the many that crowded her mind. 'When did you meet Cass?'

'Eight, nine months ago.' Rob snapped a twig off the apple tree and twiddled it between his fingers, perhaps in lieu of the cigarettes he had given up. 'I shouldn't have brought her this weekend.'

The light timed out. She stared round the garden, chasing shadows. She heard her husband's voice, somewhere in the shadows of her heart. *I love you, Sienna. I love your kindness and how you see the beauty everywhere.* She thought of him down on one knee with the Golden Gate Bridge like a promise of eternity behind him. Dark skin with a red blush rising, fingers unhesitating, sliding the ring onto hers. His smile. His face, wet with tears, as they put his daughters, one after the other, into his arms. She felt it fading, whatever they had had, becoming only a shadow, then nothing at all. The memory of a dream.

Rob spoke again, quietly in the dark. 'It was true, what I told you earlier.'

The words were like a pill offered on a palm, promising wonders. *Don't take it. Don't take it.*

'On the beach. I wanted so many times to contact you.'

Sienna turned, seeking out his profile against the damp dark, reeling with things she did not want to feel. 'Why?' she said.

He spoke very close to her. 'I wanted to remember what it was like to be right with someone.'

Oh God. Long nights and crisp days, the musty smell of radiators burning off dust, cheap wine, and Aline cooking risotto in the galley kitchen. Rob lying naked on a red and black bedcover, his room piled high with CDs and music

138

magazines, posters of Pulp and *Lord of the Rings* and old newspaper stories of Richey Edwards taped to the wall.

She said, in someone else's voice, 'You cheated on me.'

'You know I was sorry about that.'

'Do you have any idea – any idea at all – how much it screwed me up?'

'What?'

'You,' she said. 'Me. All of us. What we did.'

Long nights crying without end in her childhood bedroom. Evenings sitting between her parents, staring without seeing at the TV screen. Their faces drained with worry, unable to understand. Her friends full of well-intentioned prattling of break-ups and fish in the sea and how it would only take time. Words that were meaningless because of how much they did not know.

He stared into the darkness. 'I was screwed up too, Sienna. For years afterwards, every time I wanted to talk to someone, it was you.'

She grabbed at anger like a life raft, gripping him by the arm until he yelped with pain. She dragged him away from the watching trees, almost under the sticking-out roof of the porch, so the light sprang on again and they both blinked. She dropped his arm, scrabbling at her thick sleeves, pushed back the soft edges of the cardigan underneath and held her wrists out, vein-side up, to the light.

'Sen—'

'Look,' she said.

'Jesus, Sienna.' The words were a whisper. He slid off his gloves and took a hand in each of his, tracing a thumb over the raised scar lines. 'Did you mean it?' he said.

He let the sentence fall, closing his hands around her maimed wrists.

'I meant it enough to do it,' she said. 'Mom found me, called 911.'

God, her poor mother. Her dad too. It wasn't until she'd had her own girls, years later, that she understood how much she had put them through.

'Fuck,' said Rob.

The light clicked off. 'It took me years,' she said, 'to find any semblance of normality. And then it was only by lying.'

Her husband had told her, 'I love your integrity,' and the words had cut as no intentional insult could have done.

She said, 'We should go in.'

'I guess so.'

Neither moved. She heard the music of their youth, subdued by glass. She said, suddenly, almost angrily, 'My husband is a good man. I want you to know that. A truly decent person.'

She felt him move: a half-shrug in the darkness. 'Perhaps that was the problem.'

'Perhaps.' She looked at him, his face all planes and shadows. Her voice curled with unwilling desire. 'I always went for bastards.'

Then she was in his arms, half laughing, his breath on her lips, her nails on his back. 'Oh fuck,' he said again. 'Oh Christ, Sienna.' His fingers forced through her hair, tipping her face up to his. She tasted the whisky on his lips, and her own tears. She felt the light go on above them.

At last she pulled herself free, limbs heavy, pulse tingling. Over the music, somewhere far away, she heard Aline's voice, then Cass's.

'Not here,' she said. 'Not yet.'

'Later?'

She nodded. He chuckled, let her go, waited while she dried her eyes. At the door, she stopped him. 'Rob?'

'What?'

'I didn't imagine it.'

'What do you mean?' But his face, in the white light, was stripped of laughter and desire.

'I really saw someone tonight,' she said. 'Out there. I didn't imagine anything.'

'OK,' he said, and his voice was almost a snap. 'OK, Sen. If you say so.'

26

Darryl

Edinburgh, 2002

Wednesday 13 March

A bad afternoon. I heard Rob going out and followed him onto the stairs. 'I missed our game on Sunday.'

He frowned. 'To be honest, Darryl, I hadn't thought of it as a fixed thing.'

I pictured Aline, bright as summer in my tired flat. *Well now you can have Rob. Any time you like.* Except, it turned out, he wasn't hers to give. I counted in my head, then formulated a smile. I hoped it wasn't too desperate.

'Never mind. Did Aline talk to you about Dorset?'

I searched his face for recollection and enthusiasm, but found only irritation and borderline embarrassment. 'What about it?' he said.

'I'd like to come.'

'Why?'

I smiled, though I wanted to scream. 'I'm a geologist, you know . . .' (I was a quarter one, at best), 'and it's the Jurassic Coast.' I laughed, too loudly. 'That's like a classicist wanting to go to Rome.'

'She hasn't mentioned it.' He descended the stairs, calling up. His voice bounced off the high walls and dusty steps. 'We'd have to discuss it. No promises, though.'

When I got back the phone was ringing. I crouched on the sofa, waiting for it to stop, but it seemed to go on forever. I picked up a knight from the chess set, all cream and brown, and hurled it across the room. It hit the fireplace with a crack and rolled over the tiles, the body still gripping its horse, and the head with its long face and downturned mouth in its helmet spinning like a marble on the hearth.

Thursday 14 March

I have had a message from my second supervisor, summoning me to his lair in King's Buildings. His emails always read as though they should be written on parchment with a fountain pen, and this was no exception.

I am surprised not to have heard from you. Dr Harris has intimated that it would be helpful for you to meet with me. May I suggest 2 p.m., on one of the following days?

Several dates followed. I picked one at random.

I needed books, but they were also in the science block, where I had no desire to go. I walked instead through the Meadows, spring-warm now and strewn with students playing ball games or walking on ropes strung between trees. I knew that Gemma was lecturing in George Square.

I bought a cup of tea and stood at the edge of the gardens, leaning against the sharp-topped rail to watch the under-graduates teeming out. They squawked at each other like so many parrots, tripping down the wide steps, unlocking bikes illegally attached to railings and pulling phones out of bags. I felt the impossibility that I could ever teach them. I felt the precarity of friendship.

Gemma was at the back, looking young enough to be one of them. She was carrying a notebook and talking to a student with pink hair and ill-advised dungarees. As they came closer, I could see the girl's eager face, her exaggerated hand gestures, and Gemma's answering smile. It was the same smile she gave me, warm and kind and interested, the same one she gave the washing machine repair man.

I had planned to run into her as if by accident (something for which I am developing a proficiency). Instead, I ducked into the gardens and sat among the trees until the next lectures had started and the square was quiet again. I saw a couple sharing a flask on a bench, a pair of chaffinches rising from a rhododendron. I crumpled my empty cup in my hands.

I had thought seeing Gemma would cheer me, or at least help me to focus on my thesis, but that non-meeting was worse than not seeing her at all. Now, back here at my desk where there is never really peace, my mind is full with a line from somewhere – a poem, I think, or a song – that I *know* must mean something, but which I can neither form nor place.

Sunday 17 March

Rob did not come tonight. I stood with my ear to the shared wall, made desperate by exclusion. I could hear them there: Aline's ringing voice, Rob's lazy laugh, Michael's mumble. But not the words, not even Aline's. Phyllis watched me, judging, as she has watched all these stretched days.

'Leave me alone,' I told her.

I had no paper cup to crush this time, so I grabbed her instead. I held one thin shoulder with my left hand and pummelled the right one into her smudgy face. As I did it, I recalled a heavy male hand slamming into my jaw. I felt the urge to vomit, so violently that I almost believed it was all still happening. I reeled from remembered pain. I heard Phyllis's screams as if they were bursting from inside my own brain. I heard myself shouting.

At last I stepped back, dazed and nauseous. She was prone on the sofa with her face turned inwards, against a cushion that my mother had embroidered with pink tulips. It's not especially well done, but I cannot bring myself to throw it out. Her hair lay dull and ragged against the uneven flowers. I grabbed my coat from the wall and walked out, slamming the door behind me.

Sienna stood on the landing, an oversized pantomime fairy in a flared yellow dress. Her expression, however, was far from benevolent. She stepped back with her eyes always on me, wary and disapproving. I wanted to lift my fist, still sore from Phyllis's cheekbones, and slam it straight into her condemnatory face. Instead, I pushed past her, taking the stairs two at a time, hammering the hard stone with my thin soles.

From the bottom, I heard her knocking on my door, and her rising Californian voice. 'Who is in there? Is everything OK?' And then, more hesitantly, 'Phyllis?'

It's not OK. It will never be OK.

All the way round the Marchmont streets, skirting the bottom edge of the Meadows, I wondered how much Sienna had heard, and what she would do. Call the police? Persuade Rob to break down the door? But I am calmer now. All was quiet when I got back in, and now it is late and there has been nothing. Anyway, Phyllis will keep my secrets. She knows she has no choice.

The Second Postcard: December 2018

A lot has gone right for you, hasn't it, Michael?
Are you happy now, with your wife and children and
your adequate job? I doubt it. Some things are too hard
to forget, aren't they? Some things you won't be allowed
to forget.

27

Michael

Dorset, 2019

Nikki was asleep, the coverlet half over her, her exposed breast blue and white in the light from the door. Beside her, Rufus lay on his back in his sleeping bag, arms splayed, fingers curling. Chloe was in her nest on the floor.

Michael sat beside his wife. 'Aren't you coming back down?'

Nikki opened her eyes, then shut them again. 'You're cross,' she said, almost as Chloe might have said it.

He sighed, because it was true, and not really her fault. 'Well, it is kind of rude, leaving everyone.' In the pause, he heard all the replies she did not make. 'OK,' he said. 'Go back to sleep. I'll say you're tired.'

'I *am* tired. I always am.' She sat up in one indignant slither. 'I'm sorry if that inconveniences Aline.'

He opened his mouth to snap back, then rammed it shut again. In her exhausted face he saw the last few months of their marriage as they must have been for her. His black silences, the nights he had spent staring into space while she dragged herself awake almost hourly to feed their insatiable baby.

Instead, he rested a hand, gentle and placatory, on her ruffled head. She swung her legs to the ground, rubbing her eyes. 'Give me a moment,' she said. 'I'll be OK.'

Downstairs, Rob had made a tower of his hosts' board games on the shining floor, scrutinising each in turn with the over-attention of the slightly drunk. Cass was shaking her dyed head, tapping Brandon's arm with painted fingers, laughing unnaturally loudly. Wine splashed from her glass onto the velvet cushions.

'I knew Rob was a geek,' she said, 'but not you too.'

'I can't play them tonight,' Sienna said. 'I'm sorry. My brain's a mess.'

Nikki slumped beside her. 'Me neither.'

Aline filled shining glasses with Pouilly-Fumé. 'Fine. But I'm not letting you off altogether.' She smiled her glinting smile at Cass. 'What do you cool young people play, then? Spin the bottle?' Her glance skimmed from friend to friend, eyes dancing. 'Truth or dare?'

Cass twisted herself, apparently scrutinising Rob. He yawned, wide-mouthed. 'OK,' she said. 'Let's skip the dares.' She thrust an empty bottle onto its side on the coffee table, hands fumbling, and set it spinning. 'Aline,' she said, only slightly slurred. 'What was Rob like at university?'

Aline grinned. 'That's easy. Very much like he is now.'

'Suave,' Rob said, 'and sophisticated.'

'The second time I met him,' Aline said, 'he was wearing someone's knickers on his head and serenading a wheelie bin.'

Nikki laughed. 'What song?'

'"Wonderwall".'

'What did you do?'

'Walked him home. For some unaccountable reason, I took a liking to him.' Aline turned, grinning, to Rob. 'I suppose that was the only time in your life that you came home with a woman and *didn't* sleep with her.'

Sienna stared at the floor; Cass frowned. Rob laughed awkwardly, then shook his head. 'This isn't fair,' he said. 'It shouldn't all be about me.' He prodded the bottle with his foot, so it almost rolled off the table. 'Play properly. Ask Michael for his embarrassing memories, or Nikki how many people she's screwed.'

'Considerably fewer than you,' Nikki said.

Aline rescued the bottle and flicked it round with a long nail. It landed, round-mouthed, pointing at Brandon. 'OK, darling. What was *I* like at university?'

For a moment his expression was unreadable. 'Also remarkably like you are now.'

'Bossy,' said Rob. 'But interesting to have around.'

'You were friends,' Sienna said. Softly, unexpectedly. 'That was one of the things I liked so much about the three of you, right from the start. You truly cared for each other.'

Nikki stiffened in her chair. Michael bit his lip. Briefly, ludicrously, he thought he might cry. Aline smiled at Sienna. 'You're right. We really did.'

Rob looked across the table to Sienna, also smiling. Cass lurched forward, glassy-eyed. 'I'll have your go,' she told Brandon. 'If I may?'

Brandon winced, but said nothing. Cass got hold of the bottle on her second attempt and turned it, very deliberately, to point at Sienna. 'OK, so what's the story with you and my boyfriend?'

Sienna looked at Aline, then Michael, and finally at Rob. 'It was years ago,' she said.

The lamplight fell on Cass's face, exposing tear marks like tracks through the heavy foundation. 'Did you love him?' she said. Around them, the room was silent.

'Yes.'

'So why did you end it?'

'I'm sorry.' Sienna spoke gently, as if to a child. 'You've had your truth. The rest is my business.'

Cass slumped back against the cushions. 'By the way,' she said, staring up at the ceiling, 'there's another crack over here.' She closed her eyes, giggling unevenly. 'Not quite so bloody perfect after all.'

Predictably, Aline broke the silence. 'Your turn, Sen.'

Sienna's mood had changed, weathervane quick. She raised her glass like a challenge, not even touching the upturned bottle. 'OK,' she said, as Cass had done. 'I have a question for you.'

Her gaze was on Aline, and Aline looked back, lightly sceptical, her eyes as beautiful as a cat's. 'Go on then. What do you want to know?'

'What's your biggest regret?'

It was as if a wall had sprung up between the sofa cushions, raised by her words, bricking five of them in and keeping the other two out. Michael felt the flush on his face. Nikki frowned. Brandon watched shadows on the white walls. Rob glowered. Only Aline seemed unmoved. 'If you really want to know,' she said, 'I've never run a marathon. I've always wanted to, but the time's never been right.'

Brandon spoke as though he had been forced into it, anger flaring in his face. 'Seriously? *That's* your biggest regret.'

'*Seriously*,' Aline said, in exaggerated imitation of his Midwest accent. 'I have no regrets. How can I, when I have everything I ever wanted?' She smiled at him, quickly, intimately. 'You should feel the same.'

He didn't reply. She shifted gear. 'And you, Rob?' She too didn't trouble to move the bottle. 'What's *your* biggest regret? I guess you have a few.'

Rob glanced sideways at Cass, now soundly asleep. 'Losing Sienna,' he said. 'What else could it be?'

Sienna gasped, the colour rising like crimson paint on her porcelain face. Brandon said, 'Jesus, Rob. You really pick your moments.'

Aline laughed. Her smile was dangerous now, as bright as the diamonds in her ears. She too was drunk, Michael thought, but barely enough to show. 'How unsurprising. Well, I've got a bonus truth for you all. One no one knows. Not even Brandon.' They watched her outstretched hand. 'See that desk?'

They could hardly miss it: a huge old-fashioned piece at the side of the room, polished mahogany with ornate

carving and a locked top. It must have been her grandmother's. Aline waited a beat. 'There's a gun in there.'

Sienna yelped. Nikki's face flashed from exasperation to
anger. Brandon said, very quietly, 'I don't believe you.'

'Look for yourself. The key's in the blue vase.'

He got up without speaking, lifted the vase – cerulean
glass – from a high kitchen shelf, extracted a key from
inside it and crossed to the desk. The key turned awkwardly,
out of practice. He thrust the lid open, stared down for a
few seconds. Then he banged it shut.

'Shh,' Aline said. 'You'll wake Cass.'

When he spoke, his voice was shaking. 'What the hell is
that doing there?'

She shrugged. 'Granny had a shotgun for rabbits. Didn't
you know? It's mine now.'

Michael put a hand on Nikki's, willing her not to say
anything. Rob settled himself more comfortably on the
sofa, spoke on a yawn. 'You're American, Brandon. I'd have
thought you'd be used to firearms.'

Brandon paused: a long breath's length. Upstairs they
could hear someone – Milly? Lexie? – padding across the
landing, shutting a bathroom door. 'Yeah,' he said. 'I'm
American, so I know what happens when people get careless
with them.'

'I'm not careless, darling. The cartridges are kept
separately.'

Brandon didn't answer. He locked the desk, returned the
key to its vase and the vase to its shelf.

Rob said, 'Aline, do you even have a licence?' He sounded
amused.

'Granny had one,' Aline said. 'It's on my list.'

Brandon swung past them, marched up the stairs. A moment later, a door slammed.

Michael stacked glasses by the dishwasher, watching Aline's face for some sign of distress, or even irritation. She showed none. He said abruptly, 'I have to talk to you.'

'What about?'

He thought of Nikki, sliding into bed upstairs, trying not to wake their son. He saw the postcard, Titian's *Diana and Actaeon*, that had waited on his doormat like an unexploded bomb three months ago. He wished with a regret that was almost desperate that he had never turned it over.

'The past,' he said.

Aline was washing up. Her hands stilled in the bubbles, then moved again. 'You made a promise, Michael.'

'I know,' he said, 'but something's changed.'

Some things you won't be allowed to forget.

She watched him: a careful, assessing look. 'OK,' she said.

28

Darryl

Edinburgh, 2002

Thursday 21 March

Today Aline told me I could not go with them to Dorset. 'Sorry, Darryl. It just wouldn't work.' She stood before me on the street, as spring-like as the blossoming trees – and as indifferent. 'We're staying with my gran. It wouldn't be fair on her.'

'But I want to go. I need to.' I improvised, wildly. 'My supervisor says it's essential.'

'Then go,' Aline said. 'Why not have a field trip with geology colleagues? But I'm afraid it won't be with us.' I had no geology colleagues, or none that I spoke to.

She turned away. I wanted to punch her, but I did not. I watched the spring breeze playing with the litter on the street, lifting her summer skirt like an unfurling flag. I was panting as though I really had hit her. Then I went inside, forced my heavy feet up each scuffed step. In my head, I was back in New Zealand and my cousins were leaving without me, heading to the beach with their friends.

Not this time, Darryl. They don't know you.

But they *could* have known me. They could have liked me if only they'd made the effort.

Phyllis lay on the sofa, waiting. 'I hate you,' I told her. For a moment, I thought she smiled.

It was only much later that I remembered I had been on my way somewhere when Aline accosted me. I should have been at my appointment in King's Buildings, far from the sun, with my second supervisor.

Monday 25 March

Gemma has emailed me. I was excited when I saw her name in my inbox. I almost felt my luck change. But it was not, as I had hoped, a date for another meeting. She said my geology supervisor had telephoned her. I was mildly surprised that he knew *how* to use the phone, but not nearly so much as I was irritated by what came next.

He tells me you missed your supervision with him. I'm sorry to hear that. The truth is, I am a little concerned about you, Darryl. We both are. It's nothing to be ashamed of if you are experiencing difficulties.

How *dare* he? One forgotten appointment, *and* I emailed to apologise afterwards – at least I'm almost sure I did – and he reacts like this. Of course, I care little for what he thinks of me, bashing away at his rocks in the nether regions of the university, but I care what Gemma thinks. He has tarnished that.

I had almost decided to confide in her: tell her all about my friends and how they have let me down. I might even have shared the sorry story of Phyllis and the drag she has been on my life. (Not all of it, of course, but some.) I had pictured her leaning towards me, her soft hair, clean nails, and eyes that are not smeared and smudged like Phyllis's or hard as a precious stone like Aline's. I had imagined her holding me, comforting me. But now, when I opened my eyes to the merciless screen, I saw no offers of tea and sympathy.

I will be away for April and most of May, but please get in touch with your second supervisor, and remember that we have university counsellors and other support services available if you need them. Don't be afraid to ask for help.

I wanted to write back, *I'm not afraid*. My fingers itched to type it. *I'll ask you for help. I'm asking now*. I wanted to beg her not to go. Instead, I replied briefly, saying I was fine and working hard, and that I would look forward to seeing her in May. After that, I opened the latest thesis file on my laptop, read a paragraph, deleted half of it and closed the file.

Wednesday 27 March

The worst has happened, but I will not be humbled by it. I will hold my head high.

They are leaving for the Easter holidays tomorrow. I found this out when I heard Michael asking the old woman downstairs to water the plants if it is hot while they are gone. I crept into the flat and stood with my nails in my palms at the door to the sitting room. I had meant to go out, but I couldn't face the sunlight.

A mistake, it turned out, because Phyllis was worse than the sparkling day: a Phyllis growing every day more confident, more demanding.

They don't want you in their flat.

I walked from her and stared out of the window to the light-tipped hills.

They don't trust you.

'Shut up,' I said. I said it quietly at first. Still controlled.

They don't trust you, and they are right not to.

I clasped my hands over my face and ears, fighting myself. 'Shut up. Shut *up.*'

They despise you.

I gave up resisting. I went to the chair where she was and grabbed her by I hardly know what. The hair, perhaps. I know she came unwillingly: that I forced her through the hall and kicked open the door. I know I held her, twisted up, so her head stuck out above the banisters and she could see all the way down four floors to hard stone the colour of bubble gum and a bike fastened to the railing. I could hear her screams, filling my head, as though it was all I would ever hear. But I didn't speak. I needed all my concentration to get her over the edge.

She fell awkwardly. Her good leg hit the banister one flight down; her hair grazed twisted metalwork, and the horrible blue dress spun out like a parachute. She knew I hated that dress.

She landed at last, head-first. I felt it in my ribcage. There was one moment of complete relief, as the screams stopped.

Then reality hit. I waited for indescribable seconds, as if she might move, but of course she did not. I went down in my socks, stumbling, almost tripping. It seemed that I ran forever, taking the twists of the staircase, always seeing her lying there, still and separate, with her pink knickers on display and her hair still unbrushed. Only it wasn't forever, because suddenly I was there, on the bottom step, and she was before me, face-down with one leg sticking out at an impossible angle. Then I was kneeling on the floor beside her, speared with regret.

I put my mouth to her scattered hair and tasted the stone floor, cold and dirt-stained, through its lifeless strands. I turned her head, wanting to see it and not wanting to see it. I pulled at her, burying her ruined face in my shirt.

'Phyllis,' I said. 'I'm sorry.'

I heard nothing. I saw them only when I lifted my head, soggy with tears. They were all there: Sienna and Rob, Aline and Michael, sunglasses pushed up on their heads, the light behind them from the window above the door. Sienna was deathly pale; Michael was shaking.

'Jesus,' Rob said. 'Jesus fucking Christ.'

I can write no more of it now.

29

Aline

Dorset, 2019

She took Michael to the snug when the rest were long quiet in their rooms. He slumped on the sofa, grey-faced, and she wondered, fleetingly, how they could be the same age. She wrapped a blanket around herself, kitten-soft, perched straight-backed beside him and waited for him to begin. His voice, too, was tired and old.

'I had an anonymous message, back in December. A postcard.'

She absorbed this. 'And?'

He paused, as though he was choosing words. He had always been so bloody careful. 'I think they know what we did.'

She bit back her impatience. 'Did they say so?'

'Not explicitly,' he said, 'but I'm pretty sure.'

'Do you mean it was threatening?'

'Again, implicitly.'

'Did you keep it?'

She knew he had. Michael had always retained everything: every book, notes on all their lectures, even their long-paid gas and electricity bills, squirrelled away in a corner of his room. He probably had a plastic folder somewhere labelled *Anonymous Letters (Possibly Dangerous)*. What she really meant was, *Is it with you?*

In the event, he answered both questions. 'It's at home,' he said.

She considered a long moment. Then she slipped her own card out from the pocket of her jeans, unfolded it and settled it in his reaching fingers. 'Was it like this?'

He examined the picture first, Botticelli's *Madonna of the Magnificat*. He looked from it to her, not commenting. Then he turned it over, held it closer to the light. She studied his face, focused and almost despairing.

She watched the light from the lamp on the fluffy cream of the rug, the oiled gleam of the floor. Just another beautiful thing. Michael read the card twice, then handed it back. His fingers were ice cold. 'Is this why you got us all together?'

'It was one reason.'

'There was someone I thought of. I think you must know . . .' His voice wavered. He waited until she thought he would say no more. 'But I don't see how it's possible.'

'I know,' she said. 'But it's not possible.'

She waited for a response, another question perhaps, but he wasn't looking at her; he was staring past her to the window. His words, intentionally or otherwise, were an exact echo of what Sienna had said on the Pirate's Path.

'There's someone there.'

Aline swung round. She saw deep grey night through the half-shut curtain, and what could have been deeper shadow, or just a trick of the clouded moonlight.

'Where?' she said, and he gestured, unhelpfully, at the glass.

'Outside.'

She pulled open the snug door, wrenched at the back door and stalked out barefoot into her grandmother's garden. She could see no one. She went on with stabbing feet, feeling cold, sharp stones and wet grass. She found the high stone wall, the gate between garden and driveway. Unlocked. Behind her, she heard the thud of Michael's feet.

She pulled the gate open, stood with him looking out onto lawn and gravel, and nothing out of place. There was only the house, the trees whose branches dipped in dancing silhouettes, and the distant nothingness of the sea.

'Are you sure?' she said.

He seemed to shrink in the darkness. 'I think so. I thought so . . .' His voice trailed off, breaking into nothing. 'I don't know.'

Inside, while she bolted the door, he spoke with regained confidence. 'We can't have *both* imagined it, can we? Sienna and me.'

She stepped into the study, turned off the lights, came out again. 'There's such a thing as mass delusion, Michael. I suppose it must start somewhere.'

'And the cards?'

'I have my own ideas about them.' She steered him to the stairs. 'Don't tell anyone else about this. Not yet.'

'Why?'

'Just trust me.'

On the dim landing, she watched him go wet-footed into his room. Then, half mocking herself, she trod silently another floor up and pushed open the door of the children's room. One, two, three, four. All accounted for; all oblivious. Lexie lay on her front, one arm flailing over the side of the bed, while Jimmy, as always, was huddled into a ball clutching the bear that Clara had made for him. The twins slept with their hands reaching out to one another.

In her own room, Brandon grunted as she curled against him, borrowing warmth. She kissed his spine, too lightly to wake him.

Do you still believe that nothing can touch you?

Her unwanted correspondent had meant to taunt her, but she *did* believe it. She would make it true.

30

Darryl

Edinburgh, 2002

Thursday 28 March

I thought they would take Phyllis from me, but they did not. I sat with her broken skull and her dislocated limbs all huddled against me, her tacky dress over the smooth plastic of her torso and the cold of the floor filtering into my bones. She fitted easily, all of her, onto my lap. Her wounds were bloodless because she had no blood.

'Darryl,' Michael said. 'What's happened?'

My mouth moved of its own accord, shaping her name. I said it again, over and over, unable to stop. Sienna approached, letting go of Rob's hand. She kneeled in front of me, reaching out pale fingers, but she did not touch the broken doll. The day outside was warm, but I could see the goosebumps on her arms.

Aline said, 'Is *that* Phyllis?'

I got up on shaking legs. I sought the words that might still mend this. *My sister's. Accident. No, of course this isn't*

Phyllis. But when I opened my mouth, I was speaking not to Aline, but to Sienna.

'This is your fault.'

She gulped. Rob sprang forward, faster than I would have thought possible, and stood between us. I staggered away from them, taking the gap between Aline and Michael, still holding Phyllis against my chest. I felt them watching me, all the long, sore way back upstairs.

They left this afternoon, without saying goodbye. I don't know if Sienna has gone with Rob or with Aline, or neither.

Friday 29 March

Today is Good Friday. I have had no hot cross buns, just as I will have no Easter eggs on Sunday. Instead, I went this morning into the back bedroom, which was once my sister's, and pulled out a small suitcase from underneath the bed. It still had its label: a white card in pink plastic from when we all went to Portugal, when my sister was nine. I touched the label. *Edinboora*, she had written. She had cried when I pointed out the mistake.

I levered the case open, hinges stiff, and the dolls lay there in their row as though they were waiting for me. How old was my sister when she folded a blanket in here and laid them on top? Eleven? Twelve? Old enough to be embarrassed to have them out when her friends came round; too young to want rid of them.

There were no surprises here. The blonde with her hair half pulled out, her arms bent and broken, one eye missing after an argument with the table. The brunette with her fixed curls and ridiculous lashes, who had been my sister's favourite. She was the tallest: maybe forty centimetres from flat plastic feet to acrylic hair. From the front, she still looked almost unblemished, even her mauve silk dress still in place and untorn. From the back, you could see where the plastic had melted when I held her against the hob. I took Phyllis from the bed, where I had lain her the day before, and squeezed her in between her broken sisters.

Two remained, genuinely unblemished, still as lovingly dressed and coiffured as they had been when my sister shut the lid on them. One had olive eyes and almost black hair, very straight and shiny, just touching her narrow shoulders; the other was a redhead, wrapped in green. My sister had painted silver nails on their tiny fingers.

I made my choice, though it was no choice really. I touched the static bronze hair and the mask-white face, then slid my hand round the green dress. I held her up to the sunlight, smiling. My fingers squeezed tight on her waist.

'Hello, you,' I said.

Friday 5 April

If they had trusted me, I would not have done what I did today. I took a pencil and marked a careful cross on the wall between my flat and the one next door. Right in the corner, where I know they have bookshelves. Then I dug out my father's drill.

The new doll watched me. Her dress is already ripped, one of her fingers missing, and she has a dent in the side of her face. I cannot even bring myself to name her. 'You should be ashamed of yourself,' I said. 'The state you're in.' I turned the drill on and held it close to her skull, but there was no reaction. 'Don't worry,' I said. 'This isn't for you. Yet.'

I held it instead to the thick wall. 'I know what you are thinking,' I told her. 'But this is different. I will be careful. I have learned from what happened in New Zealand.'

I drove the drill through the brick, coughing on the black dust. I waited for the worst of it to clear, then peered through. I experienced a moment of anxiety, then relief at the dim, unfamiliar sight of the back of a row of books, dust-edged. They will know nothing. And what does it matter if I cannot see them? It will be enough to hear their secrets.

On my side, I covered the hole with my father's framed print of the skating minister on Duddingston Loch. It amuses me to wonder what Raeburn would make of the use to which his work has been put. Or the Reverend Walker himself, for that matter. The doll glared from her cushion, so I took my mother's sewing shears, cut off those artificial locks, close to her skull, and threw them among the potato peelings in the kitchen bin.

Sunday 14 April

It is truly spring now, but it feels like summer, as Edinburgh so often does in April. The flowers flaunt themselves in brilliant colours across thousands of gardens. The Meadows are a cherry-blossom absurdity.

I would rather it was winter, and I could hide.

I forced myself out, through this obscene brightness, to the university library. I seemed incapable of writing at home. But I had forgotten that it is exam season. The library was barely recognisable. Undergraduates sat in rows at tables and computers, books piled around them, in various stages of panic or exhaustion. I only wanted enough words on the screen to keep Gemma happy when she gets back. But the words would not come – no more there than in my unwelcoming flat – so I opened my email instead, still thinking of her.

There was only one message, *not* from Gemma, and that was the end of my peace for the day.

I read the one line of content. Then I returned to the sender's name, the address with its giveaway tail: *yahoo. co.nz.* My head pulsed, my eyes darkened. Sweat swelled on my forehead and I gripped the underside of the desk with both hands to keep from slumping to the floor.

I glanced from side to side, as though this thing that was happening to me would be apparent to those around. But the boy on my right was asleep with his ginger head on the desk, and the Chinese girl on my left sat frowning into a textbook while her fingers played, as if of their own accord, with the keys of her computer. Beyond her, a boy was listening to music, too loud, on headphones, drumming his fingers on a copy of *Microeconomic Theory*.

At last, I composed myself. I blocked the address (my fingers fumbled so badly that it took me nearly a minute to do it), but I could not block what the email said, for that was already carved into my brain.

I'm coming to Edinburgh. I need to see you.

Later, I heard the others arriving back. Loud voices, then David Bowie, top volume, through the wall. But I let the Reverend hang where he was, undisturbed. I hardly cared.

The Third Postcard: December 2018

Here's a quote for you, Sienna, since you like them so much. 'Truth will come to light . . . In the end truth will out. '

31

Sienna

Dorset, 2019

He came to her in the night, as she had known he would, and her alcohol dreams gave way unprotestingly to blurred reality. His sharp-boned body, painfully familiar, desperately the reverse. His warm mouth and cool fingers: half felt, half remembered. The tears, which were all real, and which he must taste on her.

She whispered, 'I'm still married.'

Rob murmured, close against her ear, the Hyde side of her own conscience, 'Only technically.'

She choked, somewhere between laughter and pain. 'And Cass?' she said, weaker still. 'Is she a technicality too?'

He kissed her shoulder, then her neck. 'She's temporary,' he said.

She wanted to stop then, fling him from her bed, tell him that no girlfriend – no woman – deserved to be dismissed as a stopgap. But she wanted him more. She would be ashamed of that later.

'I was yours first,' he said. 'And you were mine.'

His kisses moved along her collarbone. Her lips shaped words. *We shouldn't . . . I feel bad . . .* But they would be just that: words without the actions to make them true.

'Sienna,' he murmured, as he used to do. The same amusement, the same desire. Then his mouth was on hers; his fingers were on her waist, sliding under silk. Memory ripped at her; desire contorted her, so hands and limbs and lips moved of themselves. His whisper was soft and triumphant. 'I knew you'd come back.'

This isn't what I came for.

She did not say it. But afterwards – long afterwards, when they had loved and slept, and stirred drowsy in each other's arms – she found other words.

'Rob?'

'Hmm?' He shifted, settling her closer against him. She felt his thin frame where for years she had felt the sturdy muscles of another man she had thought she loved. Another reason for guilt. But they were all entwined now. She closed her eyes and saw a painting, clear as if it lay before her. Bold oil colours, flesh and muscles, and the hard metal of a sword.

'Rubens,' she murmured, as though it was a mantra she was condemned to repeat.

'What?'

Until the postcard had arrived, she had known her lies for lies but she had tried to pretend she could live with them. She had almost succeeded.

'Nothing,' she said. And then, because she had not come here to tell more lies, 'It's just . . . Do you ever think about that night?'

'Which night?'

She moved sharply against him. 'You know which.'

He groaned, not as he had groaned before. 'Sen, do we have to do this now?'

Her face turned, salt-wet, into his chest. 'Yes,' she whispered. 'Yes.'

'Well then,' he said, 'I try not to.'

'I've never stopped thinking about it.' The words, now they had come, came fast and desperate. 'All the time, even when I should have been happiest. Every piece of luck, my husband, my children, I thought how I didn't deserve them.'

Rob rolled onto his side, raising her face to his. 'Enough,' he whispered.

She spoke blankly, into the air behind him. 'Today,' she said, 'when Astrid ran into the water—'

'She's fine, Sienna. Nothing happened.'

'If she had drowned,' Sienna said, 'that would have been my fault too.'

He cupped her face in his thin hands, spoke with a firmness she had not expected. 'No, Sen. Stop that.' He kissed her hair. 'Enough guilt.'

She wept into his bony shoulder. 'Is there ever enough?' she said.

Cretaceous

Sea levels fall, mudstones and chalk form. Tectonic plates shift. Megalosaurus roams by swamps and coastal forests. Rat-like mammals thrive and spread and wait their chance. Sauropods lay huge feet on the living earth, leaving their tracks for a wondering posterity. The jar has been tipped, and the settled lines are tilted east, eroded down, forming a new permanent. Apparently immovable.

32

Darryl

Edinburgh, 2002

Tuesday 30 April

Calton Hill was firelit for the Beltane Festival, at once wild and claustrophobic. It is every year, but I have never been before. So many people, with their faces painted or masked, cloaked or almost naked, bodies green or red or gold. The pale columns that were something out of a different past. The men with thick beards and goat's horn headdresses, and girls bare-breasted, carrying torches. The watching eyes all around, excited, serious and alive. The drums with their relentless, taut energy.

I wanted to tell Aline, 'You should have been the May Queen.' Because it was true, she was lovelier than any of them, even that girl they had chosen, with her long hair and ornate robes and the firelight that flickered on her face. Only I could say nothing to Aline – to any of them – because although I went there for them, I was not *with* them. I was reduced to a follower, creeping in their wake.

I emerged from the flat when I heard the four of them leave and made my way a half-street behind, cloak-wrapped, all the long trek through the Meadows, along the bridges and across London Road to Calton Hill. Aline's hair was twisted high onto her head, wreathed with flowers, Sienna's hung like a flag down her back, and Rob had a thorny crown on his head. Those had been my guides.

On the hill, the crowd swelled, bizarre and ritualistic with the lengthening dusk. I watched it all, hidden beneath my cloak. The May dancers, weird-beautiful, with the flowers in their hair. The Green Man, young and muscular and painted, his head wreathed, sacrificed and reborn like something from a barbaric age. Except then the sacrifice would have been real, fire blackening that decorated torso, screams of pain mixing with the excitement.

As darkness crept in, I watched a row of young women with white-painted faces and strange, secret smiles. Did they look like that, the maidens laying down *their* lives, or at least their virginity, all those centuries ago? A girl was lifted high on a man's shoulders, raising her arms to the stars, breasts and buttocks bare and muscular. A man's head, clean-shaven, painted blue, was so close I could see the sweat on it.

I spotted Rob, faintly cynical, in the crowd. With that bony face and spiky crown he could almost have come as Christ. I laughed aloud at how doubly inappropriate that would have been. I thought again of sacrifice. I felt a little drunk, and yet I had had only a half-measure of Glenfiddich before I left the flat, to give me courage.

I thought of Gemma. I pictured her smiling like those girls and holding out her arms to me. I even looked for her among the swaying dancers. Then I pushed the thought aside, for steadier times.

Before the procession – the death, the regeneration, the vast bonfire awakened and blazing – Sienna seemed distracted, always watching Rob. Afterwards, she danced with him, leaning into him as though they were part of some pre-ordained ritual. I wanted to look away, but when I did, I saw Aline and Michael, also close together. The swaying flames showed me his face, streaked with green paint, borderline handsome in its brief ecstasy. I crept closer, sheltered by the crowd. They were almost embracing. I saw moving lights and the city like another world below us, and heard the chanting revellers.

I heard the drums. I hear them still.

They were so close now, my former friends. Sienna spun from Rob, her fingers still reaching back for him, her skirt billowing. My hand went out and I felt her warm skin. My fingers gripped her arm, pinching into flesh, tight enough to bruise. It was wonderful, and fearful.

If she screamed, it was lost in the noise about her. I moved away, heart thumping, and when I looked again, sheltered by numbers and distance, I saw the four of them together, leaning in and talking fast. Rob and Aline each had an arm around Sienna. Michael was scanning the crowd, his head rotating like a meerkat's. I pulled my hood closer.

Later, someone piled more wood onto the bonfire. Sienna and Rob clung tight again, kissing by the leaping red and

orange flames. I turned from them in disgust to watch the
man with the blue head, now performing a strange acro-
batic dance. I saw Aline spinning round and round with a
young giant in a stag's headdress. Michael was nowhere to
be seen.

I left them dancing and walked home with the cloak held
tight about me. In the flat, I laid piles of paper and card in
the grate I had not used since my parents died. I poured
whisky into one of my mother's best glasses and raised it to
the flames.

There were drums in Auckland too.

It was my aunt's birthday. She wasn't really my aunt, but
she told me to call her that and for a while I did. Her
husband had 'made reservations', as he put it, at an
expensive restaurant in town. My cousins were going to a
party at a friend's house. 'You'll take Darryl?' their mother
said, and all day I was anticipatory, almost delirious. But
when I came downstairs, in a shirt I had changed three
times, they had already gone.

I went after them. I thought I understood them by then,
in their alternating friendliness and indifference. I told
myself that this half-hour's walk was a task they had set
me: one of many by means of which I would prove my
worthiness to associate with them.

The drums carried down the suburban street, so that
neighbours appeared disgruntled at curtains. There was a fast
beat and a woman singing, bodies everywhere and a fairy-
thin girl at the door who held a pink drink in her hand and
looked through me as though I was less than nothing. Then

she turned her head and shouted into the melee, 'It's your freak cousin. I thought you said he wasn't coming.'

I wanted to vomit in the street. I wanted to run, but my cousins were there now, parting the throng, seeing me on the doorstep. The girl's wrist was in the hand of her weightlifter boyfriend, her skirt hitched up her long bare legs. Her brother was beside them.

I waited for kindness, welcome, praise. I waited for them to defend me to their friend who had been so unkind. I saw them balance their options, consider their audience. The girl said, 'Oh Darryl, we only said we'd bring you because Mum insisted. We didn't mean it.' And then, with mock pity in her drink-glazed eyes, 'Are you stupid? Did you really think we were your friends?'

33

Brandon

Dorset, 2019

When Brandon was nine, a five-year-old in their town had found her mom's Smith & Wesson in her bag. She'd hurtled into the kitchen, wanting to play, with the gun in one hand and a Barbie in the other, and shot her mother in the head.

He remembered the moment he had found out, as vividly as his parents said they recalled hearing that Kennedy had been shot. The football he'd been carrying slipping from his fingers, shaping its muddy arc across the kitchen floor. His own mom's face, so empty of colour it was like the damp dishtowel she held in her hand. His dad with his head on the table, saying over and over, 'Oh God, that poor kid.'

Now, in the dawn stillness of their Dorset bedroom, he dreamed of that afternoon, but somehow he was both his younger self and the girl's father. She was Lexie, then Chloe, then another, unnamed child, running bloodstained through his own house with a gun that was too big for her. He went to the body and tried to turn it, expecting Nikki, and saw Aline's face instead, simultaneously dead and laughing. He leaped up, in the bed, and woke still hearing that laughter.

He sat with his back against the wrought headboard, the duvet slumping from him so the cold hit him full in his arms and chest. Aline still slept beside him, her face turned on the pillow. He experienced an almost overwhelming urge to run upstairs to his daughter, just to check, but that way lay paranoia. Instead, he swung his feet to the carpeted floor, pulled the blanket from the bed and hugged it around himself. He stood at the window, drew the curtain back and gazed out at the early light, thin silver over a still-black sea. Behind him, the radiator clicked on.

Aline turned, murmured, 'Where are you?'

He didn't reply. She spoke through the dimness, sharper and more awake. 'What's wrong?' She sat up in the bed, dragging the covers with her.

He turned reluctantly from the quiet dawn. 'You have a gun, Aline. How could you not tell me?'

'I'd forgotten it was there.' Immediately, indifferent to contradiction, she added, 'I didn't think it was important.'

It is to me.

He put a hand on the windowsill, forcing his fingers hard into the paintwork. 'Our kids are in this house.'

She considered him a moment, then changed tack, smiling tenderly. 'Come back to bed, darling. We can talk about it later.'

He didn't move. She said, less tenderly, 'The kids are completely safe, Brandon. The gun is locked. The cartridges are kept separately, also locked.'

'Where?'

'That little cupboard above the back door. And I know how to use it properly. I'm a good shot. My gran taught me when I was a teenager.' He pictured bloodied rabbits and limp birds hanging from her hands.

She got up despite the wintry room and came to him at the window, wrapping her arms round his waist. 'Trust me,' she said, and he saw the images of his dream, like grisly cartoons, dancing across the grey sky.

'I want you to get rid of it.'

She sighed. 'Darling, you're being ridiculous. At least give it a try first. You might enjoy it.'

'Please, Aline.'

'Or what?' She touched warm lips to his cold neck. 'Or you'll leave me?' She laughed, soft as a caress. 'You know you could never do that.'

He unpeeled her hands, pushed her from him, pulled out shorts and T-shirt, found last night's fleece thrown on a chair. She sat on the edge of the bed, sculpture-calm, with the blanket about her. 'Where are you going?'

'Running,' he said. 'Alone.'

It was a grey morning, clouds hanging like a threat. He took the coast path, reversing their route back from the Pirate's Path the night before, then going beyond it, breathing in damp air, treading long wet grass. He took fast, full-legged strides, feeling his muscles come alive. Far beneath him, the sea shivered into the new day.

I need this.

Once, in the Meadows, stretched out on the grass, still panting from a fast 5K, Aline had told him, 'This is the only therapy anyone should need.' He doubted that, but it was all either of them had had.

He ran faster, tasting salt and his own sweat.

They had become engaged on this path: further along, closer to Durdle Door, on a breezy summer day shortly after graduation. She had kissed him, and it was as though she had entrapped him in that spectacular, terrifying place, giddy and desperate for her and for it. 'We should make this permanent,' she had said, and he had replied with a groan that was half a laugh, pulling her back against him, tugging at her T-shirt like an oversexed adolescent.

Afterwards, hidden among bushes off the path, giggling and gasping, still three-quarters dressed, she had said, 'I'll take that as a yes.'

'A yes to what?'

'To our future.'

He had not been able to say no. And afterwards with her family – her grandmother, her parents, Clara and Clara's girlfriend – all drinking champagne from the same glistening glasses they had used this weekend, she had gripped his hand in hers and told them all, 'I have news. We're going to be married.'

His foot landed awkwardly, but the pain was nothing: barely a distraction. He was deep in memory now, hitting each one like a gong with each step on this mass of earth and clay and stone topped with its veneer of green. A month into their engagement, when he had insisted that he didn't want kids.

'Don't be silly,' she'd said. 'You'd be a wonderful father.'

'It's not what I want,' he'd said, and it was half true.

'OK,' she had said. 'It's no deal-breaker. We're young. We'll work it out later.' And she had.

Another pace: a rock beneath his sole. Their first major row, a year after their lavish wedding, when his dad had just gotten sick. He had wanted to apply for a job in Cleveland; Aline had refused. 'We belong here,' she'd said. 'My family are here. We can go visit.'

Another step, sore on his twisted foot. He'd applied for the job anyway, and been invited for an interview. 'I won't go,' she had said, 'and I won't let you.'

'Perhaps you can't stop me,' he had said.

'I can.' She had taken his face in her hands, smiled her loving triumph into his eyes. 'I'm pregnant.' She had kissed him then, warm and sweet and deep as if there had been no quarrel, no qualms heard or uttered.

'I love you,' she had said. 'I know it's a little sooner than we planned, but we're both doing well. We're going to be so happy.'

He allowed himself a moment's pause, atop a rise, taking in the coast ahead. White chalk cliffs, dark green grass: brown-edged, rising and dipping. The dark blanket, white-flecked, of the sea. He heard the liquid cry of a willow warbler; the first this year. Somewhere inland, the cows were returning from milking, issuing a low, intermittent mooing. He didn't want to go back, so he went on.

When his dad died, Brandon had not been there. They had flown out for the funeral and he had held baby Lexie to his chest all through the service, poleaxed by love and grief. At the wake, eating hash brown casserole, surrounded by family, he had watched Aline work the room in her Bond Street clothes. Universally charming, particularly attentive to his mom.

'You've done so well,' his aunt had said, hugging him and the baby close at once. 'Your dad would have been so proud.'

He had taken another mouthful, felt it hot and salty in his mouth. Comfort food; the taste of home. Now he tasted sea air and his own hangover. His chest burned. He slammed his still-sore foot into the dirt and flung himself forward. If his wife needed therapy, he thought, she would never admit it. She would never even know it.

An hour later, when he was running on nothing, almost back to the house, he was accosted by a man coming the other way with a walking stick and a cap low on his forehead. Brandon nodded, managed a panting 'Hi' and would have gone on, but the man planted his stick firmly in the path.

'You're the American that married that Linden girl.'

'I am.' Brandon managed to smile. 'Nice to meet you.' He paused for breath. 'Did you know Aline's gran?'

The old gent ignored these pleasantries. He regarded Brandon steadily, through watery red-flecked eyes. 'I wrote to her,' he said, 'when she started her crazy renovations, but she's as stubborn as the old woman was.'

'I'm sorry, I don't—'

'I told her what I thought of them. Told your builders too.' He peered closer. A vein throbbed on his temple. 'She didn't even tell you, did she?'

185

Brandon sought in vain for an appropriate response. His interlocutor stabbed at the ground with the stick. 'Well, I can see I'm talking to the monkey, and I want the organ grinder. You just ask her what I said. I'm down there most days.' He gestured down and westwards, towards the beach. 'No doubt I'll see her.'

'OK,' Brandon said. He thought suddenly, absurdly, of Sienna, and how much she would have appreciated this costume-drama dialogue.

The man raised his stick – in threat, or salutation? – and stomped on before Brandon could say more.

Brandon walked the rest of the way, his lungs easing, his calves stinging and a twinge in his knee that had not been there when he ran round the Edinburgh paths and streets with Aline. Perhaps he should have defended her, or himself, but he had not had the heart.

He thought, as he had thought so often over the years, of that little girl who had almost been his neighbour. For years, until her father moved the family to another state, he had seen her from time to time, trailing at the end of the line coming out of the elementary school or trembling at the back in church. He had always looked away. She had been like an image of herself, traced on tissue paper; too real to vanish, too thin to survive. What kind of a life had she had?

If he had told Aline that story this morning, would she have answered him differently? He didn't know. And if he had meant to ask her about the old man's words, that intention vanished the moment he entered the house.

34

Darryl

Edinburgh, 2002

Monday 13 May

I have neglected my diary this past fortnight. I have neglected everything. I watch from the window as they wander out in the summer sun. Sometimes it's all of them, carrying cans, a portable barbecue and a cricket (or rounders?) bat. Other times, it's just Rob and Sienna, or Aline alone in running kit or denim shorts and vest top, fast on the pavement with her sunglasses and her long, tanned legs, alive with youth and confidence. Some nights, when she is out, I see Michael coming back alone from the shop, carrying a microwave curry.

If I had less of my own to worry about, or liked him more, I might pity him.

I take further confidences by stealth, lifting the Raeburn print down from my wall. I shut out memories: a girl sprawled on a pile of cushions, a telephone receiver on its curly wire pressed to her head; a gaggle of them together, talking in

New Zealand accents. I pull up a chair and sit with my ear like Pyramus's eye, hard against the chink.

In this way, I know that Sienna is leaving on Friday to spend a fortnight with a friend in France, and Rob is annoyed that she won't take him. I know this last because she told Michael last night, when Rob was late home from the pub. I know too that Michael has confided in her what she had almost certainly already guessed: his unrequited adoration of Aline. Sienna has done her best for him: a best composed of anodyne New Age philosophy and the odd literary quotation chucked in, like a dash of antiseptic, to sharpen the mix. But she cannot give him hope. You'd think with her literature major, as she persists in calling it, she would have known better than to try. The course of true love, sometimes, is a one-way ticket to despair.

Do *I* have hope? I do, despite everything, because I still have Gemma. The one true, lovely thing in my life. She will be back soon. And there have been no more New Zealand emails. That, at least, is a negative kind of good.

Saturday 25 May

Something has happened, and I must decide how to use it.

Sienna has been gone eight days and Rob does not appear to have stayed in and wept for her. Last night, their flat was full: a loud impromptu party. The sound was so abrasive that I put in earplugs and retreated to bed, like a very old man. I wanted to dream of Gemma, but instead I dreamed of Phyllis, falling, falling, only she had my sister's face. She lay in a broken heap on a concrete floor and all I could hear were my New Zealand cousins, standing with their arms round each other. *Oh Darryl, did you really think we liked you? Were you really glad – and don't pretend, we know everything – were you really almost glad that it had happened, if it got you us instead?*

The dream shifted, as they do, so I had my eye to a hole in a wall and a woman was dancing for a man on the other side, and the woman was Gemma, in my mother's silk dressing gown, and the man was Rob. I woke sweating and crying and wished, improbable and bizarre, that I had Phyllis lying undamaged beside me.

I did not sleep again.

In the morning, I opened my door to the smell of beer on the landing and to a sight that had once been familiar enough: Rob, greenish-faced, letting a girl out of their flat. She was a stranger, curly-haired, with last night's thick make-up spread like battle scars on her face. She turned as she left, clung like a beetle, kissing him on the mouth. For a moment, I thought that too was a dream. Then I knew it was not.

'Morning,' I said, very loud.

The girl jumped, giggled and scuttled away down the stairs. Rob looked at me as though he would say something. I thought of all the things *I* could say, and uttered none of them.

The Fourth Postcard: December 2018

So many years, Rob, and so little to show for them.
One mediocre job and a score of disposable girlfriends.
Do you know you can't escape, in your constant replay of
a misspent youth? Not even from yourself.

35

Rob

Dorset, 2019

It was an unpropitious morning. Rob came down last and unwillingly to find Nikki feeding Rufus on the sofa, the kids squabbling round the table and the nanny pouring batter into a frying pan. And Sienna – of course – sitting quiet between her daughters.

'We have to talk,' she had told him before he left her in the early hours. 'All of us.'

Now she met his eye for one tense moment, then turned back to Astrid, who was tugging at her arm. Behind them, through Aline's pretentious windows, he could barely make out the sky from the sea.

We all have to talk. But not, apparently, right now.

God, he wanted a smoke. Instead, he sipped his coffee, which was delicious, and contemplated adding that to his Brandon List.

'Where are the others?'

'Outside,' Nikki said. She looked dog-tired; even worse

than usual. If ever there was an advert for remaining child-free, it was the state of near-collapse in which she and Michael seemed perpetually to exist. 'Brandon's gone for a run.'

'After last night? He's insane. And the rest?'

'Out the back.' Nikki's face twisted as she said it, and he realised, with interest, that she wasn't just tired; she was furiously angry.

He looked a question, but she glanced from him to the kids still stuffing pancakes, and said nothing. Sienna gave an infinitesimal shake of her head. He made for the garden. The back door stuck, and while he wrestled with it, Nikki addressed the assembled children, sharp as a whip. 'You all stay here. Remember? None of you is going out there.'

Lexie gave an exaggerated sigh, and her mother's shrug.

Outside, between the high stone walls, where rain hung on the apple trees and beaded the long grass, he found Aline, Michael and Cass.

Michael was at the far end, arranging two Coke cans on the branch of a tree, maybe a metre apart, shifting them one way or the other under shouted instruction. Cass watched with folded arms. Aline stood on the remains of the path, looking the part in a Barbour jacket and the kind of wellington boots you needed a mortgage to buy, with the shotgun open in her hands.

'Want to join us?' Her voice was bright. Too bright.

'Sure.'

He stood by Cass, trying to smile. 'How are you feeling?'

She looked sideways at him. 'How should I be?'

Hung-over. But perhaps he need not ask. She was very

pale, un-made-up for once, with bags under her eyes and hair scraped back in a ponytail. It made her look plainer, but also (oddly) even younger. She was taking long breaths of the cold air.

Aline retrieved two cartridges from her Barbour pocket, loaded them expertly, clicked the gun shut, set it on her shoulder and fired twice. She barely seemed to notice the recoil. The cans vanished like hit birds from their branch: one, then the other.

'Fuck me,' Rob said.

Aline glanced at him, while Michael scurried forward with new cans. 'Surprised?'

'I suppose I shouldn't be.'

She loaded the gun again for Michael, positioned it on his shoulder, issued instructions, warned him of the recoil.

Cass said quietly, 'Perhaps I should ask how *you* are? Or how Sienna is?'

'What do you mean?'

Aline stepped back. Michael stood there a moment, fumbling, his finger lurching over the safety catch. Then he sighed and lowered the gun. 'I can't,' he said.

'Really?' Aline sounded contemptuous, but also as though she was only half attending.

'I'm not firing it.'

Rob finished his coffee, grateful for the distraction. 'Scared of your wife?'

'I just don't want to.'

Cass said, 'Perhaps he cares what Nikki thinks. Is that a crime?' She straightened, unpeeling from the stone wall. 'Can I have a go, Aline?'

'Sure,' Aline said, without noticeable enthusiasm. 'Don't tell me. You're a stalwart of your local shooting club, waiting to show us all up again.'

'I doubt I could show you up, even if I was. Anyway, I'm not.'

The two women stood together, close as conspirators, while Michael slumped against the wall beside Rob. Aline repeated her instructions, her voice as cool and detached as the voiceover on an aeroplane safety demonstration. Through the kitchen window, Rob could see Milly putting the frying pan in the sink and Lexie and Jimmy bickering. Beside him, Michael looked even worse than Nikki had.

'What's up?' Rob said. 'Lose your nerve?'

Michael seemed to be staring past the two women, the cans on their branch, even the high stone wall at the back of the garden. 'I told you. I just didn't feel like it.'

Cass was lifting the gun to her shoulder now, Aline's fair head against her faux-red one. Suddenly Michael spoke again, in a sharp whisper. 'Rob, do you think Sienna was right about seeing someone on the Pirate's Path?'

'I don't know.' Rob frowned, remembering Sienna's face as it had been in the garden last night. *I didn't imagine anything.* 'She sounded certain, but it's not exactly probable, is it? Why?'

'I just wondered.'

Rob saw Aline's long fingers indicating trigger and safety catch, Cass asking a question, Aline moving away.

Cass said, 'I've never shot anything before.' She turned her head so her eyes met Rob's: a steady, contemptuous look. The gun moved with her. 'It feels powerful,' she said aloud. 'As though I could do anything I wanted.' And then, mouthing the words, saying them only for him: 'I know where you were last night.'

Rob saw blue letters on white card, almost for the first time since he had ripped it into pieces and thrown it into the bin. *Do you know you can't escape . . . Not even from yourself.* He felt the beginnings of fear.

He should have equivocated, feigned surprise. Instead, he heard his own voice, with a panicky edge.

'*Don't.*'

'Don't what?' said Cass. She laughed, too high, turned back to the tree and fired.

The first shot went wide. The second struck the left-hand can. 'Well done,' Aline said.

Cass shrugged, ceding the gun. 'Beginner's luck.'

She walked to where Rob still stood, pretending he hadn't been afraid. Beside them, Michael stared conspicuously the other way. 'I heard you through the wall,' she said. 'You and her.'

Rob opened his mouth, closed it, opened it again. He said, 'I'm sor—'

She shook her head. 'Fuck you, Rob.'

She strode to the door, pushed it open and marched inside, leaving it swinging behind her. Aline raised her eyebrows, seemed about to speak, then didn't. Instead, she wrenched open the gun, reaching in her pocket for more ammunition. 'Do you want a turn, Rob?'

Before he could answer, Brandon came out through the still-open door and stood in the porch, staring at her, red-faced, dripping sweat and shaking with anger.

36

Darryl

Edinburgh, 2002

Sunday 26 May

I watched Rob all along the street from my window. I watched him on the path in his sunglasses and T-shirt. I counted from when he passed out of sight into the tenement and opened my door at exactly the right time.

'Hi,' I said.

It must have been another heavy night, because his face was the colour it was that September morning when Aline first brought him to my door. His T-shirt was powder blue with a white box containing the words MANIC STREET PREACHERS and EVERYTHING MUST GO and, inexplicably, a pair of brackets with nothing between them. He smelled of cigarettes.

'Chess?' I said.

He glared, as though I had insulted him by asking. Then he turned away. 'I'm busy,' he said.

'Really?' I waited a moment. 'Because I think we should talk.'

He stopped. It was as if I could see through hair and skin and skull to the moving cogs of his brain; as though that curly-haired girl stood between us on the landing. At last, he shrugged, not very graciously, and followed me into the flat. He kept glancing about. Perhaps he was looking for Phyllis. Well, he wouldn't find her now. Or maybe it was just the mess that bothered him. I hadn't really noticed it until then.

He wrinkled his nose, apparently confirming this. It has been a while since I emptied the bins. He said, 'Did someone die in here?'

I thought again of Phyllis. Perhaps he did, too.

'Beer?' I remembered that I didn't have any. 'Coffee?'

He shook his head. In the sitting room, the first thing he noticed was the knight, mended with superglue but still obviously scarred. 'What happened to him?'

I picked up the piece and held it tight in my fist. 'Nothing.'

Rob didn't ask more. He sat at the other end of the sofa from the chess set, so I sat down too.

'How've you been?'

'Fine. Darryl, what is this about?'

I smiled, and kept on smiling. *I am in control here.* I said, 'I was thinking about Dorset.'

'What about it?'

'Now that Sienna won't be going, maybe I could.'

He was already still, but he seemed to freeze at that. 'What the hell are you talking about? Sienna's coming with us.'

I met his eyes, all innocence. I was almost enjoying this. 'I just assumed you and she were over, after yesterday morning.'

I thought he might walk out; he looked angry enough. 'Sienna and I are fine.'

'Is that what she'll think when she knows?'

He swallowed. His knuckles were stretched smooth. At last he spoke, in a very different tone.

'To be honest, Darryl, we've been keeping away from you for a reason.' *To be honest.* His go-to phrase for disingenuous cruelty. 'You've been behaving very strangely. Even if I said you could come to Dorset, the others wouldn't go for it. Michael and Sienna think you need help.' He paused a moment, eyeing the room. I saw what I had stopped noticing: the plates of half-eaten food, the wine bottles it was easier not to throw away. The scratch in my grandfather's desk. Oh God, that print of Duddingston Loch, hanging crooked over the hole.

'*I* can't help wondering,' he said, 'if the university knows what's going on with you. Your supervisor . . .'

I thought of Gemma, whom I will see this week. I gripped the knight so tightly that the horse's ears stabbed into my palm.

Rob stood up. 'Of course,' he said, 'it's none of my business.'

'No,' I said. 'It's not.'

'And my love life is none of yours.'

So that was it. No chess game, this. No equivocation. Just a straightforward threat to match my clumsy attempt at manipulation. *You tell Sienna, and I go to the university authorities about that business with the doll.*

After he had gone, I took the redhead from the kitchen floor and forced her back into the suitcase with the rest.

Wednesday 29 May

'I'm sorry,' I said. 'I've been reading a lot, but I haven't managed to get much down.' It was a lie, of course. I have not been reading at all.

Gemma and I stared at the single sheet of paper on her desk, and she sighed as though she was sad for me but not reproachful. She was prettier than ever today. Her skin was tanned gold. (Weeks in the sunshine with the boyfriend? I didn't want to think so.) Her hair was much longer now than Phyllis's had been, and loose. Her dress was floaty, with little black birds darting across a deep red background. Her ankles and calves were bare, and she had painted her toenails the same red as the dress. I imagined her getting ready, preening herself for me.

She said, 'How are you, Darryl?'

'Fine.' I pictured myself holding her hand, walking among the fallen cherry blossoms on the avenue in the Meadows with the breeze raising that soft hair, then letting it fall.

When she had made what she could of my jumbled notes, she played awkwardly with a blue biro. 'Are you sure you're fine?'

I said nothing. My hands were suddenly clammy in my lap. She said, 'I was hoping you'd been able to access the support services I recommended.'

I stared at my shoes. 'I'm not sure they're right for me.'

'It's not my business, I know . . .'

Oh it is. It is.

'. . . but like I said in my email, your second supervisor and I are both a bit worried by the deterioration in your work.'

He's not.

'He says you haven't been in touch to reschedule your meeting with him.'

'I've been busy.'

We both looked at the one sheet of paper that was all I had produced from this alleged busyness. Gemma sighed. 'I'm not *blaming* you, Darryl. I just think you might need to talk to someone. You've been through a lot.'

'It's true,' I said. 'I have.' I looked past her to the window, the summer-blue sky, and knew the time was right. The *person* was right.

'Yes,' I said. 'Thank you, Gemma. I *would* like to talk about it.'

I went on fast, immediately, my words jumping ahead of each other. She started to say something, tried again, then fell silent. I told her about my parents' last evening on earth. I told her of the police officers knocking at my door in the middle of the night, of sitting on my sofa with the woman officer beside me, being asked over and over if there was anyone they could call. In the end, a friend of my mother's had come, stayed with me at the hospital until Mum's cousin could get there from Auckland. I told her of the three days and nights by my sister's hospital bed.

'I'm so sorry,' she said.

I said, 'The other driver was an American. He walked out of hospital, got a taxi to the airport and went straight back to the States. I don't know if the cops were just incompetent, or if he bribed someone.'

'Jesus,' Gemma said.

'He killed them,' I said, 'and he got away with it.'

She said it again: 'I'm so sorry.'

'I had to tell you.'

Outside, someone opened and shut a door. Voices progressed along the corridor, loud and then quiet again. Gemma said, 'Thank you for trusting me with this.'

'There's more,' I said. I heard myself babbling, and could not stop. 'My family in New Zealand were unkind. They were cruel. I should never have been sent there.'

She raised her voice, just a little. 'Darryl,' she said, 'I can't begin to imagine what it has been like for you. But I'm not qualified to help. If you would let me refer—'

'No.' The word came out like a cry: far sharper than I had intended. *That's not why I told you.*

'I'm so sorry, Darryl, but I have another meeting now.'

'My friends here,' I said. 'They've let me down too. They've betrayed me and I know they will tell lies about me.'

Someone knocked on the door. 'Darryl,' she said. 'Please go to the counselling offices. Go now. Or to your GP.' She smiled, very gently. 'Promise me,' she said.

'Thank you,' I said. But I did not promise.

I opened the door and her next student scuttled past me. A scrofulous, unappealing boy, but she gave him her generous smile.

I walked down the stairs with my feet like rocks and the sunlight flickering through the intermittent windows, over the laminate floor. I knew now what the lines were that had taunted me, months ago, from the edge of consciousness. I could quote them, word for word, but I could not say where they were from.

> She smiled, no doubt,
> Whene'er I passed her; but who passed without
> Much the same smile?

Gemma could place them for me. So, no doubt, could Sienna. But for obvious reasons I cannot ask either of them.

Friday 31 May

I have done it.

I didn't decide until I saw Sienna tonight, and then I acted on reckless, reactive impulse. I heard her constant delighted chatter through the wall. I heard Rob's indolent replies. They stopped to kiss, disappeared to the bedroom, re-emerged after a long interval, and she rattled on more about her French holiday. The peace, the atmosphere, the food, how she had 'recharged'. I heard her asking about Michael and Aline.

Then I froze.

She said, 'And what about . . .?' I could almost see her gesturing to the shared wall. Rob seemed to hesitate. Then he replied lightly – lying, of course, but confirming my suspicions – 'No new weirdness. I've barely seen him.'

'Thank God,' she said. 'I've been thinking, you know, he really does need help. He must be seriously disturbed.'

'Very possibly,' Rob said. 'But right now, I'd rather not think about that. I want to concentrate on you.'

I got up. I felt the chair judder against the wall and hoped they had not heard it. But I was too angry to stop. I went out as I was onto the landing and hammered with both fists on their door. At last they came to it, disordered, post-coital and halfway back to coital again.

I was dishevelled too, but not like them. Sienna saw that at once. She clocked a three-days-old shirt, pulled back on and never properly tucked in. There was a button missing. My socks had been on longer still.

I hated her for noticing. I hated her again for the pity in her eyes.

'Good trip?' I said, before she could speak. 'How was France? Get up to anything exciting?'

Her hand wavered on the open door. She turned in a little, towards Rob. Did she think I was drunk, dangerous or merely disgusting? Maybe all three. 'Yes, thank you,' she said. And then, as the pause stretched, 'Was there anything you needed, Darryl?'

'Oh no.' I smiled. I felt my lips stretch. 'Just checking in.'

She started to shut the door. 'It was great, thank you. Goodnight.'

I rammed my foot into the narrowing gap. The pain was like brandy: sharp and invigorating. 'Rob did,' I said.

'What?'

'Rob had a *great* time.' I turned my cadaver grin on him. 'You mean you haven't told Sienna all about it yet?'

She made a strange little sound. It was the noise I imagine someone might make if they had been shot but hadn't felt it yet. Rob slammed the door so hard that I only just got my toes out unmangled. I sent my last jibe through unyielding wood. 'Or rather, all about *her*.'

As I limped away, I heard Sienna's voice, oddly calm, from behind the door. 'What did he mean?'

I checked my listening hole, but they must have gone to another room, so I went to the window instead and looked down onto the street. Students chattering, a woman weaving past them on a bike. Trees vivid green, and a man stopping outside our gate. Dark brown hair. Wide shoulders. White T-shirt.

I dived back behind the shutters. I expected the buzzer, but when it came, the sound made me crouch on the ground, clutching with cold hands at my hot face. I did not answer. And when I looked out again, minutes later, peering like the village busybody round her lace curtains, he was gone.

37

Milly

Dorset, 2019

It is quite a scene. We follow Brandon to the back door: Nikki, Sienna and me (even though I should probably stay with the kids). Cass has already stumbled off upstairs, her face all crumpled as though she was about to cry. Lexie tries to come with us, but her dad shouts at her to stay put. In all these months, this is the first time I've heard him raise his voice at either of the children, but it is nothing to how he yells at Aline and their friends.

He should look ridiculous, giving out like that in his shorts and muddy trainers, with his face still beetroot red from running, but he doesn't. His anger is too real, too raw for that. Even Aline winces, though she has herself together in seconds.

'Darling, what a fuss.' She comes to him, across grass and stones, and puts a hand to his face. 'The kids are all safe inside. The gun hadn't been used for years. I just wanted to test it out before I decide what to do with it.'

He pushes her hand away. He doesn't do it hard or

violently, but I am watching her expression and she *really* doesn't like it. 'We've already decided,' he says. 'We're not fucking keeping it.'

She lifts her eyebrows. Then she smiles. 'Well, we can discuss that later.' She turns to her guests: the ideal hostess, covering her husband's awkwardness. 'Sorry you didn't get a go, Rob. Maybe another time. Let's have more coffee.'

Inside, with the gun locked away and the cartridges in the cupboard above the back door (*not* particularly secure, I'd have thought), Brandon goes off, still furious, to the shower. I cuddle Rufus while Sienna and Aline discuss dresses for that evening and the other kids play Snakes and Ladders. Rob and Michael read their phones; Nikki drinks her coffee in silence. I think that might be it for the drama, at least for now, but then Cass comes marching downstairs. Her bag, too quickly packed, is bursting with belongings. Her face is blotched with tears. She stops when she sees the rest of them, though I'm not sure where else she thought they would be.

'I'm leaving now,' she says.

Aline sets her cup down. 'I'm sorry to hear that. Can't I get you a coffee first?'

'No thanks.' She pauses. 'Thank you for having me.'

'Any time.'

Cass turns towards the door, takes a step, then swings back again. 'He's all yours now, Sienna. And you're bloody welcome to him.'

I want to look away, but I can't. Rob whispers, '*Shit.*' Sienna goes red. Luna makes a strange, puzzled little movement.

Astrid says, 'What does she mean, Mama?'

Aline jerks her head at me. 'Milly, *please.*' No *darling* this time, which shows how preoccupied she is.

I wave them towards the stairs. 'Let's get ready for the beach, shall we?' But Luna slips from me, runs to her mother and buries her head in her lap. 'Upstairs,' I tell the others, and Lexie lifts Chloe, wriggling, into her arms. Jimmy puts his arm round Astrid.

Nikki goes to Cass, which none of the others do. 'I'll help you with your stuff,' she says.

Cass shakes her head. As she lifts her bag higher on her shoulder, a creamy bra slides out and lands on the floor. Lexie gives a stifled giggle. Nikki picks it up, shoves it back in and walks with Cass to the door. From outside, I hear her saying, 'Are you sure you're all right to drive?'

She's kind, Nikki. I've noticed that. But I wonder if she is worrying about Cass's tears, or her alcohol content.

From halfway up the stairs, Chloe speaks over Lexie's shoulder. 'Why is she leaving? Has she been naughty?' Lexie starts to giggle again, tries not to, and almost chokes.

We wait, not speaking, until the engine starts and Nikki comes back in. Aline gives a long sigh and picks up her coffee. 'It's a good job we'd planned the local beach for today,' she says. 'We're a car down.'

Rob says, 'I suppose I'll have to get the train home now.'

Perhaps he means to be funny, but no one laughs. Sienna cuddles Luna, the girl's head on her chest. Nikki says, 'Aline was right, Rob. You really *are* a shit.'

I go upstairs after the other children. If I'd come from a proper agency, I'd have something to say about this job.

38

Darryl

Edinburgh, 2002

Saturday 1 June

I slept little last night, made restless by impatience and dread, and rose heavy-headed at the first creaks and flushes from next door. I saw Sienna come out, warped by the peephole as if by an illusionist's mirror, but still unmistakably her. Her hair hung dank and sweat-soaked. Her dress lay limp over breasts and thighs. Her sobs were so loud that they reverberated through the closed door, so violent that her whole torso shuddered.

Aline was with her, in running gear, and so abundantly, glossily well that the contrast was almost preposterous.

I put my thumb in my mouth and bit down hard to keep from laughing.

Rob lurked in the open doorway, bare-chested, jeans half undone, mumbling something. Sienna shook her head. Aline replied for her, chime clear, with an arm round

Sienna's shoulders. 'Let her go, you imbecile. She needs space.'

I found a clean towel, got into the shower. As the hot water hit me, I wondered how Sienna smelled after a night of frantic tears, jealousy and last-ditch coupling.

Tuesday 4 June

This afternoon I had an email from the professor in charge of postgraduate students: a man who has never, as I recall, spoken a single word to me, but who wrote of my 'behaviour' as though we were long acquainted.

. . . causing some concern. Of course, your private life is your own business. But any impact on your academic progress, or the well-being of other students, is something we take very seriously. As your primary supervisor returns from maternity leave in mid June, I would like to invite you to meet with her, your second supervisor and myself as soon as possible thereafter, to discuss how we can best proceed. I would like to reiterate my best wishes for your successful progress, and to reassure you that our students' mental and physical well-being . . .

Etc. etc. All commitment-less gobbledygook that he must have picked up on a half-day management course. Now, hours later, only two things seem to matter. The mention of *other students*, confirming Rob's perfidy, and the reference to my primary supervisor. That discouraging cow is *not* my supervisor. Not any more. Gemma is.

I have decided not to reply.

Thursday 6 June

It is all collapsing about me now. I am so upset, so outraged, I can barely write. Firstly, after all that – all I have been through – the witch is back.

I heard by chance: footsteps on the stairs this morning when Aline and Michael had gone out. I saw her through the peephole, red hair brushed, yellow dress clean. I stood bent with my ear to the hole in the wall because I didn't even have time to get a chair. I caught her words, clear as Rob must have heard them.

'I hate myself for it, but I can't be without you.'

I thought, *I hate you too*. I should have cast her likeness, her poppet, into the trash while I had the chance. I should have put her in the fire and burned her up until there was nothing left.

Second – and even worse – Gemma emailed me. My heart lifted, until I read what she had written.

> Dear Darryl,
>
> I hope you are well. I'm not sure if you know this yet, but I've been in touch with Caroline, and since she will be returning from mat leave at the start of July, she'll be taking over your supervisions again. I think you said you were on holiday sometime in June, so that should work perfectly! I'm sure our paths will cross at the odd departmental seminar, but in the meantime, let me wish you the best of luck with the rest of your fascinating project.
>
> With best wishes,
> Gemma

PS I'm keeping my fingers crossed on the journal submission. Hopefully you'll hear soon.

I read it twice, then a third time. The blood is still in my face and hands, throbbing in my chest. I wonder if this is what a panic attack feels like. Even the music through the wall has faded to nothing. I can hear only the desperate churning of my own body.

Later

There is more. So much more. After a long while, I got myself out of the chair and walked as though I was sleeping. I hauled out the suitcase, creaked it open and leaned over the dolls. There they lay, broken and reproachful. The first two, names almost forgotten. Then Phyllis, who had had Gemma's hair and had once had her features; and the red-haired one, who had never had a name because whenever I looked at her I saw only Sienna, laughing her American laugh and stealing my friends. Even deformed, she seemed to mock me.

I lifted them out, shutting the lid on their unmaimed companion. 'This time,' I told them, 'I'll be rid of you for good.'

I took them to Dean Bridge, so high above the Water of Leith that it makes tourists gasp to look over. I stood by the wall, gazing down over sharp spikes to the trees like a living canopy, and the dark brown thread of the burn. The little white eddies where the stones clustered and the buildings piled higgledy-piggledy behind, rising from the deep rift. Behind me, the traffic slipped relentlessly past. At one end of the bridge the church loomed, square-towered and sharp-topped, brown and dirty cream against the blue sky. Far below, the tourists looked – ironically enough – like so many walking dolls.

A couple were taking a selfie across the road. I waited for them to go, clutching my carrier bag, then I waited again for the tourists beneath me to thin out. I extracted my little bundle and stood on tiptoe, holding it above the narrow strip of the stream. Thirty metres up. I let it go. Then I walked away before it could hit the water, before anyone could call out or complain.

I had tied them together, all four of them. I had bound them with ribbons at waist and neck so that they would go into their watery grave together. Deformed Ophelias, reed-draped and clasped in each other's arms, fit for a particularly macabre Pre-Raphaelite painting. That would suit Sienna's alternative sensibilities. In my head, I saw them floating away, turned by the stream, choking in the relentless wet.

And in that split second of clarity, the traffic about me as insignificant as gossamer, the sacrifice paid off. I understood it all. Gemma's superiors had made her write that email. University protocol. Or maybe it had been her boyfriend. He was jealous. Yes, that was still more satisfactory. He had stood over her laptop while she wrote. Perhaps he had even held her there, twisting one of those smooth arms until she cried out with the pain. The main thing was that she hadn't wanted to let me go. She had been made to do it.

As soon as the thought was complete, I was so sure I was right that I could have danced. I laughed instead, and a woman walking towards me with her toddler drew him almost into the car-heavy road to keep away.

Giddy with relief, I left the bridge and walked down through Dean Village and so by circuitous turns to the same strip of water that I had just been watching, and followed the raised path north.

It is an attractive route, dipping far below the busy streets and omnipresent cars, hidden from the city. It is especially so at this time of year, with the lush green of the trees and the promise of summer in the air. There, among the families and runners and cyclists, I might have found normality. I had already forgotten the dolls, making their dead way along that same strand of water. But I barely saw it: the beauty or the peace. I could only pace alone, thinking of all those in my life who had let me down, and of Gemma, who never would.

I left the water at Arboretum Avenue and made my way to the thin cobbled street with its nose-to-tail parked cars and handkerchief-sized gardens, filled now with flowers. It wasn't until I was there, outside her door, that it occurred to me either that Gemma might be out, or that her boyfriend might be in.

I checked my watch. Six o'clock and, on this June evening, still brightly sunny. I saw a fifty-pence piece lying on the pavement, picked it up, tossed it and caught it covered by my other hand. Heads I would go to her, tails I would go home. The last time I saw anyone do that, it was my father, a week before he died. Whichever way it flipped, it didn't work out for him.

I peeled back my fingers. Heads.

39

Sienna

Dorset, 2019

While Rob talked, Sienna scanned the shore for her daughters. Astrid was running in circles with Milly and the other kids. Luna was kneeling on the shingle close by, making a sculpture of seaweed and broken shells. They at least were happy.

Resentments threaded, unspoken, through the adults. Brandon and Nikki stood side by side, as though setting themselves deliberately apart, while Michael jiggled Rufus in his sling. Aline had been accosted by an old man with white hair that stood up in the wind and binoculars round his neck. Above them, a steep mass of geological scar tissue had apparently folded in on itself: brown and white and scattered underneath with broken rocks. The man's expression was intent, pointing at the stony debris. Aline was serene, even amused.

Rob raised his voice over the tiny gusts of wind. 'What do you bet they'll be on speaking terms by the time we go on this mysterious outing tonight?'

'Brandon and Aline, or Nikki and Michael?'

'Either. Both.'

'I'm not sure.' Sienna watched Astrid, feet flashing, utterly at home; the intense look on Luna's little face. 'Aline usually gets her way. Anyway ...' she allowed herself one sideways glance, 'you can hardly talk.'

He grimaced. Astrid stopped running and Milly stopped with her, stooping to listen. Sienna could see the liquid curtain of the young woman's black hair, the narrow lines of her body, and only a toe, a sticking-out curl, of her own child.

Rob said, 'Where are you going tomorrow?'

'I don't know.' She should return to California; the girls wanted that.

'Why not come to Edinburgh with me?'

The words, utterly unexpected, shook her into recollection. Rob's hands on her skin; his mouth everywhere. Real as the salt breeze. She said, 'I nearly went in January. I didn't know you lived there then.'

'So go there now. Stay in my flat.'

'With the girls?'

'Of course.'

But he had hesitated. It was fractional, but she saw it. She glanced at the rolling sea, then back to her daughters. Astrid was running again.

She found the words she had not said in the night. 'That's not what I came back for.'

'No?' He stepped closer, eyes laughing, almost touching her. 'But maybe it's what you've found.'

She shook her head, turned away, flailing for words.

He stepped back. 'So what *did* you come for?' He scowled at her, elation gone, defiant and slightly sulky. 'What was so new and important, Sen, after all this fucking time?'

215

She swallowed. She had flunked it once, and she'd intended to wait until the five of them were together again; shock them into taking her seriously. But she had started now, so she might as well go on.

She picked her words like stones from the shore. 'Have you had anything in the post?'

There *was* shock in his face, but there was a kind of recognition too. He turned away and she put out a hand, forcing him back. She saw Aline, all wind-strung hair and polite detachment, humouring the agitated stranger. She saw Nikki and Brandon pacing the shore, and Michael watching them. She saw her own girls, vulnerable as thistle-down between stones and sea.

'Just tell me.'

'Yes,' he said, into the wind. 'If you must know.' His voice was a sullen teenager's; his words brought a feeling that she could not stop to analyse, somewhere between relief and dread.

'A postcard?'

He nodded. 'It meant nothing, though. Just some nutter.'

'I had one too,' she said. 'I think it meant something.'

He scowled. She heard a child shout, as from a great distance. She watched them, counting heads, and asked, 'What was the picture?'

'I'd never seen it before. Some Venetian artist.' Rob kicked the broken shells at his feet, then added drily, 'The caption was: *Don Giovanni dragged into hell.*'

Sienna laughed, then couldn't stop. It went on and on, bubbling from her, choking her, rising uncontrollably until she was bent double, ribs burning, tears hot on her cold face, and Rob was tugging at her arm.

'Sen, stop it, for fuck's sake, please stop.'

When at last she straightened, limp with hysteria, she saw Luna standing before them, quiet and unreadable as a sibyl.

The old man had gone, stamping off alone across the strand. Aline had opened her backpack, digging out snacks: crisps, protein bars, little sandwiches for the children. Sienna took a deep breath, then gripped her daughter's hand.

'Come on, darling. Show me what you've made.'

Luna had crafted a mermaid with Medusa hair and a downturned mouth. She showed it to her mother, bit by bit, between solemn bites of bread and cucumber and ham. Sienna examined the rows of shells, the waving seaweed, giving each part due attention. Around them, the other children devoured their picnic. Rob sat on a rock, eating Kettle Chips and being scolded by Aline.

'Look at her eyes, Mama. Do you like the blue?'

'I love it.' Sienna touched the azure pieces, all their sharp edges rubbed off. 'It's called sea glass,' she said. 'She's a beautiful mermaid, darling. But I'm sorry she's so sad.'

Luna wrapped an arm round Sienna's neck, cuddling close. 'It's OK, Mama. It's not your fault.'

Aline's voice sounded above them. 'Personally,' she said, 'I think you got off lightly. If I'd been Cass, I would have shot you.'

They walked slowly back up, brambles catching and clinging, hedgerows flecked with spring flowers, and stones sinking into the muddy earth below them. Nikki and

Michael lagged behind, arguing, while Rufus screamed in his sling. Brandon strode in front with Milly and the children; Chloe, radiant with smugness, was on his shoulders.

'I'm so tall! I'm taller than on Daddy.'

Rob asked Aline, 'What was the old guy talking to you about?'

She shrugged, her eyes on her husband. 'Oh, nothing important. He just wanted a moan about the renovation. I think he's a bit obsessed with geology.'

'He looked serious.'

'Yeah, well. You know what locals are like about second homes. I don't suppose he understands architecture.' She paused, then called to Brandon, 'He said he spoke to you this morning. You didn't say.'

Brandon gave no sign that he had heard her, though Chloe twisted, wobbled and waved.

Aline grinned, defiantly. 'He knew my granny, for what that's worth. He said she was quite the local legend.'

'I expect she was,' said Rob.

Outside the house, he caught Sienna's hand, drew her aside. 'Think about it,' he said. 'Edinburgh.'

'And after that?'

'I don't know. We'd work it out.'

Seventeen years ago, they had kissed in a snowy doorway and she had almost danced down the Edinburgh street. Just then, she had been entirely sure that the world was beautiful and would be good to her.

She thought of Luna's whimper that morning, Astrid's expression. *What does she mean, Mama?* She thought of what she would have to tell her husband, when they were not yet even divorced. She felt Rob's hand, cool and dry round hers.

She said, 'My children belong in California, and I must be with them. I need to be with them.'

'I know.'

She tilted her face, looked into his eyes. 'Is *that* what you want, Rob? Life as a stepdad, thousands of miles from home? Because that's what you'd commit to.'

She felt the pause, counted it in seconds in her head. From inside, Astrid was calling her. Rob looked away, to the grass and sea. 'I don't know,' he said.

In her room, hair damp from the shower, with Luna curled like a kitten on the bed, she heard a knock on the door. *Let it be him. Don't let it be him.* But it was Aline, wrapped in a velvet robe, with a silver dress draped over her arms. 'You said you didn't have anything smart with you for tonight.' She held out her arms like a priestess. Sienna hauled herself, with an effort, from her multiple preoccupations. 'Brandon's mum got me this. I think it's more your taste than mine.'

'That's so kind.' Sienna regarded Aline's slender waist, then giggled. 'I hope it's more my size, too.'

'Probably. She always gets that wrong. Try it.'

In the dress, long-sleeved and low-necked, Sienna stared bewildered at her own reflection. Perhaps it *was* too small, although it would have been loose on Aline, but it managed to be intensely flattering, simultaneously clinging and flowing.

'My God,' she said.

Aline grinned. 'I always wanted to dress you.'

'Thank you,' Sienna said. 'But isn't it worth a fortune?'

'I doubt it. It looks it on you, though.' She ruffled Luna's hair, headed for the door.

Sienna said, 'Where are we going?'

'I told you: it's my last surprise.'

'Aline,' Sienna said, 'I need to talk to you all.'

'Do you?' Aline said, with a witch's smile. 'Maybe later.'

When they were alone, Luna said, 'Now *you* look like a mermaid, Mama.'

'Do I, darling? A happy one, I hope.' She leaned forward and began to apply eye make-up.

Luna sat up, her little fingers making pleats in the bedspread. 'Is Rob going with you tonight?'

Sienna's hand jolted, landing a streak of eyeliner somewhere near her temple. '*Frick.*' She rubbed at it with a tissue. 'All the grown-ups are going, honey, and you kids get pizza and a film with Milly. Won't that be great?'

'I suppose. Mama?'

'Yes?'

'When will we see Daddy?'

Guilt sliced at her: familiar as her own body. 'Oh darling.' She went to the bed, kissed her daughter's smooth cheek, pulled her against the new dress. 'Soon. I promise.'

She found the rest already downstairs: the men in suits; Nikki in a skirt and what was too obviously a nursing top; Aline in a velvet cocktail dress, cut low, with her hair swept back and emeralds at her neck.

'What is it?' she asked Sienna as they followed Brandon to the car. 'You're staring.'

'Your sister once said you looked like Grace Kelly. She was so right.'

40

Darryl

Edinburgh, 2002

Thursday 6 June

Gemma answered the door wearing denim shorts and a floaty purple top, with her hair newly trimmed and still slightly damp. I hadn't made a sound when I dropped the dolls, not even when they hit the water, but I gasped at the sight of her, sexy and off-duty, as though she had been waiting for me.

I said, 'I have to talk to you.'

'I'm sorry Darryl.' The boyfriend had coached her well. Even her smile was not as it usually was.

I spoke again, before she could say more. 'Can I come in?'

'I'm just going out.' She kept her hand on the door. 'Could you come to my office on Monday?'

'It's important.' I pushed past her into the sunny hallway, straight into the little sitting room. No sign of him.

'Didn't you get my email?' Gemma said. She was trying to sound normal, but I could tell she was nervous. 'I'm not your supervisor any more.'

'Obviously I got it.' I smiled at her. Her face was piquant, puzzled, irresistible. 'That's why I came. I had to tell you I understand.'

'I'm sorry?'

I wanted to shake her, to yell at her to look at me, hold me. I said, 'I know he made you write it.'

'Who?' she said. 'What?'

'Him . . .' I gestured at one of the photos. Venice like a film set in the background, the peeling walls of the palazzos mirrored up from the canal, and Gemma with her boyfriend's arm about her shoulders. Now I thought about it, he looked overly possessive even there. 'I know he's jealous.'

'Darryl, I think you're—'

'It's OK.' I couldn't stop now, rushing my words out as I had once before. Suddenly I was sure it *would* all be OK. 'I get it,' I said. 'It makes sense for you to stop supervising me.'

'It was only ever temp—'

'We couldn't be together then. You'd get into trouble. But now you're not working with me, it's fine. The university can't object. So I came to say I'll help you face up to him. I feel the same way as you.'

She said, 'I really doubt that.' Her voice was high, very unlike the gentle one I was used to. But the words only registered on some distant plane, while the rest of me was focused on getting hold of her hands, pulling her towards me.

'I love you,' I said, and I put my mouth to hers.

222

I felt pain, sharp as ice. Then fury. She'd pushed me from her, shoving me so hard that my coccyx slammed against the edge of a table. I bit my lip, to stop from crying. She glared at me. 'I need you to leave now.'

She was breathing fast, or maybe it was my breath I could hear. Outside, a car started, revved violently, then fell silent. 'You've made a mistake,' she said. I didn't speak. My hands were clutching one another, fighting down the screams. 'I don't want to call the police,' she said, 'but I will if you don't leave right now.'

Who was I kidding? There was no desire in her face. There was fear, but not enough of that. There was not even Phyllis's sulky contempt. There was the same expression I had seen and resented in Sienna's grey eyes. She pitied me.

I released my hands. I had gripped them so tightly I could feel the blood returning hot and sore to my fingers. Gemma moved towards the corridor, fast and sudden but not fast enough. I had her by the throat, like she was Phyllis, or one of the others. I held her so hard I almost lifted her by it.

Then she was afraid. She screamed. Once, twice, three times: strangled yelps before I swung her as I had swung Phyllis, so her head whacked against the framed photos on the wall, breaking the glass. Her body went passive in my hands, as though she too was only a doll. A rag doll. The blood flowed over my hands, thick and warm. I gasped with revulsion, but I didn't let go. I squeezed and kept on squeezing until there was no breath left. Then I squeezed a little more, just to be sure.

I washed my hands in her basin, leaving it pink-tinted, and dried them on a clean white towel. When I left, I saw that she had left the door open. It made me sad that she had trusted me so little and everyone else so much. And then, blinking in the evening light, it came back to me. The lines I had quoted were from Robert Browning, 'My Last Duchess'. And I had remembered what came after.

I gave commands
Then all smiles stopped together.

Gemma had placed them for me after all.

41

Michael

Dorset, 2019

They drove in convoy along the high-hedged lanes, then the A road, jarringly restored to the everyday world. Then smaller ones again. 'Where are we going?' Nikki said.

'I don't know, but I'm sure it will be worth it.'

Michael's tone was placatory; he despised himself for it. Nikki flipped down the sunshade, frowned into the mirror, then delved in her bag for lip gloss and comb. 'You look great,' he said.

'Not great enough.'

They trembled on the brink of words that both would later regret. In the back, Rufus dozed: another bone of contention. She had said she couldn't leave him, would stay with him – and in the end had brought him with her.

She rubbed pink gunk into her red lips, mumbling something that might have been 'Sorry.' She began to smooth her already-brushed hair, then gave up and put a hand on his knee instead.

'Michael.'

'What?' It came out sharper than he'd intended. She winced, pulling her fingers back.

'I *am* sorry,' she said, 'but I wish we hadn't come.'

Earlier she'd shouted at him, alone together in the tasteful room that Aline had given them (now cluttered with clothes and baby paraphernalia). 'How could you, Michael? That fucking gun?' She hardly ever swore, so he knew she was furious. 'Is there nothing you won't do to please Aline?'

'I'm sorry,' he'd said. And then, truthfully, 'I didn't fire it, for what that's worth. I couldn't. I knew you would hate it.'

'You might have thought of that sooner.' But she had stopped yelling. 'This place scares me,' she had said, softly. 'And I know there's something you're not telling me.'

He had been silent then; he was silent now, thinking of all the things he was not saying. Nikki said, 'I just want to be back home. Our little family. I want to be normal again.'

He wanted that too. More than anything. He thought of their crammed house with its toys in IKEA boxes, plates that didn't match and pictures worth nothing except to them. It was so different, their London, to the one Aline and Brandon inhabited. A life of second-hand clothes, takeaway as a once-a-month treat, and searching for special offers in the supermarket. But he had been content with it, until December.

'We will be home. We'll be back there tomorrow.' He matched tone for tone, put a hand on her thigh, despising himself for his hypocrisy. 'Promise me you'll try to enjoy tonight first.'

She looked at him, then ahead. He saw the rear lights and flashing indicator of Aline and Brandon's car, and

Sienna and Rob's heads in the back seats, disconcerting as a photo from long ago.

He thought about the confrontation with Aline, buffeted by questions. It had resolved almost nothing. He had been so sure there had been someone at the window: he could see it now, a pale face, blurred against the glass. Had that really been the product of his imagination, fed by Sienna's? What had Aline meant when she said she had her own ideas about the postcards?

And why, after all this time, when he wanted the life he had built with another woman, did she still have the power to control him?

'I will if you will,' Nikki said.

She was no fool, his wife.

'I told you it would be special,' Aline said, and it was. A lighthouse, dramatic white against the falling light, settled on rolling stone-flecked grass. Before it was a scattering of expensive cars. Beyond it, the land dropped away and the sea was a navy mirror.

Michael said, 'It looks incredible.'

'Decommissioned,' Aline said. 'It's a restaurant now. I've been longing to come.'

Inside, they had a glimpse into a big room to the side of the tower, which the maître d' (hovering inevitably, deferentially around Aline) told them had once been the lighthouse-keeper's cottage. Tables glistened with white cloths, candles and polished glass; the voices of early diners rose and hummed. Somewhere in the back of the room, a fire burned in a vast dark grate. A waitress moved past them, balancing a tray of seafood soup. It smelled incredible.

A waiter hurried their group past the open door, through a short corridor and into the foot of the tower itself. 'Where are we going?' Michael said, and Aline laughed.

'Up.'

They followed twisting stone steps, shiny with wear, high curved walls dropping away below them. At the top, the waiter opened a heavy door with a flourish, revealing a small, round room. Clean white walls were adorned with black-and-white prints. There was a round table, damask-covered and laid with silver, Moët & Chandon in an ice bucket, and bottles of sparkling water. Three windows were set into the deep stone, exposing the glowering sea.

'Bloody hell,' said Rob.

'I thought a private room would be nice,' Aline said. 'Make an occasion of it.'

The waiter fluttered round, lighting candles. Nikki set Rufus down still sleeping in his car seat. 'What a lovely idea,' she said, and Michael knew she was thinking of their tiny house with its windows in need of painting; their stretched mortgage; her almost payless maternity leave.

'Our treat,' Aline said. 'Obviously.'

Michael glanced at Brandon, who had barely spoken all afternoon. 'Obviously,' Brandon said.

Michael considered protesting, then didn't. Sienna made a series of embarrassed exclamations, Nikki said a quiet 'Thank you,' and Rob, already reaching for his champagne, said nothing at all.

Nikki refused the Moët. 'I'm driving.'

'Me too,' Aline said. 'But I'll have one.' She gestured through the thick glass to the panorama beyond. 'I know it's early to eat, but I wanted to be here in time for the view.'

'It's spectacular,' Michael said.

'I know. Even better than ours.' It was the same, faintly dangerous smile that she had worn the night before. 'It'll be dramatic later, too, but in a different way. Have you seen the forecast?'

Michael shook his head.

'I think I can promise you a storm.'

'So?' Rob swigged champagne, spoke into the silence. 'Make an occasion of what? What are we celebrating?'

'Do we need an excuse?' Aline raised her glass. 'But if you want one, we're celebrating friendship.' She gazed at each of them in turn. 'Friendship and loyalty.' There was a pause, so infinitesimal that Michael wondered if he had imagined it. Then the glasses clinked.

He took a long sip, tasting a life that had never been his. He looked at Nikki, tired and almost frumpy. He glanced, despite his best intentions, at Aline, seeing again the brilliant girl who had slipped into the row beside him in an Edinburgh lecture theatre, as glitteringly unexpected, as life-altering, as a sapphire dropped from the sky.

Would he have undone that meeting if he could have gone back? He didn't know.

And Sienna? Freckles on ivory, a smile like moonlight, and that heavy hair, still red, coiled at the back of her neck. Older, yes, but still herself. Her borrowed dress was the same silver-grey as her eyes. What would *she* have changed?

Rufus whimpered. Nikki broke the circle, set her water glass on the pristine table and crouched beside him. On the stairs, the waiter's footsteps faded away. Sienna whispered, so quietly it was as though the stones of the tower were saying it, 'We have to talk.'

Michael saw only the flash of annoyance on Rob's sardonic face, something harder to diagnose on Brandon's, before Nikki was back among them. Their son squirmed in her arms. Aline, of course, gave nothing away. She wrinkled her eyebrows, just fractionally, as though Sienna had said something in bad taste. Then she turned, cooing, to Rufus.

Through the window, far below, the sea was still calm. A single sailing boat, late out, appeared to hang suspended on dark glass. Michael watched that instead.

42

Darryl

Edinburgh, 2002

Thursday 6 June

I seemed to float in my exhilaration. Perhaps that is what taking drugs is like. I took off my pullover somewhere in the New Town, and thrust it into a council bin. It had Gemma's blood on it. In Marchmont, I went up the tired stone stairs as though I didn't feel them. When I put my key to the lock, I realised my fingers were shaking.

Then I heard the voice, behind me. The New Zealand accent.

'Hello, Darryl. Long time no see.'

The ground lifted and dropped about me. Sickness welled and ebbed. I gripped the banister, tried to speak, and succeeded on the second attempt.

'How did you get up here?'

'Your neighbour let me in.' He smiled. Beneath the new, big beard were the white teeth I remembered. 'He didn't seem especially security-conscious.'

Idiot Rob. Aline had said that, in her cut-glass English, through the intercom.

'Are you all right?' my cousin said.

'I'm fine.'

'Then can I come in?'

I put my hand out, backwards, to my door. I thought of the last time I had seen him.

There are two things that should be said in my defence, although I never got to utter them at the time.

The first is that I didn't make the spyhole between his sister's room and mine. I found it, weeks after I had moved in and months before I used it. I moved the cupboard looking for something I'd dropped, and saw a gap in the plasterwork, the light coming through. It could have been years old. I didn't look through it then. I didn't even see if I *could* look. I put the wardrobe back and tried not to think of it. It wasn't until after the party that I did a little more furniture-moving, and made it my friend.

The second thing is that I didn't use it voyeuristically. It was a balm for my loneliness. I watched her reading, drawing, chatting endlessly on the phone extension that she had made her parents install. I liked to imagine that she had asked me in there with her, just to hang out. It was pure bad luck that *that* night, months later, was different. The boyfriend was there, their bodies, half naked, clinging and groping, but I didn't want to see that. I was backing away, but it was too late.

I don't recall my own door opening, although it must have done. I remember only a man's voice – the man I had been told to call my uncle – strident behind me. 'What the hell do you think you are doing?'

I turned. I saw his face, empurpling, and a can of beer open in his hand. I still don't know if it was for me or himself. In two steps he was across the small room, pushing me aside. He put his eye to the gap in the plaster and recoiled, staggering, as though he would vomit. Beer flew out, splashing on the floor. He flung the can after it. 'You bastard,' he screamed. 'You little pervert.'

I saw his fist rise, before it hit my face. Moments later, they were both there with him, dragging me downstairs: the boyfriend topless and sweating, and the brother. They were all big men, muscular and capable of violence. They stopped shouting after the first angry accusations, because they were keeping their energy for fists and feet. But the girl yelled enough for all of them.

'How dare you, Darryl? How bloody dare you. You freak. You fucking creep.'

Afterwards, I thought her words stung more than their blows, but that can hardly have been true, because there was so much pain. There was blood, too, as there was tonight, only that time it was mine. There were bruises that stayed for weeks.

They left me on the floor of what they called their lounge, with the blood inching out across the beige carpet. My so-called aunt came to the door, hours later, and put towels and ice there, at the edge of the room. I could not look at her, for she had my mother's face.

'I don't know what to do with you,' she said. 'I just don't know.'

I saved her the trouble of deciding. When the night was thick and quiet and the bedroom doors were closed, I crawled upstairs. I cleaned off the worst of the blood. I changed my clothes. Then I took the credit card from her handbag and booked myself the first flight back to Scotland.

Can I come in?

I had no will left to refuse. This was the low, I suppose, after my killing high. I turned the key. I went into the sitting room and slumped onto the sofa. My cousin followed, shutting the front door behind him. He turned on the overhead light. I thought he looked oddly at me, and I wondered if there were flecks of blood on my shirt or trousers, or whether the pullover had absorbed them all. But the flat still smelled of bins; perhaps it was just that.

I didn't ask him to sit, but he did. He spoke abruptly, as though from a prepared script. 'My mum is dying.'

'Oh,' I said.

He waited for more, and when it didn't come, he went on. 'We were going to come here together,' he said. 'But then she got sick, so I came for both of us. I promised I would speak to you face to face.'

My plate from last night was still on the coffee table, a bluebottle crawling over the remains of cheese on toast. Or perhaps it was from the night before. I thought of Gemma's body, wondered how soon the flies would come for her.

He said, 'Mum's always felt terrible about how things turned out. We both have.'

'This is the first I've heard of it.'

My cousin leaned forward, his large hands on his knees. 'She and Dad aren't together any more.'

Did he think that made it OK? *Did* it? I recalled the angry father who crashed his knuckles so hard into my skull that I thought I would die. I thought of myself curled into a carpet that had once been clean, with this man's feet thumping my chest. I decided it didn't.

He said, 'It's been a tough time, for all of us.' His tone was matter-of-fact; explanatory rather than self-pitying. 'My sister has struggled to . . . find her path. I suppose we both have. But for the last few years Mum and I have been involved with the local church. They've been kind. It's helped me to think. I suppose that's what's brought me here, to you.'

I saw Gemma's face, swollen out of its prettiness, her body hitting the floor. 'If you're looking for redemption,' I said, 'you're in the wrong place.'

'I'm not,' he said. 'But I do want to apologise.'

I said nothing.

'The night you left,' he said, 'we lost our tempers. We shouldn't have done what we did. I'm truly sorry.'

I wondered how it would have been if he had come six hours or six months ago. I wondered what would happen if I closed my eyes, then and there, and let myself sleep.

'Mum wants to apologise, too,' he said. 'She knows she should have helped you. She wants to know you're OK, before . . .' He looked at me. I wondered if he expected pity, along with the forgiveness. 'You know,' he said.

I saw a dark red mark, the size of a teardrop, on my trousers. I said, 'You can tell her I'm fine.'

'And that you forgive her?'

I shrugged. 'Her, perhaps, if it makes her feel better.'

He quailed, just slightly. I stood up with an effort. All that walking had made my limbs sore, or maybe it was the memory of that much earlier pain. 'Anything else?' I said. 'Before you go.'

He paused, as though he wanted to get the words right. At last he said, 'My sister said I can tell you that she forgives you.'

'I'm sorry?'

'It's been hard for her. She doesn't have the church like we do, but she said it. Mum and I forgive you too, of course, but it's easier for us.'

He smiled. The anger I had thought satiated in Stockbridge was with me again. It leaped, twisting like smoke in my throat.

'Perhaps you've forgotten,' I said.

The smile dropped. 'Forgotten what?'

I could hardly breathe. 'How the pair of you tormented me, played with me, *humiliated* me, almost from the day I arrived.'

He shook his head. He looked sad in the face of my anger. 'It wasn't like that, Darryl.'

'Oh really? So how *was* it, exactly? Because that's the way I remember it.'

'We tried,' he said. 'Our lives were upturned too.' He held up a hand, anticipating my rejoinder. 'Not like yours. I know that. But suddenly there you were, a stranger, and we had to make space for you in our lives.'

'How tragic for you.'

'I told you,' he said. 'I know it wasn't the same, but it was still hard. We wanted to be kind and welcoming, but we had our own friends. When we tried to include you, you froze them out. They started saying it felt like they had no right to be in our house.'

'I just wanted to spend time with you. Is that so wrong?'

'Of course not, but it was like you wanted *us* to have no one but you.'

'I was grieving,' I said. 'You destroyed me. You and your bitch of a sister . . .'

'Don't call her that.'

'. . . and now you come here and say *you* forgive *me*. You changed me,' I said. 'You turned me into what I am now.'

He stood up, tall even in this tall room. I felt his control slip, his burgeoning rage, just as I had felt Gemma's pity – and then her fear. 'We didn't change you,' he said. 'Oh Darryl, you were already you.'

'*No.*'

'Dad didn't want us to take you. Did you know that? Our mum had heard things from your mum, how she worried about you.' I put my hands to my ears, but I could still hear him. 'How possessive you were, how jealous. How you used to steal your sister's toys and break them. How you watched from corners, as though you resented them loving each other.'

I heard my sister screaming at me, the last night she spent in this flat. *I hate you. I hate you.* I felt Gemma's skin, satin smooth beneath my tightening fingers. I saw my cousin's neck, strong as a bull's, and his arms heavy with muscle. I sought about me for a weapon and, finding none, I punched out, hard and fast, so my knuckles burned and I heard his nose crack.

He staggered back. More blood, this time running from his nostrils into moustache and beard. I waited for the counterpunch. I think I almost wanted it. But it never came. He put one hand to his nose and held the other out, warding me off.

'Don't,' he said. 'Don't make me hurt you.'

'Again,' I said.

At the door, he turned. 'I shouldn't have said that about your mum. I didn't mean to. But you need help, Darryl.' He stepped away, looked back. 'I'll pray for you,' he said, but it wasn't clear from his tone if he intended this as threat or reassurance.

I yelled after him, down the stairs, 'Pray for yourself.'

The Fifth Postcard: December 2018

You don't know me, Brandon, but I know a lot about you.
A golden life, with a golden wife. But you sold your soul
to the devil to get them. I know that too. Count your
blessings, while you still have them.

43

Brandon

Dorset, 2019

While Nikki was with them, they were trapped in a strange suspended reality; a pretence of normality, although he only realised that later.

Rob and Aline ate oysters, the discarded shells gleaming on their plates. The cooler held Sancerre; their glasses filled and filled again. Outside the window, the sky was darkening fast. The wind was getting up. The sea would be rising too.

They talked of the lighthouse. Of other lighthouses, other restaurants. Of London, Edinburgh and San Francisco; films, music; work. The safe topics of dinner-party strangers. Starters were replaced by mains, the Sancerre by Cabernet Sauvignon and Chardonnay. They spoke of the children. Brandon saw worry quivering at Sienna's lips, the tension about Michael's eyes. He kept a polite lid on his own enduring fury.

His wife, of course, was the queen of the evening.

Earlier, she had come to him in her black dress and her jewels, and kissed him long and languorously on his set mouth. 'Truce,' she had said. 'I want to focus on our friends.' She had run light hands over his hair, stepped back and smiled at him in his suit. 'My handsome husband.'

'The gun, Aline.'

'Forget it, please. Just for tonight.'

He hadn't forgotten, but he had let her take his hand, call Milly from the snug to take a photo of them. He had put his arm round her waist, faked a smile for the picture. 'Do you have any idea,' she had said, as they waited for their friends, 'how much I love you?'

Yes, he had thought. *I believe I do*. But he hadn't said it.

After the main course, Rufus became so loudly angry that the tower echoed with his screams. Nikki glanced at Michael, and when he made no move, she got wearily to her feet, Rufus in her arms, reaching for his spotted snowsuit. Her movements were heavy with resentment and her parting words, wryly spoken, fell heavily into the white space.

'I may be some time.'

The door closed behind her, and the silence was absolute. They sat so still that they could have been there for a seance, the circle broken only by Nikki's pulled-back chair. Then Sienna spoke, and the past was with them.

'Someone knows what we did.'

No one replied. Michael sat forward, as though he would, but didn't.

She said, sharper still, 'That night, that summer.'

Brandon said, 'What do you mean?' His voice creaked.

Sienna's eyes were steadfast, looking straight at him; an amber pendant shifted on her clavicle, catching the light. She said, 'I've had an anonymous letter. Well, a postcard. So's Rob.'

'*What?*'

In the tense stillness, Brandon became gradually aware that something else was wrong. Aline and Michael, who should have been as shocked as he was, were not. Michael glanced at Aline, as though for permission. At last he said, flatly, 'We've both had them too.'

The wine shivered in Brandon's glass, then lay still. Aline sat with her knife and fork neatly together, her plate filmed with blood from her steak. She raised her water glass to her lips. Michael said, 'You didn't know?'

'No.' Brandon controlled his voice. 'I didn't.'

'And you've not had one?'

'No.'

Sienna said, quietly, 'That's strange.'

'Yes.' Brandon gazed across candles to his wife's flawless, unreadable face. 'It is.' Her lips tightened just a fraction, then were still again. 'Aline?' he said.

She shifted her knife, laying it infinitesimally straighter. 'Actually,' she said, 'you have. It came the morning after mine.'

He would not shout at her. Not now, not again. He took a swig of wine, and it tasted sharp in his throat. He counted to five in his head, then spoke.

'What did it say?'

242

Aline rose with all her usual grace. She lifted her evening bag from a side table, extracted two postcards and handed them to him without a word. He read the one to her first, then his, finally turning it to examine the painting on the back. Light and dark; a woman's face at once detached and implacable; a man's dead head, open-mouthed, held up by its long dark hair. He flipped the card again. *Salome with the Head of John the Baptist.* He drank the rest of his glass and poured more with a hand that would not stay still.

A golden wife. He watched her, marble carved. *You sold your soul to the devil.* He thought, *You don't know the half of it.*

'Why didn't you tell me?'

'It wasn't worth worrying you.'

'But apparently it *was* worth getting everyone together, staging a reunion. That is why you did this, isn't it?'

She shrugged. It was almost a yawn. 'Sienna contacted me. It made sense. I wanted answers.'

'But you didn't ask for them.' Sienna's voice came as a shock. She had been sitting very still, turning her glass so the wine slid almost to the rim, then back again. Now she was leaning forward, all red hair and creamy flesh in the candlelight. She said it again. 'You didn't ask the questions.'

The door opened. The waiter came in, collected plates in awkward silence, asked if they wanted dessert menus. 'Later,' Aline said. 'Give us ten minutes, please.'

When he had gone, she spoke to Sienna. Her voice, for the first time, was sharp.

'What do you mean?'

'If you'd wanted answers,' Sienna said, 'you could have said so. You could have asked us openly that first night, when Nikki and Cass had gone to bed.'

'So could you.'

'I know. I wanted to. I wish I had, but I was nervous. I thought maybe I was the only one. And seeing you all was so . . . Well, I flunked it. There's no better explanation. I suppose I thought there would be plenty of time.' She paused, her eyes settling on Aline's face. 'Somehow I don't think that was your reason. You weren't afraid.'

No, Brandon thought. *Aline has never been afraid.*

They waited. Aline watched, impassive. '*Oh*,' Sienna said. 'My God.'

'What?'

'You didn't want to consult us. You wanted to *watch* us.'

The rising wind whined at the window. On the table, a candle flickered and went out. Brandon thought of Nikki and Rufus, willing them back inside. Sienna sounded like a prophetess now, foretelling an unwelcome destiny. 'You think one of us sent them. You don't trust us.'

Michael put a hand to his face.

Aline laughed. 'I haven't seen you for nearly seventeen years, Sienna. How do I know if I can trust you?' She paused, letting the words land. 'After all, none of us knows why you came back.'

'Because *I* got that bloody postcard. But not only that. I told you. I wanted to talk.'

Aline leaned forward across Rob, tipped the last of the white wine into Sienna's glass. The movement was calculated, insolent. 'Then talk,' she said.

Sienna said, slowly, 'The postcards can only hurt us because they should. Because we did something terrible.'

Michael choked. Rob scowled. Aline raised her eyebrows. Sienna went on, quickly, 'Oh, I know it's obvious, but none of us said it. Not then, not now. And it needed saying.' She took a mouthful of wine. 'You don't forget something like that, or I don't. I tried, but I never could.'

'So?'

'So then that card arrived, and it was like I'd been waiting for it.'

'Ah yes, *your* card. Just out of interest, do you have it with you?'

Sienna stared. The glass swayed in her hand. 'It's at your house. Jesus, Aline.' She put the glass down and moved her hand slowly back. 'Are you suggesting I didn't get one? Or that I wrote it myself?'

'I'm suggesting nothing. I'm just wondering about the timing. You have your little crisis of conscience, then we all start getting these *reminders* in the post, then you turn up here. It seems . . . surprising. Some might say convenient.'

'It wasn't a little *crisis of conscience*, Aline. Not some minor psychological blip. It was – and is – guilt. Shame. And it's not new.'

No one spoke. Sienna was shaking. Michael looked as though he might cry. She said, 'I can show you later. I can show you the postmark. London, in case you're interested. West Central.'

'Oh, I'm interested.'

The tears ran down Sienna's wan cheeks. 'Do you know what it said?' Her mouth worked, forming the same angry rectangles that Rufus's had earlier. 'He, she, whoever the hell it was. *Truth will out.* Of course it bloody will.'

She dropped her head into her hands, almost knocking over her glass, contorting with sobs. Michael put his arm around her. Brandon saw Aline's face – apart, dispassionate – as he had seen Caravaggio's Salome. The lighthouse walls seemed to close in, constricting him, and he made an enormous effort to push them back. Over the words of the card, he wrote new ones in his head: a promise to himself. *Whatever happens tonight. Whatever they say or don't say – whatever* she *says – this marriage is over.*

Aline found his gaze and held it. He thought of his children, and bit down on despair.

Rob's voice, sharp with malice, brought Brandon back to the rest of them. 'Is that it, Aline? Is it enough to upset Sienna, or are you going to accuse me of sending these bloody things too? Or how about Mike? Why not him?'

Michael jumped, his arm flopping down from Sienna's shoulders. Aline spoke over Sienna's broken sobs. 'It's not his style.'

'Still too much your puppy dog, I suppose.'

'For God's sake,' Michael spat. 'I've been tearing myself inside out ever since that horrible thing arrived.'

Aline said, 'I think that's true.' She studied Rob as if he were a museum exhibit: interesting, but slightly unsavoury. 'He has too much to lose. You, on the other hand . . .'

'Oh, my life is a mess. Whatever. I agree. But it's not my style either.'

'What happened to *your* card?'

'I chucked it.'

'Now that *is* in character.' She half smiled, considering him. 'And you're hardly the *crise de conscience* type, are you? So you'd have to think there was something in it for you, and I really don't see what that could be. I think you're in the clear.'

'Fucking hell, Aline.' Rob flipped from indignation to apparently genuine laugher. 'Coming from you, I don't know whether to be insulted or complimented.'

'Be whatever you like.' She sat back, her face hardening. 'If it wasn't one of you,' she said, 'I need to know who you told.'

44

Darryl

Edinburgh, 2002

Friday 7 June

I woke on the sofa in bright daylight, still clothed, sweating from impenetrable dreams. I heard music from next door, Aline's laugh, and for a moment I was cast back seven, eight months. I was made happy by the promise of new friends. Then the recollections of yesterday swamped me, dragging me into horror. I looked at my watch. Ten o'clock, which seemed impossible. I closed my eyes again, and begged for sleep.

Next door, the music clicked off. I hauled myself up and made a cup of tea, my hands operating like someone else's. There was no coherent plan in my head, only jumbled calculations. How long until the police thought of me? Had Gemma discussed me with her boyfriend, friends or colleagues? *What* had she said? What exactly had the perfidious Rob written in his email? What had my cousin told the nurses when he took his broken nose, as he must have done, to A&E?

Everyone was against me.

I went back to the sitting room, yanked the Reverend from the wall and listened. I heard Rob complaining of lost sunglasses, Michael saying he'd check the hall. I heard Aline, disembodied, a character in a radio play. 'You'll have to leave them, Rob. We've got to go.' My whirling brain stilled, settling on one irrefutable point. They were leaving today, now, and I should have been with them.

I heard Sienna, her Californian vowels distinctive and disconcertingly close. 'Can I just grab some of those books, Aline? For the beach.' I froze. Was it ridiculous to care what they thought of me when they had let me down so badly? Or to worry about the repercussions of one hole in the wall, when Gemma was a corpse with bruises on her neck from my closing fingers?

Probably, but I still did.

Aline saved me, decisive and impatient. 'You won't need them, Sen. Granny has all the books in the world. Come *on*, we've got to load the car.'

I punched out thoughts, hammering them straight. Aline and Rob weren't taking me with them, as they should have done, but they couldn't stop me going. Aline had as good as said so, those weeks and months ago.

If I had run away from Auckland, I could run from here too.

I went to my door, weighing options. If they went straight to the car now and didn't come back, I couldn't follow without being seen. If they returned just once more to the flat, I had a chance. I watched them out, one after the other, carrying rucksacks and suitcases, chattering as they went. They were all in shorts except Sienna, who wore a long floating dress she had probably tie-dyed herself. Warped by the peephole, she looked like a circus act. Michael pulled the flat door closed and I held my breath.

He did not lock it.

I located my car keys, barely used, in the same drawer that my parents kept theirs in. I found my sunglasses, a light tweed jacket that had been my dad's and a cap so clearly designed for a geriatric that it was probably his father's. A basic disguise, but it would have to be enough. I grabbed wallet and diary from my desk and waited by the door like a sprinter at the gates.

In three minutes, they were back. 'You'd better go to the loo,' Aline said, 'because I'm not stopping before Tebay.'

'Yes, Mum,' said Rob. Sienna giggled. I counted them back inside, then dashed down.

Outside, the day was dazzling. I pulled the sunglasses down from the top of my head and stood a few seconds in the doorway, blinking. I looked up and down the street and saw the tenements, tall and understated, the parked cars like mirrors in the light, as though I would never see them again. A man strode along the pavement from the Meadows end, and I had a moment's panic, picturing plain-clothes detectives. Then I dismissed it. CID officers did not carry heavy rucksacks. Anyway, they came in pairs.

I got into my own car, oven-hot, and opened the windows. The man came closer and closer still, eventually stopping by our front gate. I saw then that he was young, probably a student, certainly too young to be a detective. Tall as my cousin, but with a Brad Pitt jaw. There was something oddly familiar about him, or perhaps it was his navy T-shirt, emblazoned with the Detroit Tigers logo. I felt sure I had seen it before.

He turned, as if my staring had been obvious. I looked away from him, over my shoulder, and reversed onto the wide road, the wheel alien and slippery beneath my pulsing fingers. I pulled up on the other side, dragged my cap lower, extracted the road map from behind my seat and pretended to flick through it.

At last, the front door opened. Aline was framed there, briefly: an advert for the street, the city, or even the summer weather. The waiting boy called, 'Hey,' and she spun, hair flying, reaching out her hands.

'You came,' she called. 'I hoped you would.'

Hoped, not *knew*. It was the only sign of insecurity I had ever seen in her. I looked at him again, with more interest. He grinned back at her, only just not goofily. 'Are you sure this is OK?'

Another bloody American.

'Of course.' She turned to her friends, emerging behind her onto the hot street. Sienna was wearing a hat the shape of a fried egg and a puzzled expression. Michael looked anxious; Rob faintly amused. 'Guys,' Aline said, 'this is my running buddy, Brandon. He's at a loose end this week, so I asked him to join us.'

I might have laughed at Michael's stricken face if I hadn't been so angry myself. What had she said to me? *We're staying with my gran. It wouldn't be fair on her.* But this

handsome American, apparently, was no imposition at all.
She drew him along with her as though she owned him and
waved a key fob at a lime-green Skoda, which I did not
recognise. Had she hired it? Borrowed it? It didn't matter.
People were always doing her favours.

'You can ride shotgun,' she told Brandon. 'You're too tall
for the back.' Sienna peered sideways at Michael, under her
hat, then looked away.

The lurid car reversed into the road. I waited a few
seconds, then followed less smoothly. As I did so, a police
car turned into the crescent from the other end. I wondered
if my chest would explode.

45

Sienna

Dorset, 2019

The waiter returned, glanced round at the set faces, put the menus in a pile by Brandon – 'For when you're ready' – and slid silently out of the room. Aline's sea eyes skimmed Michael, hesitated on Sienna, then landed on Rob.

'Let's stick with you. A woman scorned? There have been enough of them.'

'I kept your secret, Aline.' Rob's voice was as cool as hers now. Indifferent, impossible to match with the man who had shared Sienna's bed, kissed every inch of her in the flickering moonlight.

'*Our* secret,' Aline said.

'OK, ours. But you said it yourself. I'm too interested in my own preservation to do anything else.'

'Even from Cass?'

'I just fucking said. Cass is like all the rest. I've said nothing to any of them, because as far as I'm concerned, that night never happened and I'd like it to stay that way.'

For a moment, neither of them broke eye contact. Then Aline sat back in her chair. She reached for a dessert menu, flipped it over, then shifted her inquisitorial gaze, returning to Sienna. 'You have a husband, Sen.' The abbreviation felt like a weapon. 'I don't suppose he's been feeling especially loyal while you've been getting ready to leave him.'

When Sienna found the words, her voice was surprisingly calm. 'What are you implying?'

'I'm asking, not implying. How much does he know?'

'Nothing.'

Once, at a San Francisco dinner, a fellow guest had confided a minor past offence. Sienna couldn't even remember what it was now. Shoplifting, perhaps, or snorting coke at a party. The woman had made a jest of it and some of them had laughed. But Sienna's husband, who was then her boyfriend, had not laughed. Afterwards, hand in hand on the cobbled street, she had told him, 'You judged that woman.'

'*Judged* is harsh,' he had said. 'But I can't help seeing her differently, now I know.' Sienna had stared down at their feet on the grey stones, felt the warm California rain through her thin blouse, and shivered.

Now, in Aline's dress, under Aline's gaze, she shook again. She thought of the years of wanting to confide in her husband and dreading what would happen if she did. She thought of those last weeks when he had asked her over and over what was wrong and it had seemed less awful that they should separate than that he should know she had lied.

'It destroyed my marriage,' she said. 'Either way, telling or not telling, it would have been the same. But I *didn't* tell him.'

Michael looked sideways at her, then away. She swallowed back hysteria. 'Even if I had,' she said, 'he wouldn't have written those things. He might have told the police. He probably would, but he'd have gone straight out and done it. He would never threaten anyone. He's a good man,' she said, her voice cracking. 'An honourable man. A fucking Jane Austen hero.'

Outside, the rain started. Aline regarded Sienna as if reserving judgement. Rob said, 'What about you, Mike? You have a wife too. How much have you told her?'

'Jesus,' Michael said. 'You can't suspect Nikki.'

'Why not?' Rob gestured at Aline. 'She's suspected every-one else.'

Michael looked as though he would punch him, but just didn't. 'Well, for your information, I haven't told her. I've lied, for years, to the woman I love. And it's like Sienna said, at least since that bloody card arrived. It's destroying us.'

He crumpled a napkin in his fists, dropped it to the table. 'Anyway,' he said, more calmly, 'I think there's another option. I said so last night . . .' He glanced at Aline. 'But you said it was impossible.'

Sienna's fingers found her glass, slid round the narrow stem. 'Go on,' she said.

Michael reached out for the two cards that Aline had brought with her. Brandon, wordless, gave them to him. Michael pressed his finger into the blue ink. 'See? Brandon's message says, *You don't know me*. But with the others,

I don't think that's true. That quote for Sienna, Aline's, mine. It was someone who knows us, or knew us. But they're anonymous, so it's also someone deranged.' He glanced from face to face. 'Anyone spring to mind?'

Rob swore. Sienna whispered, 'But he couldn't know. *Could* he?'

Rob said, flat-voiced, 'I don't know, but he was in Dorset then. I know that.'

Michael let the cards drop.

46

Darryl

In transit, 2002

Friday 7 June

I drove after them on autopilot, passing indifferently through the wide, beautiful streets of the Grange, up through suburbs, across roundabouts, past the Pentland Hills beyond the city, with their dinosaur spine. The towns and villages were place names to skim through. Carlops, West Linton, Dolphinton. It wasn't until Biggar, with its wide market-town street and memento mori obelisk, that I breathed without wanting to choke.

They were still there, two vehicles ahead of me, as I emerged again into the derestricted zone. I put the radio on and the *William Tell* overture pulsed through the car like a promise of adventure. I watched the green car like a beacon, and when I put my foot down, I started to enjoy it. Now, at least, I had one immediate, concrete goal. I would follow them, if I could, all the way to the Jurassic Coast. It would be my distraction, and my challenge to myself.

I barely thought – then or for many hours – of what I would do when we got there.

On the motorway, all through the southern uplands and across the border into Cumbria, I was grateful for my rediscovered concentration. Aline was a fast driver, showily competent, skipping between lanes and keeping a steady eighty, eighty-five miles an hour. Several times I would have lost them if their car had not been such a ludicrous colour.

I parked a row from them at the Tebay services and sprinted in, bladder bursting, with my cap and sunglasses still on. Back on the M6, I imagined them laughing and singing in the car ahead. I pictured Sienna exclaiming over the mountains of the Lake District, probably quoting Wordsworth. I held tighter to the wheel, fingers twisting, and thought of Gemma's swelling face. I pictured her flat, clean and light, turned into a crime scene. Men in plastic suits, gloves poking at her body, and the boyfriend, not grinning now but crying, begging them to tell him it was all a mistake.

Enough. Stop. Concentrate.

And I did concentrate, even as the sun beat on the assembled metal and I had to turn the air conditioning up and up again so I could keep my jacket on. I had them in my sight through the almost static queues that began just south of Preston, got briefly better, then worsened again. I watched them at the Stafford services, then across the shifting, jumping lines of traffic moving from motorway to motorway.

I grew complacent, in my minor triumph. Then, just after Birmingham, a coach pulled out between us, a car hooted, there was almost a collision. I thought of my parents and experienced a brief, almost overwhelming fear. Then it was over. No one had crashed, no one was dead, but the green car had gone. I had lost them.

I stopped at the next services. I bought a double espresso, something I never drink, and drained it, hot and bitter, until my heart shook. I filled up with petrol and drove on, rigid with rage, because this was all I could do now. I passed Cheltenham, Gloucester, approached Bristol. The traffic thinned, then thickened again. The sun dropped in the sky, and behind me, suddenly, where there had been only an innocuous red Fiat, I saw the blue and yellow and white of a police car.

I saw Gemma's prone body on her landlord's floor. I saw the blood streaming from my cousin's nose. I saw a sign for a service station and considered swinging into it, making my escape on foot, then abandoned the idea. I waited for the indicator that would bid me pull over, the questions to which I would have no adequate response.

They signalled, pulled out. But then they sailed on past me, past the van in front, without even a sideways glance. I laughed until I cried and then, through my tears, I saw the green Skoda again, coming out from the services.

Fate was on my side.

It was almost dark when we left the motorway together, and I was so drained that my eyes felt distinct from my body. I never play video games, but it seemed to me that I was in one then: a strange, artificial world of high hedges and stone walls, shielded by the dark; and our two vehicles the only things that mattered. I crept closer and closer until I could see the three heads in the back.

Until then, I had been content to follow them. Now, in my tired anger, this was no longer enough. I took off my sunglasses and tugged the cap lower. I pulled a scarf from the side pocket, musty with age and being used to wipe windows, and twisted it one-handed round my neck and chin. Then I accelerated, almost into their rear bumper.

Aline flicked her brake lights on and off, trying to shake me. Then she sped away. I gave it a minute, then advanced on them. I did it again and again. I could not make them like me, I thought, but I could make them afraid. One of the men in the back turned his head, trying to get a look at me. I think it was Michael. I was glad of cap and scarf.

They were going faster now, more erratically. Once, they stopped, pulling into a lay-by to let me pass. I saw just in time and got myself half off the road, well behind them. I turned off my lights and watched for the two red glowing spots that would tell me they were back on their way. I imagined them sitting there surrounded by darkness, second-guessing me without knowing who I was.

They pulled out faster than ever. Again, I followed, the suspension scraping on rocks as the car climbed back onto the road. I gave them maybe three minutes, to think they had lost me. Then I stormed up behind them, even closer than before, and waited for a reaction. They swung right unexpectedly, taking the next junction off the main road and diving deep into nothingness. A wrong turn, or an attempt to get rid of me?

I followed, but fell back a little. It was all I could do to concentrate on the driving. Besides, Aline had taken it up another notch, roaring along far too fast for those shrinking lanes. She drove as though she would get away or kill them all in the attempt. I'm not sure how I would have felt about that, but it was not what happened.

Instead, they killed someone else.

I saw it all. I saw the green car muted by darkness, flashing too close along high hedges. I saw the gap in the hedgerow where a house was, the tall bins by the road, and the woman *they* did not see until it was too late.

The brake lights went on. They skidded slow with a screech of tyres and metal that carried even to where I was. I heard the woman's scream too, piercing through the summer night. I saw her thrown onto the car and off again. I saw the Skoda shuddering, finally, to a stop.

I stopped too, my feet hard on clutch and brake. I switched off my headlights. I saw car doors thrust open, feet swinging onto tarmac, bodies unbending into the night. Someone crouched, disappearing in front of the car, where the broken thing must be. I knew by the slim curves of her body and by the hair, silver-gold in the headlamps, that it was Aline. She stood again: a perfect silhouette, the kind Victorian children used to cut out and dress with paper clothes. She shook her head.

How long were they there for? A minute? Less? I didn't hear what she said. But I saw her slide into the driver's seat, the others pile back in around her. She reversed, accelerated, and then the car was gone.

I flicked my lights on and inched forward until I could see the body sprawled on the tarmac like Phyllis in the stairwell, Gemma on the floorboards. The spread hair and the blood dark as treacle beneath her head. I hooted loudly. Once, twice, three times. Then I slammed my foot on the pedal, swerved too fast round bins and body, and went blindly on.

Dorset, Saturday 8 June

I slept a few hours in the car by a farm gate, somewhere the other side of Dorchester, and this morning I drove to Durdle Door. I don't know why, but I had to go somewhere. I nearly stopped at a petrol station for something to eat, but there was a police car outside. I pulled out again and away. It was still morning-cold, but I was sweating. In the car park at Durdle Door, I saw a man in dull clothes holding an Alsatian on a lead, watching me. Perhaps I am growing paranoid. Perhaps I am not.

I stood a long time atop the shallow sandy steps, gazing to where the sea had forced its way through the limestone, leaving that precarious arch. I thought of my family, and of the man who had killed them living his life, untroubled, on the other side of the Atlantic. I pictured my former friends, so hard I could almost see them. I pictured my hands on their backs, Aline's hair, corn-bright, spun out like a halo as she twisted and tumbled, falling past the cliff.

I smiled.

Then I came down here to the beach, where there are only a few early-morning walkers, and sat where I am now, at the edge of the scrappy crag.

They say a diary is not a true record unless you keep it only for yourself. Well, mine is true, for I am still writing it now.

I just spotted them at the top of the steps, conspicuous in the growing sun. Two men and a woman. Two of them are in suits, and one is in police uniform. In a moment – before they can get here – I will walk to the shoreline. I will stand at the water's edge, where the foam catches at my shoes, and I will throw this journal far into the waves. Perhaps my pursuers will abandon their already inadequate incognito, come charging down the last steps and across the heavy shingle. Perhaps they will fear that I will throw myself in too; rush forward so that the rip tide will punish me before they can do it.

I will not. There are other things I have still to do. But I will destroy the diary, and I will keep no more, because I will have no privacy now, and I will not give more of myself than anyone is entitled to. Instead, I will sit quiet in my next imprisonment, making metaphors. I will wait, and I will think of this layered and irredeemably fragile land, for that alone is real.

Gemma would be proud.

47

Rob

Dorset, 2019

Rain pounded the windows. Outside their tower, the wind was like a harpy, screaming to get in. Rob looked round at his friends, defensive in the face of astonishment. 'He was arrested here. I read it online.' He quoted the still-remembered text: '"A joint operation between Lothian and Borders and Dorset Police".'

Aline said, 'Why didn't you tell us this before?'

Rob shrugged. The truth was, he didn't know. Perhaps it was because Darryl had always been more *his* friend than any of theirs; he had, in a sense, brought him into their lives. 'We never talked about the trial, did we?' He glanced at Aline. 'I thought it might be on the proscribed list. But I was interested, OK? I looked things up.'

I knew him, or thought I did. Those Sunday evenings, week after week, watching how someone's brain worked. What should that have told him? What had he missed that could have stopped it all from unravelling?

Michael pushed back his chair: a long scratch of wood against wood. 'It was him in that car. Christ, Rob. It was him all the time. And you never told us.'

Rob stared at him, jolted from the past. 'What do you mean, *It was him*?'

Michael looked as though he might hit him. 'How can you not remember?'

'Rob was asleep,' Aline said. 'Him and Sen both. It seemed incredible at the time.' For a moment, she appeared about to laugh. Then she didn't. 'Someone chased us, Rob. That was why we were off route and going so fast. We told you afterwards.'

Dimly Rob recalled words thrown at him from the front of the car, on that drive he had made a point of forgetting. 'You said it was some crazy local. I thought you meant an angry farmer or something. I never made the connection.'

Brandon looked up, bleak-faced and quiet. 'How could you?' he said. 'And we never talked about it again.' His voice was barely audible, but it was bitter sharp. 'That too was proscribed.'

'Fuck,' Rob said.

Michael made a noise that was half howl, half snort, and got to his feet. Aline snapped, 'Where are you going?' but got no answer.

'But he was in prison,' Sienna said. She repeated it like a confused child begging for clarification. 'He *is* in prison.'

Behind her, the door opened a crack, then shut quietly again. That poor bloody waiter.

'Do you *know* that?' Michael snapped. 'Do you know for sure they didn't let him out? Because Sienna thought she saw someone on the Pirate's Path, didn't she? And I saw someone looking into the snug window last night.'

'*What?*'

Michael glanced at Sienna, then pointed at Aline. '*She* said not to tell you. She said it was nothing.'

They were watching an illusion, Rob thought, as it finally shattered.

'If you want to know,' Michael snapped, 'I'm going to find my wife.' The door handle turned. Aline made a silencing gesture. Michael ignored her. 'Because she and Rufus are out there somewhere, in the car or the bloody rain, and how the hell do we know that psychopath didn't follow us here too?'

'*Who* didn't follow us?'

It wasn't the waiter. It was Nikki in the doorway, her hair soaked, her expression furious and Rufus in her arms. His face was shiny with rain. Sienna murmured, 'Thank God.' Michael dived towards his wife and child. Nikki stepped away from him.

'What the hell's going on?'

For a moment, Michael hovered ridiculously, arms outstretched. Then he dropped them. 'It's nothing,' he said. 'Just someone we used to know. Don't worry.'

Nikki snorted. Aline raised her voice: a teacher with an unruly class. 'As it happens,' she said, 'they did let him out, but I know for sure that he can't harm us.' Her gaze, meeting Rob's, was clear and hard as glass. 'You're not the only one who can use Google. Darryl Arniston died of lung disease five months before those postcards were sent.'

The silence held, then broke. Michael reached out for Rufus, but Nikki closed her arms tighter, as though she could no longer trust him with his child.

'Sit down, Nikki,' Aline said, still in her teacher voice. 'You're just in time for pudding.'

Nikki stared at her. 'Are you crazy?' she said. 'Are you all crazy?'

'I don't know what—'

'Don't bother lying, Aline. I know there's something going on – something that has Michael lying awake half the night when he thinks I won't notice, and has just made Sienna cry – and you're *all* hiding it from me.' Nikki stared at her husband as though she hated him. Her voice had a cracking clarity that was worse than shouting. 'And now I find there was someone on the cliff yesterday, stalking you, and someone in the garden last night, and you *knew* this, Michael, and you left Chloe and the others in that house, with only a kid to guard them.'

Sienna whimpered, scrambled to her feet. Michael started to speak, gulped, and was silent.

'I'm going back,' Nikki said. 'I'm going to my daughter. You can come or not come, talk or not bloody talk. I don't care any more.'

They went.

In the car, Sienna spoke. Rob wondered if she was afraid, or egged on by Nikki to righteous anger.

'You know, she said, 'that woman had a name.'

Rob shivered, waiting for the heating to kick in. Aline put her foot on the accelerator and said nothing.

'We keep saying *that night*,' Sienna said. 'As though we can make it impersonal, abstract, *the accident*. But it wasn't impersonal: a woman died.'

'Sienna,' Aline said. 'I don't think this helps.'

'Yeah? Well maybe it helps me.' Sienna was crying again now, shouting through her tears.

Rob closed his eyes, lulled by the car. He wanted nothing more than to be back in his Edinburgh flat with its games console and old leather sofa, a bottle of adequate whisky in the cupboard and the dating apps back on his phone.

If he could only get there, he could relearn to silence the memories.

'She had a name,' Sienna said, 'and I looked *that* up. Did any of you bother? She was called Beth Taylor. She was a mother. Like you, Aline. Like me. She had a child.'

Winter

The rain falls heavy and hard and often. It hits the salt surface of the sea, the broken shells and gleaming shingle of the beach. Further up, it sinks into the soil, filters into the Cretaceous chalk and broken rocks beneath, filling them like a sponge. There is rain every year, so you could be forgiven for forgetting that one day – this year? next year? ten years hence? – it will be too much. The porous rocks will be saturated. The water will thread down, pushing and breaking, until stones crack and slide. And as the foundation yields, the resting layers above will slump in their turn, taking everything with them.

48

The Daughter

Edinburgh, 2018

I have never been to a hospice before. Why should I when the only death I have known was immediate and unexpected? This is a quiet place on a suburban street with a young woman in a nurse's uniform at the door. She smiles – a nice blend of efficiency and kindness – and asks who I am there to visit. No doubt she thinks me someone's grand-daughter, wan with sorrow, but my pallor is for something else. Fear and anticipation and all the words I cannot say aloud.

I am here for the truth.

I am here to see a murderer.

'Darryl Arniston,' I say. Her face changes. She is very professional, this woman, but not quite professional enough. The smile returns, with an edge to it. She asks me to wait while she gets someone. Her supervisor, perhaps.

'He asked me to come,' I say.

She scuttles off into her world of flowers and antiseptic and peaceful death, and I sit on a cushioned chair and drag from my pocket the postcard I received two days ago. I twist it in my restless hands. I crush the edges. I think.

I never had a father. Or rather, I must have had one, but I never knew him. He isn't on my birth certificate. I don't know what my mum would have told me if she had lived long enough to do it, because she was killed when I was four years old.

I found her. People assume I don't remember that, but I do. I remember a car horn, blaring away sleep; the carpet under my feet as I ran to the window. I remember the overturned bins, spilling out all the bits of our life that we had thrown away, and that strange, crumpled thing on the tarmac. I hear my light footsteps on the stairs, feel the sharp gravel, and my mother's skin still warm to my hands. I hear my voice, begging her to wake up. I see car lights and the teenager from the farm along the road crying with me while she phoned for help. I see her dress with flowers on it and feel the warmth of her chest against mine, for I was very cold by then.

Afterwards – days? weeks? – there was a closed casket, carried away on a conveyor belt not unlike the one I had seen once at an airport, the only time we had been abroad. I remember my shoes, which were new and blistery, and my uncle's hand, tight and unsympathetic on mine.

Then there was the rest of my childhood, or what passed for it.

My aunt and uncle fed me and bought me clothes, all new and hard-edged and scratchy with chemicals. They kept my room hoovered and gave me clean sheets every week and played me an audiobook, picked at random from an age-appropriate list, for exactly ten minutes every night. 'You are so good,' my aunt's friends told her, drinking their coffee or sparkling wine while I listened from the corner of the kitchen or garden. 'So good to take her on.'

At first, when I crept out of the shadows of my grief, I wanted to please them. I drew them pictures and smiled when they spoke to me. I tidied my room and pretended to like the toys they had got me. At school one year we made clay animals for Mother's Day. I told the teacher I had no mother and she said why not make one for your aunt, so I did. I made a cat, smoothing the clay with care, painting it glossy black. I put it in the paper bag my teacher gave me, and drew two kisses on the outside. When I gave it to my aunt, she said, 'Thank you, but I don't like cats. And I'm not your mother.' She smiled and my uncle laughed, as though they would make a joke of it.

How old was I then? Six, seven? I don't know. But after a while, I stopped trying.

When I was fourteen, I dressed for a school friend's party, fancying myself grown up in a short, borrowed dress. My uncle said, 'You can't go out like that. You look like a slut.'

I went upstairs to change, and from the stairs I heard my aunt, as she must have known I would. 'Like mother, like daughter.'

Before then, and for long after, school was my escape. Words to learn and numbers to lose myself in, and a route out of there. When I got my place at LSE, my aunt's friends said, 'She's been very lucky. She must be so grateful to you.'

~

I got the postcard at the end of my second year, when I had almost learned not to mind when my friends went home for the holidays. I opened it over toast and marmalade in the dining room of my student halls.

There is a picture on the front that I know now by heart but did not recognise then. It shows a sharp-faced woman on a bed and a little girl – blonde, nothing like me – watching the viewer with her hands to her head. According to the small print, it is Munch's *Death and the Child*. On the back, in spiky cursive, I read the sender's name, *Darryl Arniston*, the address of this Edinburgh hospice where I sit now, and one line of text.

I know who killed your mother.

Even as I sit here, where it has taken me – after the train journey, the night in a hostel, discombobulated by this magnificent, unfamiliar city – I am wondering if I should just have thrown it away.

A voice sounds quietly, then louder, as though it is breaking through wood. 'Do you have ID?'

It is the young nurse, back with an older colleague. I show them my passport and the older woman nods. 'Mr Arniston has confirmed that he asked you to visit. Come with me.' On the way along the very clean corridor, she says, 'Do you know—'

She stops, suddenly, and I wonder what she was going to say. *Do you know what he did?* Or perhaps, *Do you know what he wants?*

274

'I know he was in prison,' I say. 'I know why.' I found this out so easily – thirty seconds on Google – that he must have known I would.

She looks me up and down. 'You're very young,' she says. 'I'm not sure . . .'

'I'm twenty.'

'There will be a guard at the door,' she says. I nod, and try not to look as though this frightens me.

But when I see Darryl Arniston, I think at first how unscary he is (except, I suppose, in that the obvious proximity of death *is* frightening). He has faded brown hair in retreat around his temples, pale, opaque eyes and an ashen, sagging face, as though he's the 'after' version when the Honey Monster has been on a starvation diet. He does not look like a murderer.

'Hello,' I say, because I have to say something.

He lifts one thin hand and gestures to a chair by the bed. I sit down. He watches me with his head tilted on the pillow, and I start to feel that there is after all something perceptibly disturbing about him. Then I see the doll, and I am sure of it. She's propped up on the table beside the bed, a little taller than a Barbie, wearing a red velvet dress. Her face is a milky oval, her eyes are pale green and her acrylic hair is dark. She's a perfectly ordinary doll: nothing odd about her, except that she is here with him. There is a story there, but I'm not sure I want to hear it.

I wait for him to speak, and when he does, it is not what I expected.

'Are you happy?' His voice is a croak: an expiring frog.

'I'm OK,' I say, which is neither more nor less than the truth.

'What do you know about me?' he says, almost as the nurse did.

'What the internet told me.'

I know that he put his hands round a woman's neck, a woman who was kind to him; that he banged her head against a wall until the blood flowed fast, and then he choked the life out of her.

He opens his mouth, almost smiles. One of his teeth is missing and the rest hang from his skull, yellow and brown, as though he is already dead. 'If you'd lied,' he said, 'I'd have sent you away.'

'What is it that you have to tell me?'

He assumes an expression of didactic reproof, overlaid with something hideously close to flirtation. 'Impatient, aren't you? All in good time. Anyone would think you weren't happy to be here.'

I shudder, and try to hide it.

He says, 'There were five of them in the car.' He raises one hand and taps the digits in turn against his wasted chin. His fingers are dry-skinned, puffy and ringless. 'Brandon Miller,' he says. 'Michael Arley, Sienna Adams.' He pauses a fraction of a second. 'Robert Sutton, Aline Linden. They were students,' he adds. 'Like you.'

Each name lands in my brain and rests there, a pebble in mud, until I can know what to do with it. He goes on, stopping between sentences to force his thin breath in and out. 'The car was a Skoda estate. I don't know who they borrowed it from, but I know the colour. It was such a grotesque green that you'd think someone would have noticed, but no one did. In the papers, the police said there was no evidence.'

'If there was no evidence . . .' I stop, then go on. My voice is almost as hoarse as his. 'How do you know?'

He laughs. Spittle flies from his mouth and lands on the white sheets. I force myself not to shove my chair back, away from him. He says, 'I saw them.'

'You were there?' It comes out much louder than I intended. The big man in the doorway watches me, but does not move.

'I was following them.' He says this as though it is a completely normal thing to do.

'You mean . . .' I struggle for the word, which I have had little cause to use, 'in convoy?'

Darryl Arniston shakes his head. 'No. They didn't know I was there.' I wait, and he continues, rasping but oddly conversational. 'I knew them all, you see. They had been my friends. Except Brandon. I never met him to speak to.'

Had been. 'What happened?' I say.

He raises a hand again, tries to turn, and cannot. Instead, he makes futile grabbing motions in the direction of the doll. 'I want to hold her.'

I get up and walk round the bed. The guard moves this time, but does not intervene. I lift the doll by her narrow waist and lie her on Darryl Arniston's chest, taking care not to touch the sheet. He strokes her hair with a skeletal finger.

When I am back in my chair, he says, 'It was dark, and they had driven a long way.' He pauses. 'From here, in fact. Edinburgh. They were going much too fast for those roads.

Your mother was standing by the bins.' He closes his eyes. 'Then she wasn't,' he says.

I feel ice in my chest, my fingers so tightly curled that the nails hurt my palms. I count to five in my head. I tell myself that they may not even be real, these people. They might be names pulled from a hat to torment me. Perhaps there was no other car. Perhaps it was this horrible man who drove recklessly on narrow, tree-edged lanes and robbed my gentle mother of her life.

I want to scream. I want to puke.

'If you were there,' I say, 'why didn't you tell the police?'

He opens his eyes, grips the doll tighter. He whispers, so I must lean closer than I want. His breath is like sour milk. 'When I was a teenager, my family died in a car crash. The police did nothing.' He gives me his Halloween half-smile. 'You see,' he says. 'We have a lot in common.'

I sit up, back away.

We don't. We don't. We don't.

'Besides,' he adds, 'the police weren't kind to me, later on.' He glares as though he dares me to comment, but I do not. 'I didn't trust them,' he says. 'I still don't.'

He starts to cough, then cannot stop. I suppose I should get a glass of water and help him to drink it, but I am disgusted by the thought. Instead, a nurse comes in and does it. He does not thank her. When she has gone, he speaks almost defiantly: 'It wasn't that I didn't want them to be punished.'

I say, 'So it wasn't because they were your friends?'

He laughs so hard that I think it might kill him, but it doesn't. 'Oh no,' he gasps. He shuts his eyes, and after a bit he speaks with them still closed. 'At first I thought it didn't

278

matter. They were still young. I could wait until I came out. I could be patient.' His hand fondles the doll. 'Let them build more of their lives, so there would be more to destroy. I thought I had time.'

He opens his eyes. 'I was wrong about that, wasn't I?'

I say nothing. If he expects sympathy, I cannot offer it.

He says, 'That's why I found you. There's time for you.'

I'm not like you.

His hand, the one not caressing the doll, scrabbles upwards behind his head, but the contortion is too much for him and he slumps back, coughing again. 'Look . . .' he rasps, 'under the pillow. I need you to do something.'

I am still repulsed, but I slip my hand under and pull out an envelope, stiff with whatever is inside. He nods, and I turn it upside down so the contents fall onto my lap. They are postcards, art prints like the one he sent me, with writing on the back.

'I'll need you to get the addresses,' he says.

I lift them, leaf through them. Mrs Aline Linden-Miller, Mr Michael Arley, Ms Sienna Adams, Mr Robert Sutton, Mr Brandon Linden-Miller. 'No,' I say.

'Yes.'

I ask nothing as I skim the words on the cards. But he answers as though I had. 'I had someone find things out, while I was in Saughton. Keep a virtual eye on them.' His voice is a creaking whisper. 'There's always someone you can bribe.' He gives a sly glance past me to the guard at the door. 'It's harder here.'

I wonder, briefly, who got the postcards for him. The same bribee? Or a nurse here, seeing no possible harm.

I grip them together in my hand. I say, 'I have a question. Who was driving the car?'

He wraps his hand tighter round the doll. 'Isn't it funny?' he says. 'My friend here looks a bit like you.'

I gag, there in the warm, flower-filled room. 'The driver,' I say. 'Just tell me.'

'Not now. You post those cards and come back. *Then* I'll tell you. After that, it'll be up to you.' He starts to cough. 'I hope you're grateful,' he chokes. 'I'm giving you something I never had.'

'What?'

'A chance to punish them.'

The cough escalates. The doll leaps on his juddering chest, and the nurse hurries back in. She gives me a swift, compassionate look. 'Time to go, hen.'

I walk backwards out of the room, afraid that the guard will see me trembling. Over the nurse's shoulder, Darryl Arniston clutches the doll in one shaking fist and coughs out what, as it turns out, will be the last words he speaks to me. 'Goodbye, Milly. I'll see you next time.'

But there is no next time. I phone the following day, and they tell me that he is dead.

I check out from my hostel. I walk to Waverley station and stand a long time under the angular, translucent ceiling, watching dancing lines of light on the stone floor, stretched between possible futures.

Aline. Michael. Brandon. Robert. Sienna.

I could go back to Dorset, where I have not been since I left. I could tell the police there everything Darryl Arniston has told me. I could leave his story to be crammed away as an addendum in an 'Unsolved' file: an unprovable claim by a man both unreliable and deceased. That is what I should do. I know that. Or I could go to London. I know from a night's googling that three of the five of them live there. And so, of course, do I. I could find out the truth for myself.

I'll keep the postcards, in case I need them.

49

Michael

Dorset, 2002

There were words as they stood in that patch of horror. 'Oh God, oh God.' His voice, or Sienna's? He would never know. But he knew Aline's, sharp-edged in the blurry night, 'Get back in.' And then, as she steered the car back along high-banked lanes in the summer dark, 'We won't talk about this. Not even to each other.'

None of them answered. Michael closed his eyes, wondering if he would ever speak again, of this or anything, or if her words, their actions, had cast a web of silence that would hold them all forever. He stared out at the reaching trees, the thatched roofs and warm Dorset stone, while each mile took them further from what they should have done, making an intentional wrong of what had been carelessness.

Sienna cried quietly. Brandon sat in the passenger seat, as still as though he was enchanted. Aline put on the radio, and the presenter's voice was brash and unreal, the music a soundtrack to a film Michael did not want to see. At the end, diving steeply down, he thought for one absurd moment that she was going to drive them into the sea.

Instead, she pulled up against a wall of cracked stone and switched off the engine. 'We're here,' she said.

The door opened and an old woman stood there, straight-backed and still beautiful, smiling a welcome. She could have been Aline in fifty years' time. The real Aline turned her head, a pale gleam in the shadowy car. Her glance darted from Brandon to the three of them like sardines in the back. She touched Brandon's arm, and Michael wondered, with a kind of dim detachment, if he would ever stop desiring her.

'Promise,' she said, and he knew the word was not a question, but a command.

50

Aline

Dorset, 2019

The storm was rising. The rain was an assault on the windscreen, the Land Rover juddered in the wind, and Aline, who never wasted time on worry or regret, experienced a sliver of something that might have been either.

That afternoon, the old man on the beach had looked up to the crumbling mass of cliff and clay and shrub and pronounced a grim verdict.

'After the winter we've had, I wouldn't want to be living up there.'

Aline had laughed. 'I bet you said the same to my gran every wet winter for the last twenty years.'

The man had sighed, unoffended. 'I watch this beach. I've watched it for decades. Ask me . . .' he had gestured upwards, 'it could go any time.'

The children had been chasing each other in circles on the shingle. In the face of such joyful normality, his words had been too ridiculously portentous to take seriously. But she recalled them now, driving in this wild darkness.

She eased her foot on the accelerator, swinging from tarmacked road to rough track. She heard Sienna crying out on a fragile path, Michael staring into a dark window. *There's someone there.* She saw Nikki, furious in a white tower, and experienced an uncharacteristic desire to take the old man's warning seriously. They could grab the children, stow them all in a hotel in Dorchester or Weymouth for the night, then drive straight back to Hampstead. They could sell the house, like Brandon had always wanted. They could forget all this.

She heard Sienna again, shouting through the storm. *She was called Beth Taylor. She had a child.*

She shook her head, hard.

They pulled up on the wet gravel. The house was quiet, the downstairs windows bright. Inside, in the warm, gorgeous space she had created, her ridiculous fears would subside. She would handle this, as she had handled everything else.

Nikki and Sienna stumbled out of the cars, an ungainly double act, racing for the front door. Above them, the automatic light flashed on. Nikki tried the door, opened it a crack. 'It's on the chain,' she said, and pressed the bell.

No answer. Aline pushed past them both, her heels slipping on the wet gravel. She called out, 'Milly, it's us.' She heard footsteps inside, then the sound of breathing. The wind screamed. Again Aline stifled uncharacteristic unease. She pulled her coat around her, put her face to the illuminated gap between wall and door. 'Let us in. It's freezing out here.'

The door pulled shut. She heard the chain being unhooked, then someone – Milly – stepping back. Aline turned the handle, pushed the door in. She started to speak again, then didn't.

Milly stood in the entrance, lamp lit, with the stairs rising like a stage set behind her and Aline's grandmother's shotgun at her shoulder, levelled at the open door.

51

Milly

Dorset, 2019

It was easy to inveigle my way into Aline's life, because she is so completely sure that the rest of the world exists to make that life easier. She needed someone to keep her house running and her children alive while she juggled her City job (management consultant, whatever that is) with extensive renovations well over a hundred miles away. She'd even posted on social media about how hard it all was for her, without a touch of irony. Poor little millionaire. And there I was, right on cue, knocking on her door with my specially printed flyer in my hand, a highly respectable student (Russell Group, obviously) looking for part-time work.

She was so glossy, so monied London, standing at the top of the steps in designer clothes, so bloody respectable that it was almost impossible to connect her with the student she must have been, packed with friends into a borrowed car, spinning through the dark, careless of consequences.

After a while, though, I picked out the common thread: a self-obsessed entitlement carrying her from the girl who had left my mother dead in the road, her own life untouched, to the executive who spoke to me impatiently of 'my builders', 'my electrician'. *My people.*

I applied grown-up versions of the techniques I had once tried unsuccessfully on my aunt and uncle. Admiration, with a hint of self-reliance. Uncomplaining labour. Taking the initiative. And this time, they worked. Aline trusted me. I believe she liked me. And if Brandon didn't, if I made him uncomfortable, he never said so.

I didn't tell them I was born in Dorset. I talked of Gloucester, where my uncle and aunt lived, and let them think it had been my home. I talked of my mother as though she were alive and my father as though I had one. They never questioned any of it.

I sent the postcards at the start of December, because by then I was frustrated. Tired of spending half my time there, washing Aline's dishes, cooking for the kids, chivvying workmen, making her appointments at John Frieda and never learning anything of what might have happened sixteen years before. Worst of all, and against my will, I was learning to like her children. Especially Jimmy. Lexie has much of her mother in her, although she has a kindness that Aline lacks. Jimmy is entirely himself, or perhaps a little of his father. An anxious, loving soul.

But I cannot think about that now.

I had no grand Machiavellian plan (though Aline would have had one were the situation reversed). Not when I tracked down the addresses, transcribed them in careful imitation of a dying man's wavering, prickly script; nor when I dropped the cards into the postbox between lecture and library. It was the compulsion of a child watching an anthill who has no options left but a stick. Like the stick, though, it did the trick. It provoked this reunion.

In Dorset, of all places, where I find it easiest not to forgive.

For weeks, I waited for this weekend, for crisis or resolution. But when it came, I still had no real strategy. I sought their secrets, listening in corners, and when that failed, I resorted to scaring them. The stick again, blindly applied. I ran in the dark along the coast path while the children played hide-and-seek at home, going in and out through the garden and slipping back among them with my hair damp. I was a little worried, at the time, that Jimmy had noticed something, but he kept it quiet if he had.

Later, I pressed my face, fleeting and distorted, against the wet glass of a dark window and Michael saw me without knowing it was me. Did I think I would provoke them into revealing their secrets? Perhaps. In so far as I had a plan, that was it. Or maybe I just wanted to frighten them. But I don't want to think that, because it is too much what Darryl Arniston would have thought.

And the gun, slippery now in my cold hand? That, too, was no strategy. It was serendipity, showing me the way. Pure good luck.

He would have called it fate.

52

Jimmy

Dorset, 2019

Jimmy stood with his sister in the shadows of the landing. Lexie was so still that she could have been a model of herself, except that he could hear her heartbeat. Downstairs, they could see the back of Milly's head, her thin body, and the gun that looked like a toy she had borrowed from someone bigger. Jimmy had almost screamed when he'd seen it, but Lexie had grabbed him, gripping hard, and put her hand over his mouth.

'Keep back,' Milly called, but she wasn't speaking to them. She didn't know they were there. She was shouting it out through the open door.

Jimmy felt sick with fear. He wanted to ask if this was a joke, some weird grown-up game. There were two versions of Milly in his head and he could not get them apart. The girl who had been part of his life for almost half a year, who had cooked his meals, washed his clothes, played endless games of cards, held his hand when he had night terrors. And this petrifying stranger.

He heard a woman screaming something. Sienna, he thought, but couldn't be sure over the wind and rain. He couldn't hear what she said, but he heard Milly's reply. 'I've done nothing to them. They're upstairs. Asleep.'

In the dark, he clutched at Lexie's hand. It was cold – even colder than his – but she gave him a squeeze that he knew was meant to be comforting. Downstairs, Milly shouted, 'I'm not interested in the kids. They're just leverage. I'm interested in you.' Perhaps this too should have been reassuring. But it was not.

He heard his mother's voice, carrying easily. 'Milly, stop this.' She sounded so much as normal – impatient and in charge at the same time – that for a moment Jimmy really *was* comforted. 'I know it's not loaded,' she said.

Instead of answering, Milly tilted the gun up so it pointed high into the air, and fired.

The house seemed to shudder. Milly was flung backwards, almost falling. Jimmy felt Lexie go tense beside him, but Milly was steady again before either of them could move, holding the gun straight.

'Believe me now?' she called.

Lexie was moving backwards, quiet as a cat, pulling Jimmy towards the upper stairs. Over renewed voices, the drum of the rain, he whispered into her hair. 'What's happening?'

He wanted her to say it was all OK, but he knew she wouldn't, and she didn't. 'I'm not sure,' she said, 'but I think we're hostages.'

He felt cold all over. He thought of the twins still sleeping on the floor upstairs; of Chloe, who had hugged Milly so tight at bedtime that Milly had laughed and said she couldn't breathe. He longed to climb back under his duvet, where his bear, Cuthbert, waited for him; to curl up and lose himself in sleep.

'What do we do?' he whispered.

Lexie shook her head. He stood on the bottom step, gulping back tears, while she chewed her lip like their dad did when *he* was thinking. At last, she stretched out icy fingers and took his hand again. She grinned, and it was his mother's expression: suddenly sure of herself.

'We get out,' she said.

53

Milly

Dorset, 2019

I watch them in the arc of the light, still as gargoyles, gaping at me, all in their Sunday best, with thick coats on top of them. I, too, am wordless. I've got very good at that.

At last Aline calls through sheets of rain, 'Who *are* you?'

I smile, though I don't know if she can see it. 'My mother's name was Beth Taylor. You may have heard of her.'

For an instant, despite everything, I think I have got it wrong. There they are: six outraged, respectable adults, shut out in the downpour, faces too blurred to read. Then I hear Sienna. 'Dear God,' she says (moans, really). 'Oh dear God.'

I take a breath. 'Thanks,' I say. 'That's one question answered.'

Nikki says, 'What's happening? Why will no one tell me what's going on?' Nobody answers, and she scrabbles in her coat pocket for her phone, jabs at the screen. Her voice is halfway to a scream. 'I'm calling the police.'

She'd be lucky: the reception is terrible here. But Aline grabs at the phone anyway. Nikki wrenches it back.

'Aline's right,' I say. 'I really wouldn't do that. Not unless you want someone to get hurt.'

Aline stares at me, icy calm. 'You little bitch,' she says. 'I trusted you.' Sienna gasps. Brandon makes a noise that is somewhere between a groan and a sob.

'That's interesting,' I say. 'I don't trust anyone.'

Nikki is crying now, horrible, ugly gulps, so I can only just make out what she is saying. 'I don't understand. Why are you doing this to us?'

I feel the gun cold in my hands. I try not to remember that Nikki has been kind all weekend. I remind myself that they are leaving tomorrow: this is my last chance to make them talk. I gesture with the barrel at Michael. 'Oh, didn't he tell you?' I say. 'They killed my mother, him and his friends.'

She freezes, stands there with her mouth open and the rain streaming down her face. 'Michael?' she mouths. He starts to speak, then doesn't.

The wind lifts the heavy sheet of Aline's hair and she pushes it away. 'What do you want?' she calls.

What *do* I want?

My aunt didn't want me. She never liked kids, and if she had wanted them, she would have had her own. I know this because I heard her yell it, the third week I was there, just as I heard my uncle talking her down. Did she think he didn't know that? Did she think *he* wanted me? Did she think they had a choice?

I had no choice.

Rufus cries from the back of the car: a short, furious noise that we all hear even though the wind is like a banshee. Nikki sways towards him, takes a few steps, then strains back towards the house. I feel sorry for her. I don't want to, but I do.

I call out, 'Go to him,' and she stares at me, not moving, like she can't take in what I am saying. I raise my voice. 'I don't need anything from you.'

None of this is your fault.

'You have my little girl.' It is as though she says the words aloud to make herself understand them. Then, suddenly, she seems to collect herself, throws everything into her plea. 'Please, Milly, let her go. What they did . . .' she gestures wildly at the rest of them, 'whatever they did, it's nothing to do with me.'

Michael flinches. I think of Chloe with her dark eyes and confident smile, her fat, sticky fingers, and how she chases the bigger children, desperate to keep up. I feel her hugging me goodnight. I wonder if my life would have been easier – if my aunt and uncle would have loved me – if I had been cute like that.

I *wasn't* cute. Part pixie, part ghost. But my mother loved me.

I am struck by a memory that is like a photograph. A woman with my eyes and dark hair, and a smile that could hold you and keep you in its heart. I try to imagine hurting Chloe, hurting any of them, and it makes me want to throw the gun from me and run out up that steep, hard track away from this horrible house, all the way to the safe, lamp-lit roads. It's true, Nikki is just a victim. Like me. But it is too late now.

Again I use the gun to point at Michael. 'Sorry,' I say, 'but she's his daughter too.' I nod towards the car, with its escalating cries. 'One for you.' Then to the house behind me. 'One for him.'

Michael whimpers. To be fair on him, I think it is my words that prompt it, not the fact that the shotgun is now directed his way. Nikki wails. Aline said, 'Nikki, please.' Michael tries to hug his wife but she jerks herself away.

'Don't touch me. This is because of you.'

He shrinks as though she had hit him. Rufus screams even louder. She stumbles to the car and the door slams behind her.

Then it is easier. Just me and them. My personal police line-up. Brandon, so still you would think he was a manne- quin; Michael with his head bent, already in the dock; Sienna pale and trembling; Rob watching me with arms folded. I supposed he can afford the detachment. And Aline, straight as a warrior.

I speak clearly, over the wind. 'Which of you was driving that car?'

Brandon moves, Michael does too, but Aline is faster. She takes a step towards me, then another. I angle the gun straight at her, and she never bats an eyelid.

'OK,' she says. 'You can have your confession. But let us in first.'

'It was you.' My voice is a squeak, but she hears it. She gives a tiny shrug. I feel the rain, ice-cold against my skin, seeping through inadequate indoor clothes. I stare into her clear eyes along the barrel of the gun. I hate her more than I have ever hated anyone, and I am a good hater. I want, almost more than anything else, to pull that trigger.

54

Sienna

Dorset, 2002

She sat alone and early on the ragged ground. The grass, dew-damp, seeped through dress and cardigan. The sea, far below, was like dark ice.

When she had thought of Dorset, before they came, she had imagined Avalon. Merlin and Vivien, nymphs dipping out of glens, silver branches that twisted and grasped, layered with magic. But that magic, if it had ever been here, was gone. Instead, there were gin and tonics overlooking the sea, picnics conjured daily by Aline and her grandmother. There were hot walks along coast paths and up and down to beaches. There was sand and shingle under her bare feet and water so cold it made her gasp. There was Rob, and there was her. It should still have been wonderful, in its way, but it was not.

She gazed across flat water to the long spine of Portland, then left to chalky crags. Her fingers plucked at the grass, stripping thin, curled leaves from the stem. She thought of

Beltane, holding tight to Rob beside the dancing fire and throbbing drums, and wondered how that could be only six weeks ago. She closed her eyes and heard brakes screeching, pulling her dream-heavy from her sleep in the back of the car. She heard Brandon yelling, and another scream, outside: higher and harder to forget. She saw Aline, calm-faced, dragging them out of bed to wash the car together. Confirming complicity.

Oh, there was magic here after all, but they had brought it with them. A dark curse, twisting at her soul as she moved through crowds of shrieking holidaymakers. Merlin trapped alive in the tree. Vivien laughing through the storm. It was all blood, sacrifice, retribution.

She rose, rubbed her eyes, walked with new determination. She went down the steep track with its inlaid stones and its thick line of grass along the middle. Past thrusting fern, bracken, nettles and brambles. Past ash and oak and sycamore, heavy with ivy, and back at last into the silent house.

Rob lay curled on his side with only a sheet pulled over him. She wriggled in, hauled the duvet up and watched his sleeping face.

'Rob?' she whispered.

He stirred. She touched his cheek, feeling the sharp bone. Something lurched inside her, so violent that she thought it would cast her down through mattress and carpet, through boards and a whole floor below, into the clay-hard earth.

He blinked his eyes open. 'What?'

'I'm going home,' she said. 'I'm going home and I'm staying there.'

He looked at her a long time, then closed his eyes again. She watched his face, waiting for tears, and felt them, fast and plentiful, on her own.

55

Jimmy

Dorset, 2019

He stood by the open window with Chloe in his arms, listening to the rain and watching his sister as she sat on the sill and swung her legs out. In the night, the garden below them was a different place: terrifying, with silhouette trees shaking in the wind. He thought of Milly's kindness, her stories, the way she wrote their initials in syrupy loops on pancakes. He wanted to say something, then didn't.

He thought of the gun.

The twins sat on the edge of the double bed, hands clasped, blurry with sleep and fear. They had barely spoken since he and Lexie had shaken them awake, whispering that they must be quiet, it was a game, an adventure.

'I don't want to,' Luna had murmured, and Lexie had said, in their mother's voice, 'Well, you must.'

She smiled now, and slid her feet down to the porch roof. 'Not so far,' she said. She skidded, gripped tighter, and looked frowningly down, as though her limbs had disappointed her.

'I'll have to sit,' she said. 'I'll need both arms.'

Jimmy's stomach tightened. 'What about Chloe?'

'I need them *for* Chloe, idiot.' Chloe giggled, startlingly loud. Jimmy hushed her. 'You'll have to pass her to me,' Lexie said. 'Lean out.'

He hated the idea. He hated this whole plan. But he had nothing better to suggest. He felt the rain on his neck and Chloe's arms sliding under his tight fingers. He saw her trusting smile, and felt sick with fear. He thought he heard a shout downstairs, but it was almost impossible to tell over the wind.

'Got her,' Lexie said. 'You can let go.'

She held Chloe with one arm against her chest, perched on folded legs. She did it all easily, like it *was* a game, and grinned up at Jimmy.

'Now you.'

Jimmy reached into his pocket, where he had put Cuthbert when Lexie wasn't looking, and squeezed his woolly arm. He thought of his sister and how fearless she was. He thought, *I can't be sick now*, and just wasn't. He thought of his aunt Clara, who had made Cuthbert for him. 'You're brave too, Jimmy,' she had told him once. 'It's not about what you do: it's about how hard it is for you to do it.'

'Just watch us,' Lexie had told the twins, five minutes before. 'Then you'll know what to do.' But that wouldn't help if he fell.

He gripped the wet windowsill, wriggled his legs over and turned to face the wall. It might have been OK, he thought, without the cold and the storm and if he hadn't been terrified that he would topple Lexie and Chloe from their precarious perch. He slipped down, hands cold on the wet wood. His feet flailed, slamming against the sloping tiles, finding nothing to grip. He wanted to scream. He heard Lexie, still calm, sounding very close to him. 'It's OK. You're OK. Use the drainpipe.'

Where *was* the drainpipe? The wind tugged at his fleece and pyjamas. A monster, trying to drag him from the wall.

Take a deep breath, his dad always said when they got angry or panicky. Jimmy took one now. He saw the iron pipe, out to the right of him. He got hold of it, gripped tight and let his feet slide.

Chloe whimpered. Lexie hushed her. The wind howled, rattling the trees below. One of Jimmy's feet was wedged painfully against the drainpipe; the other pushed its way into the corner between the house and the bottom of the tiled roof, just finding friction. He took another deep breath, unpeeled his left hand from the window ledge and began slowly – painfully – to climb down the pipe.

He thought he heard his dad's voice. *You'll be OK, dude.* And, somehow, he was. Hand, foot, hand, over and over, ignoring the storm, the cold in his fingers and the twisting pain in his toes, until the ground was chill and sharp beneath his feet. The light came on and he froze for a second, then remembered that it was automatic. He looked up, gasping with relief. Lexie and Chloe were still there on the shallow roof, like mermaids on a rock, hair flying, illuminated by a thousand light-sparked raindrops.

'Well done,' Lexie said.

He hobbled closer. There was a slither, a rustle of clothes on wet tile, and Chloe was on his chest again. She gripped his neck, her little legs wrapped round him, and he was desperately glad of the warm, solid reality of her, even though he was shaking so much that he could barely hold her.

56

Milly

Dorset, 2019

I cannot do it. I cannot pull the trigger. And in that realisa-
tion there is regret, frustration and even shame, but there
is also overwhelming relief. I am not Darryl Arniston. I am
nothing like him.

I step back. I'm still levelling the gun as they troop
silently past me. Brandon, Rob, Michael, with the bottoms
of their suit trousers soaked by the storm. Sienna, stumbling
in heels, her long dress clinging wetly to her ankles. Aline
last of all, cool as though she were walking into the Ritz,
shutting the door behind them. I stand with my back to the
stairs, between them and their children, forcing them
further into the big room. I step forward. I'm still in
control.

And then, suddenly, I am not. There's a sound from
upstairs. A laugh, perhaps, or a cry. Sienna moans. Michael
says, '*Chloe.*' I turn my head. I look up, and Aline acts.

~

I had not thought she could be so quick. I swing back on the instant, but she is already beside me. Her hands go round the barrel of the gun, forcing it up. I feel her hair, like wet silk, and the strength in her arms. I smell her perfume. I hear her voice whispering in my ear, and it too is smooth as silk.

I get my confession after all.

'I'm so sorry it happened,' she says, 'but it was an accident.' I think she does mean it, but no doubt she would say it as convincingly either way.

I want to say all the things that I have imagined saying for the past eight months. I want to tell her how this one moment, a second's carelessness in her gilded youth, was everything to me. I want to scream that she moved on, lived, was happy, but for us – my mother and me – there was no going on.

I say, like a small child, 'You broke everything.'

'I'm sorry,' she says again. It is what I thought I wanted, but it is also wildly inadequate. 'It was dark, and we were tired.'

'You didn't stop.'

'We did. We checked . . .' For the first and only moment, her voice wavers. *We checked she was dead.* But even Aline cannot spell that out to me. Instead, she says, 'There was nothing we could do.'

Is this even true? I will never know.

'We panicked,' she says. 'We were very young.'

'You were older than I am now.'

Unexpectedly, she smiles. Her voice has changed again. She is kind, almost tender, as she has sometimes been before.

'And *you* panicked tonight, didn't you, Milly? You saw an opportunity, you grabbed it and you've been regretting it ever since.'

My fingers judder. Despite myself, I feel the power shift, drop away from me. Behind her, between sofas and wall, I am aware of the others in their frozen cluster.

'Who told you?' she says.

'A witness.'

'A witness who wouldn't go to the police?'

I say nothing. Her nails lean on the gun. I scrabble at it, at them: a child clinging to a purloined toy. She tightens her hold. 'Never mind,' she says. 'I know who it was. I know everything now.' Her voice is almost caressing. 'You sent the postcards, didn't you?'

'Yes.'

I hate her, but I am mesmerised by her. Is this how Michael feels? Brandon? All of them?

'But you didn't write them.'

I shake my head. With one thumb, she flicks the safety catch back on. I don't stop her but nor do I let go. 'You have the truth now,' she says. 'Give me the gun, and leave.'

My hands go slack. She smiles again. She touches my hair with gentle fingers, as she might Lexie's or Jimmy's. She lifts the gun, carefully as a relic, and steps back with it into the bright room. I take two steps towards the door. I feel Sienna pressing past me, then Michael, heading for the stairs. I picture Aline snapping the gun open, removing the cartridge, and Nikki running in, clutching Rufus, demanding Chloe. Demanding explanations. But I will be gone. I will take my story and decide what to do with it.

Behind me, Sienna shrieks. I hear Aline's voice, with all the gentleness gone.

'Not so fast,' she says.

In that moment, I am not afraid. I am a toddler again with my feet in wellies and thick socks and my hand in a woman's hand, held tight. The ground sinks and settles as we run back and forward, laughing, and her shoes are tickled by the waves.

I turn, blinking. Aline is still holding the gun. Only now she's pointing it at me.

57

Brandon

Dorset, 2002

They stood together in Aline's grandmother's garden, glorious in the summer evening. The stone paths wove their pattern through an abundance of roses, making a collage of the pinks and reds, creams and peaches, the stems dark and lustrous. His favourite were the yellow ones, bursting out of their buds like so many pieces of sunshine.

Aline stretched out her arms, as if the whole place was hers. Not just this garden, with its flowers and fruit trees and high stone walls, the house clinging by its fingertips to crag and clay, but even the undulating coastline beyond, all the way to Swanage one way, Exmouth the other, and the rolling sea itself. Brandon could love that coast, its ancient, unreliable beauty, if he let himself.

He watched Aline, though he might have been safer watching the flowers. Her legs were long and bare, with sandals on her feet. Her hair was looped at the back of her neck, held in place with a clip like a giant butterfly. She seemed entirely light-hearted, completely at peace.

She put her hands round his neck, pulling his head down. 'Tomorrow,' she said, 'we'll walk the Pirate's Path. Just you and me.'

Brandon closed his eyes, wiped out by lust and exhaustion. He tasted her lips, cherry-sweet. 'Aline . . .'

She whispered, 'I've always wanted you.'

So many moments. A gorgeous girl in Lycra and a ponytail. His regular running buddy, sounding decidedly put out, saying, 'She likes *you*, pal.' That same unrefusable smile that she was flashing now. The same face, the same athletic body at the Fire Festival, her hand reaching up to caress his stag's horns. Her voice like a bell, beside him in the Meadows, sure of his response. 'It's a glorious part of the world, the Dorset coast. You must come with us.'

When could he have done it? When, in all those trivial incidents, had been his chance to say no? Then there was the one that was *not* trivial, and all week he had wanted to say something. Day and night and in the slipping moments between. Everywhere they went, from the Weymouth seafront to a half-dozen crowded beaches, he felt himself detached from it, wading through a nightmare. He had seen the cottage with its climbing roses, overexposed in the headlights, and the woman at the side of the road, finishing up her tasks for the day. Expecting no one. He had seen her face frozen in that instant when the car was on her and it was too late to move.

Aline smiled into his eyes, utterly confident. 'I always get what I want.'

He sought for words that, if not right, would at least be adequate. 'Sienna's going back to the States. I thought . . . if I went . . .'

'Very funny.' She moved to kiss him again. He held her back a moment, supple wrists in his closed fists.

'After what happened, don't you think we'd be better apart?'

'Oh no.' She slid her hands free. 'We're each other's secret-keepers now.' Her green eyes were wide. 'Rob, Michael, Sienna, wherever she runs to. We all are, but especially you and me.'

He shivered. How much would he give, he thought, to change what had happened?

'I'm knackered,' she'd said, as they sat in the dark in that lay-by, waiting for their pursuer to pass. Had it only been a week ago? He had thought how far she had driven, never complaining. He had put his hand down, moved by this first hint of vulnerability, and brushed her fingers on the handbrake. He had felt the startling charge of electricity, and pulled it back.

She had looked at him, half impatient, half something very different. 'What?'

'Want me to drive?' he had said.

'Yes please,' she had said. And now, in this little patch of paradise, she kissed him again, infinitely desirable, her opening lips at once a promise and a threat. Relentless as diamond, she murmured, 'We must keep each other close.'

58

Jimmy

Dorset, 2019

He carried Chloe to an old bench, half sheltered by trees. The rain seemed like it would never stop. 'I'm cold,' she whimpered, and he took off his own drenched fleece and put it on her instead. He remembered Cuthbert, a damp lump in the pocket, held him tight for a second, then put him in Chloe's arms. On the porch, Lexie was now standing with one hand on the drainpipe, and Astrid was climbing onto the window ledge. He had to squint to see them through the rain.

He thought it was all going to be OK, until it almost wasn't. Astrid dropped, was held a second against Lexie, then slithered down the tiles. She grabbed at Lexie's ankle, so that for one horrible moment Jimmy thought they would come crashing down together. Then she let go. From the window, Luna yelped. Jimmy moved, faster than he had thought he could. He caught Astrid – anywhere, anyhow – and they thudded to the wet ground together.

'Are you hurt?' Somehow Lexie had stayed upright, her feet an acrobat's on the metal ridge pole. But her voice wobbled.

Astrid stood up. Jimmy scrambled up after her. 'I'm fine,' he said, although he thought his shoulder would burst.

'Good catch,' Lexie said. She paused, then called upwards. 'Luna, it's your turn.'

But Luna, standing like a phantom at the window, shook her head. 'I can't,' she said. 'I can't do it.'

He didn't know how long they waited. Beyond the semicircle of light, the garden was whirling dark, the wind tearing at leaves and setting the rose bushes dancing. Astrid stepped away from him and stood tiny and alone, looking up at the window.

'Luna,' she said. 'Please.'

Chloe wriggled from the bench, wrapped her wet arms round Jimmy's thighs and started to cry. He stroked her head, wondering how it was possible to be this wet and cold and still have room to be afraid, all at the same time. Luna put her hands on the sill, then lifted them off again. Lexie said nothing, though she must have been freezing.

At last Luna moved. She sat sideways on the windowsill, quivering, staring down at her sister. Astrid nodded. Luna slid one leg over the edge, then the other, and inched herself down. Lexie took hold of her and lifted her to the roof. Jimmy let out his breath, all in one go.

Then there was another noise. A terrible one, which wasn't the storm.

Astrid screamed. The lights went out. Blackness wrapped Jimmy, blinded him an instant, and then Lexie and Luna were there again, still standing on the roof with their hands joined, two darker shadows against the raging night.

He tried to shout and could not. Lexie yanked Luna forward. 'Jump!' she screamed. '*Jump.*'

59

Brandon

Dorset, 2019

Outside, the wind cracked branches and cast rain like stones. It seemed to Brandon that the earth growled too, echoing the storm, deep beneath his feet. But if it did, the rest were oblivious. Sienna and Michael stood where they had stopped, turning for the stairs; Rob was another statue, close against the wall. The girl's eyes were like onyx in a plaster face, watching Aline.

'What are you going to do?'

'Nothing.' Aline lowered the gun, but kept hold of it. 'None of us are. I just want to clear a few things up.'

'About what?'

'About you kidnapping our children.'

'I didn't—'

Brandon saw Milly as a tiny child, grieving for her mother. He saw that other child, years ago in his home town, crumpled over a bloodstained corpse. And here was his wife in her beautiful dress, with her long coat hanging open and the emeralds brilliant at her throat. As comfortable as a soldier, with a gun in her hands.

Aline cut Milly off. 'Taking them hostage, then.' She smiled. 'I'm afraid I don't know if they are different charges, but I would imagine that both come with a substantial prison sentence.'

The girl said nothing. Where had she learned to keep so still?

'Of course,' Aline went on, 'I know what you'll do. You'll tell them your tragic history. I expect they'll feel sorry for you. Then you'll tell them your tale about us being involved in your mum's death, but after that, I'm afraid, they'll just think you're delusional, or dangerously naïve.'

'You confessed.'

Aline's face was exactly right: polite shock, a little concern. 'I really don't think I did.' She glanced round at the impeccable room, as though even now she could find satisfaction in it. 'I told you, didn't I? I know everything. And I'll tell you what I would say to the police. I'd tell them how Darryl Arniston behaved to us. How he was our friend until we became seriously concerned about his mental state. Rob even reported him to the university. I expect that's on record.'

The girl's mouth and chin moved, but no words came out. Sienna made a small, incomprehensible noise. Aline smiled again, very gently. 'I'd explain that he kept asking to come to Dorset with us and sulked when we said no. I'd probably leave them to figure out for themselves that he followed us and got lost along the way, but I'd stress that we stuck to the main roads. Ilchester to Yeovil, Yeovil to Dorchester. Why would we leave them, after all?'

'You said—'

'I said nothing.' Her voice was relentless, granite-hard. 'I don't think I'd need to remind the police, would I, that he had already killed one woman and would think nothing of killing another?'

'Fucking hell,' said Rob. There was admiration in his voice. Sienna gave him a miserable look, then turned away. Aline flicked at the smooth barrel of the gun, as though she was removing invisible dust.

'It's quite some story,' she said. 'A convicted murderer, about to die, hating his former friends so much that he'd manipulate a vulnerable teenager to frame them for a crime he had committed himself. I can just see the front pages.'

Brandon could picture them too. Stolen images of Darryl Arniston, appearance presumably unimproved by his years in Saughton jail, set beside paparazzi shots of this shaken girl with phantom eyes, and studio portraits of Aline, all blow-dried hair, with her arms round Lexie and Jimmy, captioned in heavy black letters: *A MOTHER'S ORDEAL*.

Milly's face flickered, as though she too saw it all. 'The thing is,' Aline said, 'we feel sorry for you.' She stood with her back to the windows, owning the room, as she always had. 'So here's what will happen, even though you've behaved terribly. You can walk out of here. If you like, I'll even drive you to a station. We'll write tonight off as a stupid practical joke and we'll all get on with our lives.'

'No.'

The girl said it quietly, but Sienna said it again, louder. 'Aline, no. This is wrong.'

Aline took a step back, almost into the windows, where she could keep her eyes on them all at the same time. Rob walked round the edge of the room, very deliberately, until he was next to her. As he spoke, he seemed to inch himself closer. 'She's right, Sen. She's always been right.'

Sienna closed her eyes. 'No,' she repeated. 'I won't lie again.'

Could they all see the moment Aline lost her temper? Brandon could. He knew what she was going to do an instant before she did it. She turned slightly, raised the gun again, but he was there first, moving on instinct, standing between her and Sienna. He faced her across the space that she had created, this illusion of an ideal life.

He saw a laughing girl who would not be told no. He saw her in his arms, surrounded by roses. *I always get what I want.* He felt a moment of bitter relief that he was free, at last, to hate her.

And in the end the words came easily. 'It's over, Aline. We're over.' *We should never have begun.* 'I'm going with Milly to the police. I'm going to tell them everything.'

'You bastard,' she said.

He watched her finger curl at the trigger, and waited for her decision.

Then, into that frozen moment, there fell a new and dreadful sensation. The ground tugged down, far below him. The rocks groaned. The glass panes dropped shattering from his sight, swallowed by tumbling earth, rolling towards the sea, and the storm was in the room with them, alive and unforgiving. Close by the lost panes, the wooden floorboards tilted like a seesaw, snapped like so many twigs, and followed them into the void. The gun dropped from Aline's hands, disappeared into the sliding rush of clay and sand and limestone.

It happened in seconds, slowed into separate steps by Brandon's freezing mind. Aline perched on the edge of the abyss: a silhouette tilted against the open night. He ran forward, reaching for her hands. But even as they touched, he knew it was too late; she was sinking, vanishing into the landslide, consumed from below. Beside her, Rob's expression changed to one of absurd cartoon-surprise, as it took him too.

Sienna screamed, and went on screaming.

Brandon pulled back. An instinct, sparked by horror. He could not save them, and he must save himself. But Aline had found some impossible strength, now that it could do no good. She closed her fingers on his. He saw her eyes, triumphant and beautiful. He thought of his children, and prayed for them. He felt her hand like a vice as he toppled forward.

'I love you,' she shouted, and she pulled him down to pain and darkness, in the twisting, roaring, inexorable earth.

Afterwards

People will forget, eventually. Human grief will ebb. But the earth remembers. In time, grass will spread and bushes and trees, self-seeded, will hide the scars. The beach will absorb its new, piled debris. The sea will sweep in and out, slowly rising. But the lines of what happened are written there in the rocks for a later generation to read and learn from. Or to make the same mistakes again.

60

Milly

Dorset, 2019

Nikki sits across from me at a plastic table, puffy-faced and alone. I study her eyes for hatred or resentment, but see only exhaustion. They are red round the edges, as if from days of crying. But she is not crying now.

'How are you?' she says.

I consider this, which I was not expecting. 'I don't know,' I say.

I know I have barely slept, because all I hear when I do is the roaring earth, and Sienna's scream.

I see Aline raising the gun. I see her and Rob and Brandon dragged into the underworld. I see the long, slow moments afterwards, while the ground settled. I see dust in dampening clouds, thrown by the wind, and Michael and Sienna running up the stairs, shouting for their children. I see the vanished glass, the broken walls above, and the rooms the children should have been in, empty and open to the storm.

I hear sirens and Sienna screaming her daughters' names. I see Nikki as she was when we found her: blank-faced and desperate, clutching her baby, surveying a world cut off short. I see the bulk of the house, still standing, with one side ripped off. I see the garden gate opening – unbelievably, impossibly – and the children walking out, drenched and shaking and unmistakably alive.

I always cry at that bit.

I cry now, and Nikki watches me until I stop. She twists her hands in her lap and I see the rings hanging loose. Her knuckles are thick like an old woman's. She says, 'I keep thinking of Chloe. You weren't much older than her when you lost your mum.'

I didn't lose her. She was taken.

I lean forward, across the table. I say, 'I wouldn't have hurt the children.'

'I believe you.' She manages a warped smile. 'Now. Perhaps, after all, you saved them.'

I think of the warning signs that no one put together: the cracks in the ceiling; doors getting stiff. I think of the wet winter and the old man on the beach whom I had once seen haranguing Aline's builders. I told her at the time, but she barely listened. She was so sure that everything would go her way.

I ask what I have been afraid to know. 'What will happen to Lexie and Jimmy?'

Nikki says, 'Aline had a sister.'

My head throbs. I remember the police officer who leafed through my mother's address book and took me

324

from the generous arms of the farmer's daughter. 'I'll call your uncle and aunt,' she said. 'They'll come for you. It'll be all right.'

I knew, even then, that it would not be all right.

Does Nikki see what is in my mind? How can she? But she says, quickly, 'Clara came straight down. Her and her wife. Lexie and Jimmy clung to them. They're lovely.' She tries to smile, and I see that her eyes are glimmering with tears. 'They'll be good to them.'

'Thank you,' I say.

In the silence, her weaving fingers find each other again, then press down into the plastic table between us. She says, 'What will happen to you?'

'I don't know.'

'We don't want to press charges. It's not up to us, but we've refused to give statements against you. Sienna too.'

I do not say that I already know this; my lawyer told me. I know, too, that the investigation into my mother's death has been reopened. Michael and Sienna have been charged with assisting an offender.

'I'll come again,' Nikki says. 'If you like.'

I shrug. I say, ungraciously, 'Come if you want.'

She nods. There's a spot on the side of her nose, sore and picked-at. I wonder how long it is since she slept. I know that she will come.

I say, 'Are you still with Michael?'

She looks straight at me. 'For now,' she says. 'Maybe not for long. It was a very big thing not to know.'

I nod. In the silence, I think of Aline, and after a long moment Nikki looks at me again. 'She made him lie,' she says. 'I'll never forgive her, and you have so much more to forgive. But perhaps you are better than me.'

Two days later, a package arrives for me. Inside, there is a box about the size of a shoebox and a compliments slip from a solicitors' firm in Edinburgh, with a brief hand-written addendum: *Our client, the late Mr Darryl Arniston, wanted you to have this.*

I feel sick. I consider leaving the box unopened, but in the end I do not. I lift the lid and see the doll lying on a bed of tissue paper. She's still in her red dress, her face dead white. Her eyes are almost black. When I lean closer, I see that they have been coloured in with a felt-tip pen. He must have done that after he saw me: the last day he was alive.

I touch my fingers involuntarily to my own face.

I think of Nikki, who has forgiven me. I think of Brandon, whom perhaps I should hate most, except that he tried to atone for the past. I think of Aline: Svengali dressed as the Snow Queen. I see Darryl Arniston's face, near death and full of hatred.

I'm giving you a chance to punish them.

Well, the rocks punished three of them, in the end. Let that be enough.

I close the lid on the doll. 'I don't want her,' I say. She can go to a charity shop, begin a new life. And perhaps – just maybe – I will get a fresh start too.

Acknowledgements

Enormous thanks to my brilliant editor, Hannah Wann, who saw the potential of this story in a much earlier incarnation, then guided me with endless tact and insight through the editing process. I'm so proud of what we have produced together! Thank you, too, to my consistently lovely agent, Camilla Shestopal, and the whole fantastic team at Constable, especially Krystyna Green, Lucie Sharpe, Peter Jacobs, Beth Wright, Jane Selley and Charlotte Ridings. Several other kind people have also read drafts of *The Weekend Guests* (sometimes several versions!): Viv and Harry Cripps, Sarah Jones, Lisa Baylay, Tom Baird and Chloe Jacquet. Your encouragement and ideas have made all the difference.

As well as my beloved Edinburgh, I have loved being able to showcase the dramatic, fragile and beautiful Jurassic Coast in this novel. I can only apologise to its many lovers for any liberties I have taken for the sake of the story. Those who know this part of Dorset will almost certainly recognise the inspiration for the setting of the weekend reunion. However, I have kept the area anonymous (or, in the case of the Pirate's Path, renamed it). This is partly because I have made slight tweaks to the topography, removed several buildings and replaced them with Aline's grandmother's house, but mainly because of what I have inflicted on it at the end of the book. Moreover, although Dorset has several stunning lighthouses (I was particularly intrigued to explore the Portland Bill lighthouse on a guided tour), I don't know of any that have been turned into expensive restaurants.

Thank you to my wonderful parents for hosting me beautifully on 'research' visits, and for introducing me to this glorious part of the world. Special thanks to Mum for added childcare and to Dad for much driving, cycling, walking and answering of questions as I checked out locations. Thank you, Tom, for testing out the night hike in Chapter 21 with me, and for being patient when (like Rob!) I wrongly accused you of getting us lost. I'm also very grateful to Dad, Tom and the very kind Dr Giles Droop for helping me get to grips with the rich and fascinating geology of this coast. I have tried to stick to the geologically possible (if not to historical fact), but any errors are entirely my own. I am also grateful (with the same caveat!) to Farrhat Arshad for insights into criminal law.

As an academic, it was especially fun to write a 'dark academia' strand. Although I have enrolled my characters at a real (and excellent) university, I should stress that all the people and scenarios are figments of my warped imagination. In particular, I owe an apology to my PhD students, past and present, all of whom have been a joy to work with, and some of whom will undoubtedly read this.

As always, huge thanks to the many friends and family who have kept me going on my writing journey. To Sarah, Emma and Zoe for Prosecco walks. To all my local pals who have provided solace or support in a million different ways. You know who you are! To Helen, the most generous friend imaginable, for providing a whole new Liza North wardrobe. To Kate and David for being perfect in-laws, Brian and Marly for feline therapy, and especially to Tom, Alice and Lily, my gorgeous little family, who put up with the highs and lows of living with a writer and always make me feel loved.

I'm so grateful to all the lovely booksellers, fellow writers, bloggers, event organisers and reviewers who have supported me since I wrote my debut novel. The crime-writing community could not be kinder. Special thanks to Edinburgh's utterly amazing bookshops. We are so lucky to have you. Finally, and most of all, thank you to my superb, generous readers. I (quite literally) couldn't do this without you.